Praise for
HERE THERE IS NO WHY

"*Here There Is No Why* is a political, poetic, and unputdownable page-turner of a novel. Graubart's dialogue sparkles with wit, his compelling characters surprise with their complex arcs, and the story continuously keeps you on your toes. But *Here There Is No Why* stands out from other literary mysteries in that it not only takes you on a narrative journey but a spiritual one as well. Graubart asks complicated, provocative, and frighteningly urgent questions about God, war, and our own complicity. *Here There Is No Why* creates a searing portrait of a survivor, an artist, and a country on the brink of change."

—Ali Viterbi, playwright, author of *In Every Generation*

"*Here There Is No Why*, like Philip Graubart's other novels, gives readers an exciting plot filled with twists and turns. But Graubart's books transcend a 'detective' label. *Here There Is No Why* offers a cast of complex characters and raises a number of provocative theological questions. Well-written and intellectually challenging. I commend it highly."

—Michael Kinnamon, author of *Summer of Love and Evil* and *The Nominee*

"Come for the murder mystery. Stay for the blackmail, forgiveness, betrayal, love, and wise insight into some of life's deepest questions. Or come for all of that, and stay for the murder mystery! Either way, Philip Graubart has given us a compelling, entertaining, and uplifting novel that will leave you inspired. Don't miss it!"

—Richard Agler, author of *The Tragedy Test* and *A God That We Can Believe In*

"From the first tantalizing text to the climactic, shattering last scene, Philip Graubart's *Here There Is No Why* is a wild and wondrous joyride filled with dizzying plot twists and fast-paced action."

—Laura Blumenfeld,
New York Times bestselling author of *Revenge*

"Graubart has crafted a compelling mystery that doubles as a profound meditation on the nature of evil, memory, and how we come to terms with unspeakable tragedy. Through the intertwining stories of Chaim Lerner and Judah Loeb, the novel explores weighty philosophical questions while maintaining a gripping plot. The importance of Holocaust remembrance shines through on every page, reminding us why we must never forget. As one character poignantly notes, 'To articulate is to free the monster'—a chilling insight into the power and burden of bearing witness.

"With crisp prose and richly drawn characters, Graubart takes readers on an emotional journey through Israel's past and present. The novel's explorations of theology, ethics, and human nature provide ample food for thought long after the final page is turned. While some readers may find the occasional coarse language jarring, it feels authentic to the characters and situations portrayed. Ultimately, *Here There Is No Why* is a deeply moving work that honors the complexity of Holocaust memory while spinning an engrossing tale of mystery and self-discovery."

—Jeffrey K. Schmoll, award-winning author of
The Treasure of Tundavala Gap

"In this captivating novel, Philip Graubart expertly weaves together history, mystery, and the profound themes of forgiveness and redemption. His dynamic writing style and the intricate plot twists evoke the brilliance of Agatha Christie. The story of Chaim

Lerner's death will keep you questioning whether it was suicide or murder—and if murder, who did it? A truly compelling read from start to finish."

—Todd Hugie, author of *House Down Dirt Lane*

"Graubart's writing is lyrical and precise, capturing the complexities of his characters. *Here There Is No Why* raises important questions about the nature of memory, the weight of history, and the possibility of finding peace in the aftermath of unimaginable trauma. It is a must-read for those who love a good historical mystery. Five stars."

—Carol Thompson, *Readers' Favorite*

"I rate the book five out of five stars for the way it tackles complex themes with grace and intelligence. The book is perfect for anyone who is open-minded to new ideas and other people's points of view and beliefs. I recommend the book to readers who enjoy mystery books."

—Onlinebookclub.org

"In this novel, Graubart, a rabbi, grapples with primal and provocative questions about suicide and trauma. . . . A gripping novel of revelations and redemption with a searching and sympathetic character at its core."

—*Kirkus Review*

"A masterpiece."

—Brandon Currence, author of *The Maine Consecration* and *Looking for the Seams*

Here There Is No Why
by Philip Graubart

© Copyright 2024 Philip Graubart

ISBN 979-8-88824-485-2

All rights reserved. No part of this publication may be reproduced, stored in a retrieval system, or transmitted in any form or by any means—electronic, mechanical, photocopy, recording, or any other—except for brief quotations in printed reviews, without the prior written permission of the author.

This is a work of fiction. All the characters in this book are fictitious, and any resemblance to actual persons, living or dead, is purely coincidental. The names, incidents, dialogue, and opinions expressed are products of the author's imagination and are not to be construed as real.

Published by

 köehlerbooks™

3705 Shore Drive
Virginia Beach, VA 23455
800-435-4811
www.koehlerbooks.com

HERE THERE IS NO WHY

PHILIP GRAUBART

VIRGINIA BEACH
CAPE CHARLES

For Livnat Kutz and Ofer Libstein. May their memory be a blessing.

Part 1

CHAPTER 1

September 2023

*R*u going to funeral

A text from my daughter. I was drinking wine and watching NBA highlights when I felt the vibration in my too-tight jeans. The buzz was lengthier, more insistent than an email alert—clearly a text. *Probably the pharmacy*, I thought, *or a Social Security senior scam.* Not urgent enough to take the trouble of removing my phone from my pocket, at least not until the second annoying reminder. I reached for the phone, winced from the pain in my wrist—a tennis injury—and saw it was from Hannah.

I took a moment to admire the prose. It was a masterpiece of literary economy. Sixteen letters, no punctuation, no italics, no bold lettering. Yet she evoked stabbing memories of the most significant moments in my life, including the horror-filled nights and days after Hannah discovered the hanging body of her own mother, my wife. Suicide. Heartbreak. Depression. Illness. Mystery. Sex, virginal and otherwise. Romance. Racism. Genocide. God. Evil. Good. Hannah's nonsentence somehow touched on all the obsessions that defined my life and career. It summoned forgotten odors: Jerusalem pine, garbage on the streets, Israeli shampoo, Time cigarettes. And distant, nearly forgotten sensations: falling asleep to the sound of breaking waves, cold nights with no heat, the erotic jolt from watching young female soldiers. I'd won a Pulitzer Prize, written eight books, dozens of long think pieces, hundreds of op-eds, a play, and even a handful of poems, and I never achieved anything as brief, powerful, painful, and to the point as Hannah's text.

I stretched, wincing again, for the remote and muted the TV. I studied my phone. Was I going to the funeral? Well, maybe, if only to make sure the old lady was really dead. Like Hannah, like thousands of others, I'd gotten the word the night before. Zehava was enough of a legend, and her family had enough clout to override the Jewish Israeli tradition of burying the body as soon as possible. Zehava's corpse would have to wait three long days until all the dignitaries could arrive from the four corners of the earth.

All the dignitaries—and me and Hannah? I texted back the first excuse I could think of. "Too expensive?" I wrote. The question mark left the door open. It was an opening bid. In a game I knew I would lose. That, come to think of it, I probably wanted to lose.

"I'll pay," she wrote back, almost instantaneously, even before the three dots danced across the text balloon.

I wrote, "new covid outbreak," thinking I could also dispense with punctuation and capitalization and still get my point across. The pandemic was officially over, but there were rumors of a new wave. Surely, that was a valid excuse for me, an asthmatic man in his sixties (all right, just sixty-one).

This time, she took three seconds to respond. The dots danced. She wrote back, "business class." And then, in a fresh balloon, "Don't worry about the money."

Was that a bribe or a counterargument? Was business class somehow virus resistant? Or was she remembering how much I bitched about the plane ride the last time we flew to Israel seventeen years before, when she'd just turned fifteen? "Probably too late to make reservations," I wrote.

Again, no dancing circles. An immediate response. "Already done. Paid for. Tomorrow."

I laughed out loud. My rich daughter. Married to a Silicon Valley venture capitalist. My son-in-law holding wealth I wouldn't be able to count. Leader of a company I couldn't describe, no matter how many times he'd explained it to me. So much had changed since the last time. But not everything. She's still telling me what to do. Anyway, I'd already decided to make the trip, coach or business class, with or without Hannah. Michal wanted me to go. She had something to tell me. That was motivation enough.

CHAPTER 2

June 2005

I exhaled slowly through pursed lips. Screaming through the phone at this flunky would not improve the situation.

"You understand then," the flunky said. His name, I think, was Saul. But it might have been Josh. Or Jeroboam. This was the twelfth assistant I'd spoken to. Two of them, I remember, had names of Israelite kings. I wondered if that was just a coincidence. "He *wants* to do the interview. He was looking forward to it."

"He promised," I offered. It was the third time I mentioned the promise. I was quieter now but angrier. It wasn't a promising combination.

"Yes, exactly. That's why he's so disappointed. Bob *hates* breaking promises."

I sighed. "Okay, I'll reschedule." It had taken two years to schedule the two days of interviews. And an additional year to get someone from Dylan's office to call me back and confirm. My deadline was barreling at me. But what choice did I have? "Can we look at this coming August?"

Silence. Was he calling up Dylan's calendar? Had he hung up on me? "Saul?" I called into the phone.

"My name is David."

"Sorry. David. Can we reschedule? August? After the tour?"

"Reschedule?" He phrased it so it sounded like a foreign word. Like a word he would never be able to pronounce no matter how often he practiced.

I inhaled through my teeth. "David."

"Yes, Benjamin."

"My name is Judah."

"Of course. Judah."

"David, I'm never going to get these interviews, am I?"

"Well, that's my point. Bob *wants* to. I know he promised. He told me he promised. He likes you, Benjamin. Loves your writing. There was that piece you wrote, the phrase you used."

"The jingle jangle morning sound."

"Exactly."

Of course, it wasn't my phrase. It was Dylan's. I just added the word "sound." But somehow, that was the entirety of my entertainment journalistic fame. The first time I interviewed Dylan, I clarified for him the kind of sound he was trying to achieve. That was the interview that launched my career. Somehow, I'd gotten Dylan to analyze his own music. The first Dylan book led to biographies of George Harrison and then Ringo Starr. Then, three *Star Trek* books, one each for *The Next Generation*, *Voyager*, and *Deep Space Nine*. It wasn't the journalism I wanted to write, wasn't the genre of writing I wanted to practice, but it kept me gainfully employed. Until recently.

"You know I got an advance on this book. A contract. I'll have to pay it back."

"Bob is so sorry. Bob likes you."

I hung up and called Stan, my agent, a friend from Cleveland Heights High School who was also married to my sister. "I'll do it without the interview."

"Judah."

"Or I'll just make up quotes. Honestly, he probably won't notice. I can get his people to hide the book from him. You think Dylan reads rock journalism?"

"Judah."

"Yes? Is that all you're going to say?"

"Judah." He waited.

"Go ahead," I said. I gritted my teeth. I knew what was coming.

"There's an alternative. You know that."

"The Lerner book."

"I can get you the same deal. Same advance. You won't have to return any money. There's even a travel allowance."

Stan was talking about a book proposal I'd written three years before, examining the life and death of Chaim Lerner, the famous public intellectual, radical theologian, and, most prominently, Holocaust survivor. I'd been fascinated by the question of his suicide for years. Did he, in fact, kill himself? There were reasons for doubt. But if he did, was it because of the Holocaust? In other words, was he one of Hitler's last victims, just delayed, done in by PTSD and not the gas chamber? Or was it connected to his bleak theology? Can thinking too much about God, good, and evil have fatal consequences? Ten years ago, for reasons too obvious to write, I found myself obsessing over trauma and suicide. So, stuck in rehab with no computer and limited TV, I went back to Lerner's books. I started with his most famous volume, *Our Imperfect God*. As I read, I could hear his slight Yiddish Polish accent—the sound of my own grandfather—and the high, gravelly, tentative voice that seemed to invite you in, to agree or argue, or to laugh because maybe he was kidding. I hadn't spoken with him in over ten years, since I worked for him when I was a student at Hebrew University in Jerusalem. But suddenly, while rereading his devastating Holocaust memories, nearly all our conversations rolled through my brain as I reacquainted myself with his argument for a limited God.

Back then, my morbid obsessions kept me on a rehab-recovery cycle, and I almost lost my daughter. But seven years later, now employed and sober, I was browsing at the Sixty-Ninth and Broadway Barnes and Noble, and I found a new edition of *Our Imperfect God* with a foreword by Nathan Rothstein, the Nobel Prize–winning novelist. I stayed up all night rereading that book and then three additional essays that elaborated on his thesis. The next evening, I missed another night of sleep dashing off a book proposal. Stan submitted my packet to every editor he knew, and they all rejected it. But three years later, a pair of Polish documentary filmmakers unearthed a twenty-five-year-old video of Lerner giving a class of high school seniors from Baltimore a tour of Auschwitz. The grainy, appropriately black-and-white footage showed him strolling through his old crumbling wood barracks, pointing to the thin bunk he shared with three other prisoners and wandering through the ruins of the slave labor factory where Lerner's knowledge of polymers and plastics doomed him to starvation and toil, but also saved his life. The Poles created a film built around Lerner's "Tour Through the Inferno" and released it in time for the sixtieth anniversary of the liberation of Auschwitz. Surprising most critics, it won an Oscar for best documentary and launched a renewed interest in Lerner, who was already fairly well known for both his theology and the mysteries surrounding his tragic death. Suddenly, there was a commercial appetite for Lerner projects. Stan resubmitted my proposal and got back five bids, one as large as the advance I'd received for the Dylan book.

"But this situation won't last much longer," Stan warned me now, as he'd warned me in the past. "There will always be a market for Bob Dylan or any of those baby boomer favorites you love. You could do a Roger Daltrey book. Joni Mitchell. Always a market. But how long do you think publishers will be clamoring for a product about a White, male, Jewish Holocaust theologian? Or, honestly, about the Holocaust?"

"You're saying the Holocaust is hot now, but it's going out of fashion?"

"Let's just say the public will lose interest in Lerner a long time before they stop caring about Dylan, McCartney, the Velvet Underground, Star Trek, or any of your other personal obsessions. If you want to do the Lerner book, you have to do it now. Listen, I'm family. I understand your sensitivities. But, just maybe, do it without the suicide bit . . ."

"Stan, the suicide bit is the whole story. The reason for the book. It's not a 'bit.'" I massaged my forehead, shut my eyes. I acknowledged the fateful truth. The Lerner project had already won. Chaim Lerner defeated Bob Dylan. The scenario clarified itself. Financially, there was really no choice. I would fly to Tel Aviv, spend a week, maybe two in Jerusalem. I would write that book. "Ilana will kill me," I told Stan. "You know that." Ilana was my sister, Stan's wife. "A book about suicide? And what about Hannah?"

"Look," Stan said. "Let me talk to Ilana. And Hannah? She'll stay with us while you're in Israel. You know she'll love it. Better than your gloomy company."

I shook my head. "Ilana," I said.

"I'll take care of Ilana."

◆◆◆

But an hour later, Ilana called. "You fucking son of a bitch," she said in greeting.

"Is that really the best epithet?" I said. "A sister calling her brother a son of a bitch? I mean, wouldn't that make you also a son of a bitch? I mean, a daughter of a bitch."

"You asshole."

Ilana swore more than anyone I knew. And I covered the entertainment industry, where profanity was essential for the local dialect, where the word "motherfucker" was most often a term of endearment. So, it wasn't her language that tipped me off to her genuine anger. It was the low, whispery voice, a register she reserved for fury. Ilana was one of those people—like several elementary school teachers I knew—whose voices grew softer yet somehow more insistent the angrier they got. The fact that minutes had gone by and she hadn't yet cracked a joke was also ominous. She hadn't even giggled at my stupid joke. You knew Ilana was really mad when she lost her sense of humor.

"Judah, seriously," she said. "What the fuck is the matter with you? Suicide? You're writing a book about some writer who committed suicide?"

"The suicide is really a minor part."

"Fuck you! Fuck you. I read the goddam proposal. Stan showed it to me. Kiss my ass."

Two fuck yous, I thought. Once again, I marveled at her facility with cursing. Where did it come from? I hardly ever swore. I don't remember our parents ever swearing. But at least she was back to higher-pitched screaming. The low gravel voice wins every argument with me.

"Can Hannah stay with you? I shouldn't be more than two weeks in Israel."

Ilana sighed loudly, a sigh of rebuke. "Suicide. Judah. Really."

My wife had died by suicide almost ten years before. She hung herself. I'd brought Hannah home from kindergarten early because of an ear infection. She found her mother's body. She screamed out, "Daddy!" and I saw Mary, Hannah's mother, my wife, swaying slowly like a wind chime. She was dressed for a workout, with tan yoga pants and the Bruce Springsteen T-shirt I'd bought her just five months before at a concert, a week before we'd received the diagnosis that destroyed our lives. Her head tilted straight down on her chest, and unbrushed brown hair covered much of her face, but I could still see the demonic mottling on her cheeks. I noticed—funny the things you notice when you see an image that's escaped from your worst nightmare—that she was still wearing her wedding ring, but the finger was swollen and blue. Predictably, I fell apart, drinking myself into a boozy haze every night for eight months. Hannah was five years old at the time. Ilana and Stan snatched her from me before I could inflict irreparable harm. Ilana, always the older sister, dragged me to rehab once and twice more. Then, twenty pounds lighter, sober for a month, Hannah and I moved in with Ilana and Stan in Scarsdale. We stayed for a year, a brother-sister blended family with three adults and four children. For that year, Ilana was by far the most healing presence in my life. She managed everything for me, making sure I showered, dressed, and showed up to work at The Times. For the first month, she walked me every day to the train station because she was afraid I'd get lost. She researched therapists and drove Hannah and me to our appointments because she knew I couldn't be trusted to show up. And she was the only one I could talk to. The only person who would really listen when I described finding Mary's grotesque body. The only one who sat quietly with me while I spun numerous self-pitying theories, trying to explain how Mary could do it—do it to me, do it to Hannah—without even leaving a note. This was especially patient of her since she knew damn well why Mary did it, and she was weary of explaining it to me, especially since I also knew. So. Ilana was sensitive about the topic of suicide.

"Stan must have told you," I said. "The Dylan book fell through. I can't afford to turn down the Lerner book. And, yes, it, well, it's partially about suicide. His suicide. I have a theory. You see—"

"Hannah can stay with us," she interrupted. The last thing she wanted to hear was another of my (*fucking*) theories. About suicide. "But *you* have to fucking tell her."

"Thank you."

"Motherfucker," she said and hung up. But this one sounded like the good kind of motherfucker. I think.

Less than ten minutes later, Hannah called. "I'm coming with you," she said.

"No, you're not," I said, without really thinking about it. The word "no" just came naturally to me in conversation with Hannah. The initial answer to any request was almost always no. Not that my no ever mattered. "How did you—"

"Izzy told me." Izzy (Isabella) was my niece, Hannah's cousin. They were born three weeks apart. "She got it from Brad." Another cousin, three years older. Word traveled fast in that household. I remembered how everyone, even six-year-old Izzy, knew what Hannah and I had argued about on any given day at the therapist.

"You're not coming with me," I said, even as I realized that it had been years since I'd won an argument with Hannah or altered her behavior in any way. A tedious, fruitless conversation ensued: my arguments, Hannah's grating, mocking laughter, my logic, her ridicule, my pleading, her humming. In the end, I agreed to take her. Which was just fine. *It will be interesting*, I thought. To introduce her to Michal.

CHAPTER 3

From the introduction to the book "Here There Is No Why: The Death and Life of Chaim Lerner..."
—Judah Loeb, 2005

Here are my questions:
Did Chaim Lerner kill himself?
If so, why?
Because of the Holocaust? Forty years after liberation?
What's at stake in this inquiry?

Let's begin with my first stark query—the suicide. Evidence against. One, he left no note. Wouldn't a writer, among the greatest writers of the twentieth century, feel compelled to explain his most consequential action, to utilize his poetic, complex sentences, his tightly structured arguments, his humor, and his poignant metaphors to say goodbye to his many loved ones?

Two, what a weird way to take his own life. According to the suicide theory, he leaped from his third-story balcony and landed headfirst on a cobblestone plaza next to Jeremiah Street. To do that, he would have had to climb over the metal railing he and his wife had installed twenty years earlier to protect Yoav, their toddler. But eight months before, Chaim underwent a failed knee surgery, making any acrobatic climb nearly impossible. Furthermore, the three-story height did not seem like a sure bet for a fatal fall. Jumping from that distance seemed as likely to cause painful injury as death.

Three, according to everyone who interacted with him that fateful week (I do mean *everyone*. I interviewed them all, some in person, some by phone), he seemed his normal, happy self those days, whistling Yiddish folk songs, cracking jokes in four languages. His car mechanic reported that Lerner told him an off-color joke in Arabic (he refused to repeat it). His house cleaner told me they gossiped about two famous Israeli singers in Yiddish. His wife recounted a week of affectionate dinners, just the two of them, no Yoav or other relatives, none of their many author friends, no cultural dignitaries or political hacks demanding their attention. His son's fiancé beat Chaim at chess the night before, a triumph that filled him with pride and glee since he had taught her the game. With Yoav, his son, he discussed with eager anticipation his film project, a chance to branch out artistically and give him a welcome break from the often lonely vocation of writing.

That was the other thing. The week of his death, he was actively planning for the future. In addition to the film, he'd signed a contract for his next book. This one would be a change of pace. He'd finally get to write about Zionism, what he claimed was now his favorite topic. He could abandon the gas chambers and Auschwitz and questions of evil for the inspiring topic of Jews returning to their ancient homeland. He was slowly branching into discussions and debates about contemporary Israeli politics, and the prospect of new intellectual horizons excited him. He purchased two plane tickets to Italy, a long-delayed, long-promised vacation with his wife. He committed to teaching a new class at Hebrew University on the history of Western literature. His dean told me she found a complete syllabus and lecture notes among the papers on his desk.

Also, everyone who knew him—everyone who ever met him—described him as a happy guy. The adjectives included "joyful," "genial," "vital," "satisfied," "loving," and "enthusiastic." He fit none of the stereotypes of Holocaust survivors. No one described him as haunted or angry; he never mentioned revenge. After the war, his friends and family told me, he sought out opportunities for joy. He didn't mourn. He looked back at Auschwitz in his writing, but in his life, his career, and his true vocation as a free Jew living in the Jewish homeland, he *celebrated*. "The last person you would expect to commit suicide." That was a sentence I must have heard a dozen times in researching this book. Why would so happy a person end his own life?

No note. An unlikely suicide method. Planning for the future. A genial, even joyful demeanor—in general and during that fateful week. Compelling, but these are trivial pieces of evidence compared to the life-affirming wisdom we find in his writings. For example, there is a scene in the essay "Moments of Reprieve" where he describes how a fellow inmate managed to steal an apple and give him a slice. "The sweetness and the mild crunch," he wrote. "That was life itself. The juice. The way it both quenched my thirst and momentarily eased my hunger. A miracle in the gullet. How could I fully deny a God who could create such an object?" Would a person who derived so much miraculous joy from an apple slice kill himself? Even the title of the essay, "Moments of Reprieve," points to Lerner's refusal to surrender to chaos. The darkness is never complete, Lerner is saying. There's always light.

And, in a previous book, there was the way he described ethics in Auschwitz. "Theft was encouraged; indeed, it was celebrated," he wrote. "Stealing meant living, which became our ethical center. But to steal without giving—that was a sin. You stole, but you paid a tax on your theft. The most admired men in the camp were the best thieves." In these sentences, Lerner defied those who insisted that there could be no irony after Auschwitz. In other words, he could look back, and instead of turning into a pillar of salt, he could laugh, or at least chuckle. Someone who could find wry amusement in abject horror—is that a person who would take his own life?

Finally, his last book, *Our Imperfect God*, the one that brought him international, posthumous fame, rescued the entire notion of religious faith. It gave everyone who could no longer believe in God a life-affirming theology.

But still, we have it in front of us, in front of me, always, that starry spring evening. The crumpled, broken body, lying only a few feet from his bus stop, the head bleeding profusely onto the cobblestone. The great man motionless, mercifully dead. Somehow, he ended up there, and the police ruled it suicide.

And maybe they're correct. In fact, the evidence against isn't ultimately convincing. No note? Most suicides don't leave notes, not even writers. Lerner himself once wrote that writing is a "subtly fraudulent art." You use it to express the truth about a certain activity, but between the act itself and the reflection and then the actual scribbling, you can't help but distort something. Maybe Lerner was wise enough to understand the limitations of writing, especially writing about your own choice to die.

Lerner's geniality the week before? Well, that's classic suicide behavior. Most suicides exhibit cheerfulness the days before; once the decision's been made, the burdens, whatever they are,

are lifted. Even the planning ahead fits a suicide pattern. I know that from personal experience.

And it turns out Lerner's vaunted geniality was something of a façade. Yes, that was his outward-facing persona: the jolly professor, the optimistic theologian. But his closest relatives described dark, bitter periods, sometimes lasting months, when he arose from his study only to snap at them for making the slightest noise. After some prodding, his wife admitted that Lerner suffered several depressive episodes in his life, even before the Holocaust. She noticed the familiar subtle signs of an oncoming dark period the week of his death. Holding a grin a beat too long. A slight tremor in his left hand. Eyes open a bit too wide.

Moreover, this was a stressful time for him. Lerner was a committed walker. He fast-walked through Jerusalem's poor, hilly southern neighborhoods most mornings from 5 a.m. to 7 a.m., often conducting press interviews along the way, meeting with graduate students, or just plotting out a new argument for a book or an essay. But his cursed right knee (he believed the initial injury came when an Auschwitz kapo kicked him) failed to heal after his most recent surgery. A year before the knee surgery, he'd injured his hip playing racquetball, and the pain never really went away. He remained largely hobbled in his office. Also, his ninety-four-year-old mother, who had lived with Lerner and his wife the last two years of her life, had died nine months before. Lerner had been particularly close to his mother.

And it's hard to remember now since Lerner's *Our Imperfect God* is currently regarded as perhaps the twentieth century's most important work of Western theology, but the initial reviews were disappointing, at least to Lerner, who, like many writers, claimed not to care about his critics but actually poured over everything written about his work. The Orthodox intelligentsia—the academics, but also the Yeshiva heads whom Lerner admired, and the many Orthodox rabbis and teachers, both in Israel and the United States—savaged the book. One of his favorite teachers, Rabbi Avram Kaplowitz, who taught an hour lesson on the Zohar, Judaism's most important mystical tract, every Sunday morning at the Western Wall in Jerusalem, talked of forbidding Lerner from attending the seminar and spoke openly about excommunicating him. Finally—and the evidence here is not conclusive but compelling—Lerner seemed to be experiencing a profound and soul-deadening disillusion with Israel and Zionism. Some of his colleagues at the Hebrew University—they prefer not to be quoted—told me Lerner was preparing a devastating statement condemning Israel's occupation of Gaza and the West Bank, calling it a "human rights disaster" and raising the possibility of an emotional and intellectual "virus" infecting Zionism that was sickening and then killing the entire enterprise. It should be noted that Lerner's family denied that he was planning on publishing anything of the sort. And they didn't hear Lerner engage in any fundamental critique of Israel beyond the normal grumbling that was the birthright of every Israeli citizen. But one particularly close colleague assured me that he'd seen a draft of the manuscript and that Lerner had basically "disowned the Jewish State."

So perhaps he did kill himself in that strange dive off the balcony, enduring the pain in his knee and hip one last time. He had reasons.

Or, if the suicide theory is true, was it perhaps the Holocaust that sent him headfirst into the street?

Many influential American writers claim that it was. Yes, he struggled with depression, with the normal ill-health associated with aging; he lost a parent, suffered a bum knee, a sore hip. These were the stuff of life, rarely motivations for suicide. But maybe, like a time bomb, the real wound had been planted years before and then erupted. Bella Shmozic, the famous American novelist, quickly published a piece in *The New Yorker*, calling Lerner "the six million and first victim, and the eighth Holocaust writer." She was referring to the morbid fact that many, perhaps most well-known Holocaust writers, ended up taking their own lives. It started with Paul Celan, the German Jewish poet, then Tadeusz Borowski, the non-Jewish Auschwitz prisoner, then Primo Levi, then several others—poets, memoirists, novelists—and then, finally, Lerner. Only Eli Wiesel seemed to have survived as Hell's chronicler. Shmozic pointed to a short story Lerner had published a year before his death about a sixty-year-old blind man who wakes up one morning with the ability to see. At first, a blessing—"colors! The faces of loved ones! Sunsets!"—it soon becomes a curse. There's too much to see, too much to process; his weary brain can't handle the sensations. He dies of a tumor. For Shmozic, the story was clearly an allegory about the Holocaust writer. Too much to see. Eventually, it kills you. "What does the brain do with what the eye sees?" she wrote. "Makes it coherent. Turns it into a story. If we're blessed enough to be born with sight, our brains have the time to practice making sense of the nonsense—the chaos—our eyes behold. But to suddenly see it all! Without mediation. Too much. The character dies. But isn't that the vocation of Holocaust writers? To see, without mediation. To open their eyes to the horror that their brains should not be called upon to process, and yet they process it anyway. That's what writers do; it's in the job description. They see more deeply than others. Lerner kept seeing, for forty years. It was too much."

Maybe. I'm not entirely convinced. But if Shmozic and others are correct, that Lerner killed himself because of the Holocaust, that he was perhaps Hitler's final victim, it raises all sorts of questions. What does it mean to survive? Did Lerner "survive" the Holocaust? Did the Holocaust writers, who are famous because they are survivors, actually survive? Does trauma never dissipate? Do any of us really survive?

CHAPTER 4

September 1982

I met Michal when she curiously chose to sit next to me on the first day of Lerner's theology class. I'd seen her a few times on Mt. Scopus—standing by herself awkwardly at the Frank Sinatra cafeteria; in the administration building waving her arms, clicking her tongue, and arguing loudly in Hebrew with the registrar, who screamed back at her; making copies in the library kiosk with aerobic energy; and smiling shyly in a crowd of Israeli women who were all laughing uproariously, but it was impossible to tell if they were laughing at her or with her. She caught my eye, I suppose, because she was pretty; women and the potential for romance took up at least 75 percent of my concentration that year. And she was my type: cute, thin, blue-eyed, tan, with sharp elbows and knees, high cheekbones, and shoulder-length brown hair. But she also struck me as exotic in ways that, thinking back, it's hard to explain.

First of all, she was Israeli. And yes, I was in Israel, so that shouldn't have stood out. But I was in the One Year Program bubble. All the friends I'd made during the first two months were American or Canadian students in the program. My wider circle of acquaintance included several Brits, a few South Africans, and a guy I played tennis with from Belgium who spoke mostly accent-free English. All my friends, without discussing it, instinctively understood when and how our English language bubble became permeable. We grocery shopped in Hebrew and hauled our laundry to an Israeli laundromat where we followed Hebrew instructions; some of us could even chat in Hebrew with bus drivers, ask for directions, barter at the Arab market, click our tongue back at the ticket taker at the movies, or argue in the dorm room if someone was hogging the showers. But socially, most of us never crossed the border. I certainly didn't. I was too timid. Israelis spoke with such loud, rapid confidence. It was too scary. I was more likely to explore Bethlehem or Hebron—Arab cities—than strike up a friendly conversation with an Israeli student living in my dorm.

But there was something about Michal. There was the bicycle—a light-blue Italian ten-speed, men's style, with the stepover bar. I'm not sure why, but bikes were rare in early 1980s Jerusalem. Thinking back, Michal's was the only one I recall seeing that year. She pedaled it up Mt. Scopus through Wadi Joz every morning, a formidable climb for anyone, much less the petit Michal. Also, I quickly noticed that she was trilingual. She joked and sometimes sang along in Arabic with the Palestinian cleaning women in the cafeteria hallway. At lunch, she sat with the Israelis, gossiping—or whatever they were doing—in Hebrew. And I heard her explain to the hapless American students in perfect, unaccented English how the laundry machines worked. One time I overheard her mutter, "Go fuck yourself," while riding away from a guy who seemed to be trying to pick her up. Facility with local languages, a bicycle, an Israeli in Israel—I understand that this should not qualify anyone as "exotic." But it's hard to overestimate the extent of my naivete that year. I'd never left the United States, never traveled any further south than Columbus, Ohio. I only heard foreign accents on TV, and then it was usually English-speaking actors. I never had a fistfight. I'd never been truly frightened of anything real. Same group of friends since third grade. Never been in love. It didn't take much to surprise and charm me. I noticed her.

And maybe she noticed me because she seemed to scope out the half-empty room before darting to the seat next to me in the front row. She even smiled shyly, teeth barely showing, blue eyes suddenly wide open. It was a look that would slay me in the months to come. "Good morning," she whispered. I was so shocked that she spoke to me that somehow my brain switched to Hebrew, and I answered in my worst American accent, "Boker tov."

The course was "Theologies of the Holocaust." I was curious about religion in those days, so "theologies" grabbed my attention, though I'm sure I didn't know exactly what it meant. Most of the other students were there for the Holocaust. Or the class fit in their schedule. Or they'd vaguely heard of Lerner, who was somewhat famous as a Holocaust survivor/writer. Overall, I was surprised at the turnout. A celebrity teacher with a reputation as an easy grader, a popular topic (Holocaust)—and still only twenty-some students in a room that could have fit fifty. Lerner himself seemed unbothered by the small crowd. A broad, toothy grin decorated his face as he limped into the room, favoring his left knee. He carried a stack of books nearly half his size. He stumbled right before he reached the desk, and I was sure he would trip and the books would tumble to the ground. I leaned forward, hoping to grab his elbow. But, for the first time,

I witnessed his odd physical grace. The books slid easily off his arms and landed piled up in the correct order. As for Lerner, he used both hands to catch himself on the right corner of the desk, then hoisted his rear end onto the front of the desk, where he sat and smiled, swinging his feet in rhythm as if dancing to some unheard music. He studied the class. The gleam from his smile shone halfway into the room.

"Kinder!" he said in greeting, the Yiddish word for children. He looked sensually eager, as if he were about to lower himself into a soothing hot bath or dig into a banana split. His adorable charisma hit me immediately. He sounded already like everyone's favorite Jewish grandfather, the one who snuck candies into your pocket and then winked or handed you six new shiny silver dollars and chuckled warmly. You couldn't help but smile in return, wait for the comforting pearls from his mouth.

"Why," Lerner began, still grinning, "did the Nazis slaughter and burn the bodies of over one million Jewish children? Why did they, as sport, throw babies at the electrified barbed wire?"

Well, what did I expect? It wasn't a cooking class.

"We'll begin with God. That's the easiest step, yes? After all, who created these monsters, evil men who herd crying mothers into gas chambers, who gather whole communities, kindergarten children, and patients at homes for the elderly into the woods, as if heading for a pleasant picnic, and then force them all, yes, to disrobe, dig graves. And then they shoot them, yes? Easy—at first—to blame God, who created these sadistic soldiers. So we'll start there. In the beginning."

In those few sentences, Lerner somehow mutated through several personas, from the genial, joking grandfather to a biting stand-up comic to a mad, grinning psycho to some creature from hell—an imp, a dybbuk. His smile widened as he spoke, revealing damaged, yellow teeth, swollen gums. He lectured with a scary enthusiasm, as if he were imparting pornographic secrets to a captive audience of perverts. He seemed on the verge of cackling laughter the whole time but let out only two or three yelp-like chortles. He never stopped swinging his feet, even when they collided metallically with his desk.

He led us through the "Three Irreconcilable Statements" about God. "They cannot logically coexist, yes? Statement one: God is omnipotent—all-powerful. You can add, if you'd like, omniscient—all-knowing. But that is assumed in omnipotence. Better, more elegant, to leave it at one word: omnipotent. All-powerful. Now, statement two: God is all good. Nothing but good. Wants only good, expects only good. Can we eliminate these extra sentences and summarize the statement with one word, yes? We can! Benevolent. So now we have two one-word descriptions of God: one, omnipotent, and two, benevolent.

"Third statement: Evil exists. Or maybe you prefer unjustified evil exists, yes, but doesn't the word evil itself imply unjustified? Some insist on the word 'innocent'—the innocent suffer. But again, I think 'evil' covers this phenomenon. Innocents suffer; that is evil, yes? So, for the sake of simplicity and elegance, it's no longer three statements. Because of our work, there are no long sentences to parse, no paragraphs to compose. We have just three words, yes? Omnipotence, benevolence, evil. So now you see the logic puzzle. If God is omnipotent and benevolent, God then has the power and the motivation to stop all evil. Yet, babies die. Evil exists. Now, naturally, if we negate any of our statements, then we protect the logic. Maybe God is not omnipotent. God wants to prevent evil but simply cannot. But is that actually God, this not-all-powerful deity, this, shall we say, shlepper God? So then we can say, as frankly most religious folk say, though I don't think they really mean it, that evil does not exist. This is what Job's friends say to the suffering Job. Everything happens for a reason, but the reasons are often beyond our puny comprehension. Suffering comes from sin, even if you can't remember the sin.

And anyway, everything balances out in the next world. These are all different ways of saying that evil does not actually exist. But I must tell you a secret, my friends. It does. Evil does exist."

At this point, Lerner thrust out his head and leaned so far toward us, I was sure he was going to topple from the desk. He kept his smiling face trained on us, so with his outstretched neck, he resembled a grinning turtle. "Or," he continued, "we can remove the word 'benevolent' from our cosmic equation. God is all-powerful. Evil does exist. God can intervene and stop the children from smashing into the electric barbed wire. Why doesn't He?" A pause and a quick chortle. "He doesn't want to. Maybe," he said, and with this, his smile seemed to grow past his face, Cheshire-like, so the grin was all we could see. "He's the one who brings the evil in the first place."

◆ ◆ ◆

I'm not sure how it happened—did she follow me, or did I follow her—but Michal and I walked together out of the classroom into the long, wide corridor connecting the Humanities wing to the rest of the Hebrew University. Still intimidated by her strange Israeliness, I couldn't think of anything to say. I was about to turn toward my next class when she touched my wrist. "I'll give you a ride," she said.

She insisted on riding indoors, through the linoleum floors, dodging students, faculty, and floor-moppers. I took the bicycle seat and leaned back. She stood, as if we were ten-year-old boys, afraid of bodily contact. She was nearly a foot shorter than me and probably forty pounds lighter, yet she was bearing the burden. The brown hair that hung from her helmet blew into my face. We must have been quite a sight. At every moment of the ride, I was certain I was going to fall. She stopped abruptly at one of the many coffee/refreshment kiosks that dotted the Hebrew

University. She hopped off the bike and removed her black helmet. "I missed breakfast," she said. I nodded. She turned away. Was I supposed to join her? As if reading my mind, she swiveled and faced me. "My treat," she said and smiled shyly. Is this really happening? I thought. An Israeli girl on a bicycle, pursuing me?

"Nu?" she said.

I nodded, followed her in.

"Wasn't he amazing?"

I pondered a reply. "Well, I was amazed," I admitted.

She ordered in a blizzard of Hebrew words. Then she turned to me, switching to English. "I think he's the smartest man in Israel."

He's an imp, I thought. I recalled his demonic chortling, more coughing than laughter, as if he was too devilish to actually laugh.

"I know him," she said softly, leaning in slightly as if she were imparting a secret. She handed me a coffee I hadn't ordered, and we found a seat next to the round window.

I wasn't interested in talking about Lerner. I thought of a way to change the subject. "You're Israeli?"

She laughed. "Everyone at the university asks me that. Like it's suspicious I speak different languages fluently." She took a bite of her cheese toast—melted cheddar on a pita, the specialty of the house. I sipped my *café hafuch*—literally "upside-down coffee," a designation I never understood. What was upside down about it? "I'm Israeli," she said, still chewing. "Well, I was born in Milwaukee, but my parents moved here when I was eight, and my dad never stopped talking to me in English. So, there's the answer to that mystery. An Israeli with fluent English."

"What language did your mom speak to you?"

"Arabic. She grew up in Iraq."

"So, Arabic," I said. "And Hebrew?"

"Hebrew . . . that just happens here. It's a miracle. It'll happen to you if you stay long enough. But wait, how did you know I speak Arabic?"

I blushed.

"It's okay," she said, laughing. "I've seen you staring at me. I noticed. It's okay. I think. It's a compliment. Right?"

Is a romantic crush a compliment? Is love a compliment? Or just a tragic curse? It was a question I contemplated often during my time with Michal.

She asked about me, and I told her my life story. Not very interesting to me or, I believed, to anyone. A bit about my parents' divorce, my father's latest accounting job, and my increasingly intense arguments with my sister. My grandmother's suicide. My mother's interesting work as a librarian. My political arguments with my father. Bourgeois American stuff. What intrigued me was that she seemed intrigued. Not so much by my story but by my fingers as I clenched or unclenched my fist or pointed at nothing, or my nose occasionally sniffling because of allergies, the elbow I scratched, the sandaled foot I tapped. I saw her face move subtly with every one of my gestures. The way she noted my body movements, she seemed like a curious first-year medical student.

When I finished my ten-minute epic tale of not much, she nodded quickly and asked, "Do you want to meet him?"

Him? Who is him? The soldier sitting next to us? The short-order cook who made her cheese toast? My father? I'd just summarized our political disagreements. But why would I need to meet my own father? "Sorry?"

"Lerner. Do you want to meet Lerner? I think he can help you."

I shook my head. "I don't understand."

"Divorce. Mortality. Politics. Suicide. All those obsessions. He's good with those kinds of things. I think he can help you."

"Obsessions?"

She laughed. I already loved her laugh. "You're pretty easy to read, you know. Listen, I've known him, like, my whole life. All of my time in Israel. Do you want to meet him?"

◆◆◆

"I think I may be getting a girlfriend," I told Charlie that night. We shared a tiny dorm room on Mt. Scopus.

"Okay," he said. "Well, in that case, our work here is done." Whenever Charlie asked why I was spending a year in Israel, I answered that it was to meet girls. He always chuckled, but really, at this point, I don't remember any other reasons. There must have been some.

Charlie reached under his bed and took out his Uzi. "Sorry," he said. "Just have to clean it."

Having an armed roommate was another example of the exoticism I craved but didn't fully receive during my first few months in Jerusalem. Charlie and I shared much in common. He grew up in the Midwest, was a big baseball fan, quick and skilled at pickup basketball, a Led Zeppelin aficionado, and drank a lot of Maccabi Beer. But a sharp line divided us. He'd made Aliyah three years before and had just completed his army service. Even though he was twenty-one, a year older than me, he was just starting his first year of college. We rarely socialized. I hung out with the less permanent Americans; he hung out with his fellow new immigrants. But, in the way of the best roommates, we'd grown fond of each other without really trying.

"Milu'im tomorrow," he told me. He disassembled his rifle, then slowly laid out the rag and cleaning oils on the cheap Persian carpet I'd bought the month before in the Arab market. "My first reserve duty. Reporting at 7 a.m."

I looked at him. "Lebanon?" I asked, holding my breath. Israel had invaded Southern Lebanon three months before. Charlie hadn't been posted there. Not yet.

"Nah," he said. "I can't really tell you, but well, let's say it's near Bethlehem. Really near Bethlehem. Okay, you got it out of me. Bethlehem. Peaceful patrol. Don't tell your spymasters."

Charlie always prefaced his army stories with the warning that he wasn't allowed to talk about it. But for our first month together, it was all he wanted to talk about. I wasn't sure if he was kidding or if his service really did involve secrecy, and he was just particularly bad at it.

"If it was Lebanon," he said, carefully wiping each gun component with the rag, "I'd find a way to get out of it."

The IDF invaded Southern Lebanon almost three years into Charlie's service. I knew his unit spent the first week after the incursion in the Negev training on some new weapons. The following week, they patrolled Ramallah and Nablus, two mostly quiet West Bank cities. He never faced combat. The next week, three years after he joined, his time was up. He was discharged—a college freshman at age twenty-one. The night after the Sabra and Chatila massacres, about a month after he'd finished his service, we got drunk together for the first time. We drank "hats on the bench," a combination of Heineken and gin that Charlie picked up from a Dutch peacekeeping soldier in the Sinai.

"They don't even know why they do it," Charlie said. I'd asked why Christian Lebanese soldiers—Israel's allies—slaughtered Palestinian civilians in the refugee camps.

"To scare them?" I suggested. "To show who's boss? So they'll acquiesce? Or just leave?"

"Believe me, there are less dramatic, more effective ways of bullying people than shooting their wives and kids. It's just, I don't know, a thousand years of hate. It gets into their blood.

No one can explain it. They certainly can't. Let me tell you, the sooner we get out of there, the better."

But Israel was still there. Charlie whistled while he cleaned his Uzi, then carefully put the weapon back together and held it up for my inspection. "Pass," I said. "Bethlehem? You're sure?"

He winked at me. "Bethlehem. Just don't tell anyone."

♦♦♦

The next day, I showed up ten minutes before class. Michal and Lerner were waiting outside the door. Michal was still in her bicycle helmet, holding on to her ten-speed. She introduced me to Lerner. He smiled and grasped my hand with his two warm fists. The wide smile displayed none of the demonic qualities I'd seen or imagined the first day. "I'm honored," he said.

I didn't know how to respond. At Northwestern, my American college, I knew none of my professors and couldn't imagine any of them expressing honor at my acquaintance. Or taking my undergraduate hand in theirs. "Wonderful to meet you," I said.

"Michal has told me much about you. Such an interesting life. We'll talk more, yes, on Friday night? At dinner?"

Was the One Year Program holding a dinner with Lerner? First I'd heard of it. Usually, I kept up on those sorts of things. "I'm not sure . . ."

Michal cut in. "Chaim, I haven't asked him yet. You just told me to invite him late last night."

"But you'll join us," he said, still holding my hand, tilting his head slightly, studying me. "Shabbes dinner. Just family. And Michal, of course. But she's mishpuche already."

Michal looked at me. Her wide blue eyes signaled expectation, but I wasn't sure what she wanted me to do. To accept or decline? She nodded slightly. "I'd love to," I said.

She told me to meet her right outside my dorm building at 6 p.m. I wore my one white shirt, my one pair of black dress pants. And sandals, which seemed slightly more Sabbath-appropriate than sneakers. I'd remembered to buy a bottle of wine right before the grocery stores on Mt. Scopus closed up for Shabbat. I held it in a plastic bag. The twilight hour was cool, quiet, and fragrant with pine. Not yet jacket weather, but coming on that season, late September, past the Jewish holidays, autumn in Jerusalem. I shouldn't have been, but I was shocked to see Michal pedaling uphill. She reached my building and hopped off, smiling. She wore a flower-patterned dress, light blue with yellow daisies. And a black helmet. Maybe a touch of lipstick, though I wasn't yet at the point where I could discern subtle makeup. I didn't see a bike lock. "You're going to leave the bike here? Come on, we can take it to my room."

She laughed. "Hop on," she said.

This time, I held onto her, not the seat. I shoved the wine bag on my shoulder and wrapped both my arms around Michal's torso. I had to caution myself not to squeeze too tightly. The problem wasn't lust; it was fear. We headed downhill from Mt. Scopus, and Michal never stopped pumping the pedals, as if she didn't trust gravity to move us forward. She screamed and pointed at various oddly shaped towers, probably mosques, as we leveled off at Wadi Joz, the neighboring Arab neighborhood that separated the university from the Jewish neighborhoods near the Old City. I realized she was playing tour guide, pointing out the sights. But I couldn't hear her clearly through the wind, and I nearly panicked each time she took one hand off her handlebars.

Just past a strip of auto-repair shops, she cut sharply right into an alley. The pavement quickly turned to dirt, and dust blew in my face like a horde of locusts. I had to shut my eyes, so I felt but didn't see, the next sudden left, where I nearly toppled off the bike, taking Michal with me in my tight grip. But she leaned forward, yanking me back onto the seat, and thirty terrifying seconds later, she screeched to a halt. She slowly removed my arms from around her waist as if unbuckling a seat belt and then hopped off. She swept off her black helmet and grinned.

"Fun, huh? We have to walk now. They don't like you riding on the street on Shabbat."

She pushed the bike through a whitewashed arch separating the alley from a different neighborhood—Geula, as I would discover, an almost exclusively religious enclave. Stepping through the arch vaulted us into a different world. The street was crowded with Black and White garbed men hurrying to shull, young head-scarfed mothers, many of them pregnant and pushing strollers, and smartly dressed children, the boys twirling their twisted earlocks, the girls holding hands. I was surprised that I drew most of the stares. After all, I was wearing a knit yarmulke, a present from my mother, and, while missing a shtreimel, coat, and beard, I was dressed in black and white, with full-length pants and a long-sleeve shirt. Surely, a short-sleeve-clad female cyclist was more of an oddity in this neighborhood than an appropriately dressed tourist carrying a bottle of sweet Shabbat wine. But when she greeted them all with a smile and a gut shabbes, I realized they knew her. Her ten-speed was part of the neighborhood. I was the stranger.

The apartment was a third-story walk-up. I offered to carry the bicycle, but Michal grunted, hoisted it on her shoulder, and stepped quickly up the stairs faster than I would have walked unburdened. A pretty, golden-haired women—looked like early-fifties, same age as my mother—answered the door. She kissed Michal on both cheeks, muttered a few quick words to her in Hebrew, then stepped neatly around the bike and held out her hand. She smiled warmly, showing her white teeth. "You must be Judah," she said. Her English was not only unaccented, but it was Midwestern American. She sounded like my parent's friends. "I've heard so much about you." As I took her hand, I wondered how that could be so. She pulled me in for an embrace. "I am Zehava," she announced into my ear. "You are welcome in this house."

I expected a crowd. Lerner was a well-known thinker, and Michal had told me that Zehava was a prominent politician in Israel's Labor Party, the opposition in Israel's Knesset, its parliament. A power couple, I thought, imagining a Friday night salon with Israel's brightest intellectuals and most powerful politicians. But it was just the four of us: Michal, me, and the Lerners. We settled first into their modest, white-carpeted living room. Chaim and Zehava shared the loveseat. Michal and I took the two stuffed armchairs, the only other furniture in the room. The odor was redolent of my childhood Friday nights: chicken, challah, candle wax. Chaim and Michal sipped bourbon. Zehava served me an Israeli favorite: petel, seltzer with a strong flavor shot.

Chaim was fully in angel mode, his smile and easy laugh reflecting heaven, not hell. Instead of regaling me with ideas and policies, which I expected, they peppered me with questions.

I offered the same boring story I'd given Michal: accountant father, librarian mother, brought up in suburban Cleveland. A younger sister—some conflict there, nothing shocking. Divorced parents. Northwestern. Never been out of the country until now; actually, never been out of the Midwest. They nodded, appeared enchanted, though Michal studied her fingernails.

"Fascinating," Chaim muttered. He shut his eyes, concentrating.

"Amazing," Zehava said.

At this point, I'd had enough. "Excuse me, I guess I'm missing something. How could anyone call my childhood fascinating? Do you mean the divorce? That's, like, half of America. I've always thought my upbringing was the most banal thing you can imagine."

Chaim opened his eyes quickly and smiled. Zehava laughed, somehow delighted. Even Michal chuckled. *What is the joke?*

"We're not laughing at you, Judah," Chaim quickly said, though they obviously were.

"It's just you said the magic word," Zehava said. "Banal."

"I think you know it, Judah. Yes? The 'Banality of Evil.' This great essay about Eichman by my late friend Hannah Arendt? Her theory of human evil?"

I was touched that Lerner would assume I'd read some famous theory. I was twenty years old, decidedly nonintellectual, a sci-fi fan, and a budding sportswriter at most. I didn't spend my days seeking out ideas about human evil. Oddly, though, I was aware of Arendt's book. When my father moved out, he accidentally left one box of books in our basement. I was searching for my sister's stash of weed when I saw a cockroach crawl across the box. I got up to brush it away and caught a glimpse of the title: *Eichman in Jerusalem: A Report on the Banality of Evil*. I picked it up, thinking it might be a mystery. But I quickly tossed it back when I saw it was an essay about the Holocaust. Later, curious about words, I looked up "banality." "I know the book," I said.

"Yes, yes, I suspected you might. So you know the theory. Evil arises through the banal motives and actions of very ordinary people. A banal society—Germans, let's say, yes, with normal bourgeois human needs and ambitions just to put decent food on the table, listen to Beethoven, normal, banal—so everyone conforms, cooperates, works decent hours at their shops and labors to make the trains run on time. This, yes, is exactly the society that breeds unspeakable evil. But I have a different theory. You see . . ."

"Chaim," Zehava said, laying a hand on his knee. "I don't think we need—"

"No, no, Zehavele. Just a moment." He gripped his cane and leaned forward. I assumed it was a signal for all of us to rise, but he stayed seated, rigid, alert. "My theory, Judah, is the banality of goodness. Your childhood explains the goodness of America.

Your ambitions, yes, to write about games. Your conflicts—petty political arguments, divorce, some sibling nonsense over minor jealousies. You don't leave Ohio for most of your life. You see this package as boring, perhaps even oppressive. I see it as the very root of goodness. Yes?" He stared at me, blue eyes smiling, waiting.

I shrugged, not sure what he wanted from me. "Makes sense," I said.

This time, I laughed with them, still not really sure I got the joke.

Dinner included homey Ashkenazic dishes—a garlicky brisket, roast chicken, overdressed salad, limp broccoli—but also common Israeli/Middle Eastern dips: hummus, tahini, baba ghanoush. The sweet challah tasted like cake. Zehava admitted that she bought it at a bakery around the corner. "I stopped baking challah when I entered the Knesset." Refusing offers from Michal and me, she did all the serving and clearing. Chaim stayed seated. *A progressive power couple*, I thought, *but still sort of backward*. But then I remembered the cane, Chaim's limp.

He dominated the conversation. "You see, Judah," he said, always directing his thoughts at me. I guessed Michal and Zehava had heard it all already. "My theory is a banal society, like your own, your Cleveland, what do you say, your Indians? Yes? Your Cleveland Indians culture, not overly burdened with complicated ideologies, simple, simple, simple baseball, allows for freer discussion, and this is the key, yes, though I haven't quite figured out how to place it just so in the lock. This banal culture is one that allows for questions. For asking why. I want to tell you a story from the *lager*—the camp. You know what I mean, yes? The *lager*. We called it *lager*, the German word for the camp. Yes?"

"Chaim," Zehava said. "Really? Is this necessary? Maybe after we eat, at least?"

"No, no, Zehava. He knows. Judah knows."

I had no idea what he meant by that. I didn't know anything.

"It was one of our first days. Maybe the first, maybe the second." He shrugged and frowned. "Not sure. Still suffering from the train ride. You know the horrors, yes, you know the trains. Bitter cold day. Snow on the ground, subzero weather, impossible to get warm. And you know the very worst torture? You know?"

Am I supposed to guess? I nodded.

"Of course, I didn't take a survey. I'm speaking for myself, though I'm sure this feeling was shared. The great torture—and this is all through the lager system—was thirst."

"Ah," I said. I wouldn't have guessed.

"I'm sitting on the bunk, the inch-thick, narrow, lice-ridden mattress that I'm to share with three other men. I'm shivering, more fully conscious than I've ever been, and my mind is focused on one thought—to drink something."

As he spoke softly, he looked just past my left shoulder to a wall decorated with what looked like family photos, marriage scenes under a huppah, formal shots at a graduation, and a picnic at the beach. It was as if Lerner was addressing the photos, the folks framed within them, not me. Or the scene was playing out on the family portraits. While he told the story, he fell into his weird, incongruous, wildly inappropriate, amused tone. He smiled slightly, and his blue eyes lit up. It was the look and sound of fond remembrance or a setup for a joke, not a tale of horror.

"And then I saw it. Through the window, I think. Or could be, yes, the barracks door was open. They would leave the doors open on the coldest days. I spotted a miracle. An icicle, extending from a branch. I acted out of instinct. Thirst. Not life, thirst. If I knew for sure that sucking the icicle would kill me, I would have snatched it anyway and sucked with all my might. Thirst, yes? I don't remember getting up. I must have, but I only remember sitting down on the mattress. I'm about to place the icicle in my mouth, like you would with, what do we call them, an artic limon? I'm about to suck my artic limon, my popsicle, when the German guard slaps it out of my hand. Then, he crushes it under his boot. I am shocked. Strange, Judah. At this point, I'd seen German boots crush innocent babies, yes? So I'm surprised that this Nazi destroyed my icicle? Yes, I'm surprised. I can't explain it. I look at him. A brave act, staring at my tormentor, but I'm not conscious of bravery. One word floats into my brain—a German word—and I say it. Warum? 'Why?' He looks at me. Eager, I think. Eager to smash his gun into my face, eager to shoot me, or simply eager to debate a young Jew. Kein ist nicht warum, he tells me and then quickly walks away. 'Here there is no why.'"

He slowly turned from the photos and, for the first time since the beginning of the story, faced me. "Here there is no why," he repeated. "It's the absolute answer to something, yes? I'm just not sure . . ." His gentle voice trailed off for a moment, and he turned back to the family photos. "I'm not sure what." He smiled.

During dessert—sponge cake, almond cookies, melon balls—I remembered Charlie's comment about Sabra and Chatila and thought up a way I could contribute to the conversation. I locked my eyes on my dessert plate because I wasn't sure where to address my comment. "Is there a 'why' to Sabra and Chatila?" I asked.

All three suddenly turned to face me. I blushed. "Sorry," I said. "It's just my roommate's got milu'im, and we were talking about the massacres. By the Falangists." I saw that Michal had gone thoroughly pale. Zehava turned her mouth down in a frown. Chaim smiled. "It's all right, Judah. Your question. Ask it."

"I don't know," I said, now unclear why I had spoken up in the first place. Was I trying to impress Michal? Was I really curious? "The anger and violence just seems like a black hole up there. Is there any rhyme or reason to it?"

"It's not a black hole," Zehava snapped. I was astonished at the change. Her eyes glared at me coldly, and she pointed at my face. She'd gone from gentle, amused mothering to controlled rage in an instant. "That's a naive American response. There are reasons—roots to this hatred. And our government knew perfectly well what it was inviting in when they urged those goons to—"

"Zehava, this is not correct," Lerner interrupted. "Our government did not perpetrate this massacre. This is a dangerous, irresponsible accusation. A blood libel, yes?"

"Oh, Chaim, please," Zehava said. And then they were off, in Hebrew, lecturing each other, gutturals flying, hands swinging to make their points, Chaim tapping his cane on the carpet several times like a percussionist trying to urge his band toward a new rhythm. I was proud to be able to understand the gist. Chaim defended the current right-wing Israeli government. Zehava viciously attacked it. Later, I found out that neither really believed what they were saying.

"Stop!" Michal yelled after about five full minutes of husband-wife combat. They stopped, like trained animals, attentive to their trainer. They all looked at me. Zehava spoke first. "We apologize, Judah," she said. "This is a sensitive topic for us."

"It's Yoav, their son," Michal explained. "He's in Lebanon. He was nearby during the . . . you know." Michal's face reddened. Yoav, I thought. Michal looked away. Chaim and Zehava still faced each other like two wary boxers after a long match, not sure if the fight is really over.

"Hard not to think of Yoav every time we hear the word Lebanon," Zehava said. "Or Sabra and Chatila."

"We apologize, Judah," Chaim said. "Yoav is stationed somewhere up there; we don't know exactly where."

"Or what he's doing," Zehava said.

I nodded and noticed my heart was beating rapidly, and I was panting. A fight-or-flight response. That's Israel, I thought. A lovely Shabbat dinner conceals landmines—political arguments, terrorist missiles, Auschwitz stories, Jewish history. A son serving somewhere in Lebanon. Fear. Exhaustion. Anger. And here, it seems, there is not always a why.

◆ ◆ ◆

Michal lived just down the block, another out-of-place secular Jew in Geula. She pushed her bike while I walked her home. We were quiet the whole way until she touched my sleeve and pointed to a three-story building. "That's me," she said. "At the top."

"The penthouse," I said.

"You'll come up sometime," she said. Meaning, of course, not this time. "It's my parents' apartment." That was true enough. It belonged to them. It was also misleading. They were away for the year. But at this point, I only held vague, unsupported feelings that Michal was hiding something from me.

"Tell me about Yoav," I said.

She laughed. "My old buddy."

"Just an old friend?"

"An old buddy."

She told me where I could find an Arab taxi for a lift back up Mt. Scopus, but I preferred to walk. Nothing in Jerusalem was more than an hour's walk away, and the night was starry and cool.

CHAPTER 5

July 2005

I promised my sister I would explain to Hannah why I needed to go to Israel. I told myself that I knew why. To investigate Lerner's suicide. To look over the balcony where he allegedly committed suicide. To interview important Israeli intellectuals about Lerner's suicide. To ask his friends and loved ones the key questions: Did he commit suicide? Why did he commit suicide? Was it a freak accident or suicide?

Suicide. A touchy subject for a kid whose mother hanged herself, a kid who found the body. But how touchy was it? She never raised the subject to me or to her aunt and cousins. Her therapist told me she seemed to have no curiosity about why her mother died. Is that normal? I asked. She shrugged. What's normal? Anyway, Hannah gave every appearance of being healthy and well-adjusted. I only brought her to that therapist because she'd gone from an A to a B in sixth-grade math. I figured from the beginning that her mother's death was a time bomb, and I listened attentively for ticking. Maybe those half a dozen hastily scribbled mediocre multiplication and division assignments heralded a psychic explosion. But after two months, the therapist reassured me, "I know this is going to sound odd to you, but she's lucky she was only five. She barely remembers her mother." She peered at me over the top of her glasses. Ilana had recommended her, and she looked like Ilana—curly brown hair, almost an afro, piled up just a little too high. A confident gaze, experienced and wise. "Five is a very flexible age," she explained. "Hannah has already assimilated the tragedy. I'm not surprised. Honestly, I'd be more worried about you. Losing a spouse is the toughest loss, harder than losing a child. And by suicide?" She waited. I told her I was worried too.

Still, I was afraid to bring it up with Hannah. The only time we really talked was over dinner, and with Hannah's packed schedule—soccer, cheerleading, debate, robotics, not to mention schoolwork—that gave us at most fifteen minutes for conversation. On my first attempt, I brought one of Lerner's books to the table—the one about the not-so-powerful God—and asked her if she'd ever studied theology. She chuckled—definitely at me, not with me—and told me about her second-place finish in the robotics competition. "We lost because we're sophomore girls," she told me. No doubt. The next night—Friday night, pizza night—I told her I wanted to tell her about my junior year of college. But that just triggered a long discussion about which schools Hannah would apply to. Was Stanford unrealistic? Would Columbia be a mistake because it was so close to home? She was thinking Northwestern, but weren't the winters unbearable?

I remembered that about two years before, Hannah ceased all interest in any subject I brought up. All I had to do to turn Hannah off a current band, movie, or TV series was get a *Times* assignment to write about it and then try to talk to her about the piece. This was hard for me because, at my core, I'm an investigative journalist with a natural curiosity about a multitude of subjects. I could see that Hannah inherited my pop-art fascinations and tenacious curiosity—she could wax eloquent about Andy Warhol, Steely Dan, and Madonna. But she flipped off all curiosity if it was something that interested me. So I gave up on raising the subject of Chaim Lerner and his suicide during our fifteen-minute dinner talks and reminded myself that we had an eleven-hour plane ride coming up where she'd be a captive audience.

Strapped in on the crowded flight, I stalled the first three hours through takeoff, the miniature meal, some stomach-whirling turbulence, and Hannah gabbing on about her next robotics tournament. She was just about to binge watch *Star Trek: Deep Space Nine*—her aunt had given her the disks with all seven seasons—when I squeezed her wrist. She looked up at me, surprised. Physical touch wasn't nonexistent in our current teen-dad dynamic, but it was rare, and I may have squeezed a bit too hard. She waited—and I did too—for the words to come.

"I have to talk to you about suicide," I said.

"Huh," she said and looked away. But she didn't move her wrist.

I told her the Lerner story. My junior year in Israel. Lerner's Holocaust tales, his dangerous ideas. His loving warmth to me. Our friendship. I left out Michal. "It's about his suicide," I said. "That's the focus of the book. That's why we're going to Israel."

She nodded three times, frowned pensively, and rubbed the wrist I was no longer holding. "Yeah, Ilana already told me. Sounds interesting," she said. She turned back to her laptop.

"That's all you have to say? No questions? Comments? Objections? It's suicide, Hannah. You can talk about it. It's allowed. Do you have anything to share?"

"Nope," she said. She pointed at her screen. "Do you mind?"

Did I? On the one hand, this was unsurprising. I was writing about Lerner; Hannah would, therefore, be wholly uninterested in him. My angle in the book would be suicide; Hannah, despite her history, would then automatically care less about suicide. On the other hand, her mother had died by suicide. I thought of Hannah's therapist. Was this massive indifference to the thing that had shaped her life really healthy and normal? I was forming a response to Hannah, thinking of pushing the topic a bit, when I saw that Captain Benjamin Sisko had already made his appearance on Hannah's laptop. I let it go.

Three hours later, Hannah woke me up by grabbing my wrist. I was startled awake, surprised I'd been sleeping that deeply in my cramped middle seat. For a moment, I thought it was Mary holding my arm. I guess I'd been dreaming about her. "There's something I have to tell you," Hannah said.

I nodded.

"I'm not a Zionist. I just think you should know."

"Okay. That's not necessary, but thank you for—"

"It's more like I'm anti-Zionist. I think you should know. Ilana said I should tell you."

"And I'm glad you're telling me. That's brave. But Hannah, your politics don't really—"

"Not anti-Semitic."

"Of course not." I wondered what was going on here. Something to do with my sister. Hannah sometimes referred to herself as Jewish, but that was only because of me, and I was a poor role model, with really no Jewish identity past my junior year in Israel. During our marriage, Mary went to Mass every Christmas Eve at St. John the Divine, for the music, she said. She told me she'd like to take Hannah with her when she got older, and I raised no objection. Of course, she never got the chance.

"Ilana told me that some people confuse anti-Zionism with anti-Semitism. So maybe don't tell anyone I'm anti-Zionist. Maybe just say I'm pro-Palestinian."

"Sure." She still held on to my wrist. It was the most we'd touched each other since, I don't know, Mary's funeral. "Hannah, did you want to talk about Israel and the Palestinians? Do you want me to tell you what I think?"

"No!" She tightened her grip. "It's just, there are some people I want to meet in Israel. I mean in Palestine. Not Jews. Palestinians. We may have to go to Gaza."

"Hmm. Who do you have to see in Gaza?"

"I'll tell you later." She released my wrist and returned to her laptop. "Oh, just one more question," she said.

But she hadn't asked any questions. She hadn't asked me a question in years. "Of course." I leaned forward, toward her.

"Did you ever think of killing yourself?"

It took some effort not to collapse back into my seat, as if Hannah had shot me in the chest. Instead, I breathed out quickly. "Never," I said. I thought of Hannah's demented scream, Mary's corpse swaying. Of struggling to explain to the five-year-old Hannah what happened to her mother. Of drinking so much I couldn't trust myself to be a father. "Never," I repeated.

"Okay. Good," Hannah said cheerily, as if we'd just been chatting about Deep Space Nine.

"Hannah," I said. "Have you—"

"Of course not," she said. She pointed to the screen. "Trying to watch."

◆◆◆

Michal picked us up at the airport. She greeted me at baggage retrieval with a surprisingly cold peck on the cheek. She's pissed off at me already, I thought. Later, I found out why. She hugged

Hannah tightly, as if my daughter were a long-lost relative or a rescued hostage. Hannah surprised me by hugging her back, almost as tightly. It was like they already knew each other, had missed each other desperately.

It had been several years since I'd seen Michal. I was struck, as usual, at how little she'd changed. Her hair was slightly shorter, but still dark brown. There was one line on her forehead forming and some crinkling around her eyes, but otherwise, her face was as smooth as the twenty-year-old I fell for. She was still slender, possibly more so. The only major difference was her dress. I'd known her as a university student, with jeans, shorts, and T-shirts. Now she wore a gray pantsuit and carried a briefcase. She dressed like a lawyer because that's what she grew up to be. An attorney, but also a political activist for right-wing causes, a polemicist, and power broker. And apparently an airport VIP because she marched us quickly through customs and security, waiving the ID card she wore as a necklace and yelling at chastened security personnel in Hebrew. It took us less than ten minutes from baggage control to the tan Volvo she'd left parked on the curb next to a row of police vehicles. Hannah stuck closely to me while we walked, as if she were again a little girl, afraid of separation. But when we reached the car, she stepped away quickly and reached for the back door handle. Michal intercepted her hand. "You'll sit in the front with me," she said.

Hannah turned to me for an explanation, but I was equally flummoxed. "I want to get to know your daughter," Michal told me. She looked at Hannah and opened the front passenger door. "Please."

"Okay," Hannah said, after a moment's hesitation, then a quick glance at me. "But I'm just going to sleep."

She didn't get the chance. While driving insanely fast from my perspective, but, of course, this was Israel, Michal peppered Hannah with questions. How old are you, what school do you attend, what's your favorite book, favorite movie, any crushes ("No." "Why not?"), favorite sports, school subjects, and hobbies. At first, Hannah stuck to one-word answers. But she seemed to catch a warmth in Michal's tone, a sense that she was genuinely interested, enough to allow Hannah to risk a few sincere answers. She told her about robotics, that she was hoping to go to MIT (news to me), and that, come to think of it, there was a boy in her math class who was sort of her boyfriend (definitely news to me).

"And when was the last time you were in Israel?" Michal asked after the boyfriend conversation.

"I've never been to Israel," Hannah said.

Michal twisted her neck to look at me accusingly. I shrugged. "You know, she's not really Jewish." Please, Hannah, I was thinking, trying to communicate telepathically. Don't say that you're an anti-Zionist.

"Of course, you're Jewish, Hannah," Michal said. Hannah winked at me.

We were passing a stretch of road surrounded by tall pines and green hills. I vaguely recalled a kibbutz Michal and I visited a few times, where her aunt and uncle lived. Lotan? Kfar Shemesh? I couldn't remember the name of the place, which surprised me. Normally, I remembered every detail of my time with Michal.

"You see the truck there," Michal said, pointing to a red, metallic ruin on the side of the road.

"That's a truck?" Hannah said.

"It used to be," Michal said. "See, there's another one." She pointed left. "These are the ruins of caravans. They were bringing food and medicine to Jerusalem during the 1948 war. The Arab armies blockaded Jerusalem, starving thousands of civilians. They shot up the trucks and slaughtered the drivers. We keep them here to remember."

"Yeah, but who started the war?" Hannah said softly, almost a whisper.

"Excuse me?"

"The Jews started the war," Hannah said, with a full voice.

"We most certainly did not," Michal said. "We accepted partition. We declared our state. They rejected the compromise. They invaded."

"No, *you* invaded. You settled in a country that already had other people living in it. You took the best land. You expelled hundreds of thousands of Palestinians."

And they were off. A blizzard of Israel Palestine propaganda. A ping-pong match of accusations and responses, narratives and counternarratives, exaggerations, facts and lies, lies and facts. I heard *nakba*, independence, occupation, liberation, massacre, self-defense, terrorism, freedom fighter, sexism, imperialism, colonialism, anti-Semitism, democracy, dictatorship, one state, two state, Jewish state, Palestinian State, compromise, justice, Holocaust, and again *nakba*. I was simultaneously bored and nervous at the disputation. My interest in Israel and Zionism began and ended with Michal, with Chaim Lerner somewhere in between. After I left Jerusalem, heartbroken and bereaved, I turned all my investigative journalistic curiosity to American popular culture: jazz, rock, country, blockbuster movies, TV, and a few bestselling novels. For me, Israel was the place of personal grief, and nothing else. I paid some attention if a terrorist attack hit Jerusalem—scanning lists of casualties—but I willfully ignored Israel/Palestine politics after the Rabin assassination and the collapse of the Oslo peace accords. It was the conflict that would never end. A black-hole war that led nowhere except to chaos, and what's more boring than that?

But my daughter dueling with my ex-girlfriend intrigued me. Even though they weren't shouting, didn't seem angry, and Michal had stopped gesticulating with both hands while driving. In fact, she even slowed down and stopped passing every vehicle on the road as the argument heated up. Hannah, for her part, ticked off her points like a high school debater (which she was), never raising her voice, but somehow pronouncing Arabic and Hebrew words with what sounded like an authentic accent. They went at it for almost half an hour. After Michal's last spitting out of the word Shoah, Hannah broke out laughing. Michal again turned to me, puzzled by my mysterious daughter. I decided to mimic Hannah; I laughed. Michal waited an instant, then joined us just as we passed the colorful, flowered "Welcome to Jerusalem" sign. We all laughed together, like a happy family. It was all a joke.

I was surprised when Michal honked three times, shifted lanes, and then turned left on King George, toward Geula. She'd told me she was taking us to the vacation rental she'd arranged. I assumed she'd choose Bakaa, or the German Colony, where most Americans stay. But she turned right on Jeremiah Street, and I realized where we were going. It was a surprisingly leafy residential road. Oak Trees shaded nearly every house, as if God or the city planners or someone had constructed this particular ultra-Orthodox block as an oasis in a desert of concrete and Jerusalem stone. I, of course, recognized the street. It hadn't changed much in over twenty years. "Chaim's place?" I asked. "You're taking us there?"

"You mean Zehava's place," Michal answered. "It hasn't been Chaim's place since you left. But no, I'm not taking you there. You'll see Zehava tonight. For some reason, she invited you both to dinner. I'm taking you to your apartment. Like I promised." She pulled up directly in front of Zehava's three-story building. "There," she said and pointed to a small rectangular structure set back in between two buildings. It could have been a garage or a storage shed or an outhouse, but I noticed the flowers in the windows and a tiny front porch. "Your cottage," Michal said. "Right next door." She hopped out of the car. Before Hannah and I could even unbuckle our seat belts, Michal had opened the truck and removed all our suitcases. Perpetual motion, I remembered. That's Michal. Particularly when she's irritated.

"You rented us an apartment right next to Chaim's place? I mean Zehava's?"

She shrugged. "I know why you're here. It seemed convenient." She grabbed Hannah's two wheeled bags and marched up the driveway. I followed with my one suitcase and small backpack. It was still early, 7:30 a.m. local time, but the sun beat down, triggering memories of scorching, parched, dry Jerusalem summer mornings. I longed for a shower, a chance to lie down flat after the horribly cramped plane ride.

"Wait," Hannah called. We turned. She hadn't moved since she got out of the car. "Let's go up," she said, pointing to the Lerner house. "We should see the balcony. You know. Where it happened."

Michal looked quickly at me, then shifted directions, lugging the bags toward Zehava's place. "I've got the keys," she said, as if that was the only barrier, the only thing keeping us from the place where Lerner took his last fall.

"Maybe we should first put the bags in our cottage," I called out. *And maybe a quick nap,* I thought. *Or maybe forget the whole thing altogether.* But neither Hannah nor Michal paid me any attention. Luggage and all, we headed to the Lerner home. Michal unlocked the front entrance and told me to leave the bags in the foyer. Hannah and I followed her up the steps, three flights. My heartbeat accelerated as I turned for the third flight up, both from exertion and anxiety. By the time we reached the fateful third-story balcony, I was thinking I might faint. Or die of a heart attack.

Without hesitation, Hannah approached the balcony. She fingered the dark metal railing slowly, methodically, as if she were blind and studying an elusive brail text. Michal and I stood back out of fear, or respect, remembering the man who'd stood as close to the fence as Hannah now stood, but who then breached the border between concrete and air, between life and death. Hannah kept her hand on the railing and studied the dirty white floor. *No furniture,* I thought, *and dust everywhere. No one comes out here,* I realized. *For good reason.*

Hannah squeezed the top railing one last time, then looked at us. She actually smiled. "I think I've got it," she said. *Thirsty,* I thought. I suddenly realized how thirsty I was. I remembered other thirsty summer days. The thirstiest I'd ever been in my life was in Jerusalem. In this neighborhood. "The man clearly didn't jump," Hannah continued. "With his injured knee? He could never have climbed this thing."

I studied the railing. Four rusting metal bars, about neck high to a man of medium height like me. A challenge, for sure. But impossible? I didn't see it. Suicide, by definition, took extraordinary effort. One bum knee wouldn't have stopped him.

"So you're thinking a fall," Michal said. "An accident?" She sounded proud, like a mother whose daughter aced a math test.

Hannah shook her head and touched the railing. "Not possible," she said. "Look over here, four bars, like five or six inches apart? And he was a short guy, right? I looked him up on the flight. The fence here would go up to his forehead. How could he have fallen past the rail? It's mathematically impossible," she said, with the assurance of a chronic conspiracy monger.

"Then what?" I asked and immediately regretted it. I knew how she'd answer. I'd been thinking it for twenty years.

"It's obvious," she said and smiled again. "No suicide, no accident."

"Hannah," I said, looking at Michal.

"Murder," Michal said, looking back at me, eyes narrowed, lips pursed, irritated, or more likely infuriated.

"It's obvious," Hannah said.

CHAPTER 6

November 1982

I slept with Michal for the first time on her birthday. I'd purchased two St. Peter's fish at the Mahane Yehuda market and cooked them the only way I could imagine: in a frying pan, pressing down hard on the spatula. Unfilleted, they came out mostly inedible—a sea of bones surrounded by mostly raw flesh. Michal pretended to enjoy hers. In our two months together, I'd noticed she rarely finished more than half a meal, but she polished off nearly three-quarters of the dreadful fish. I took that as a good sign, so I took her hand and led her to her bedroom.

I say "slept" with her, which was accurate; I slept over because we slept in the same twin bed, in her childhood bedroom. I stayed the night. We made out; we did things. We didn't, however, have sex. A month before, the first time we came at all close to intercourse—which is to say, the first time she took off her top—she told me she was saving sex for marriage. I was surprised, slightly charmed, a little disappointed, and also relieved. Like Michal, I was a virgin and nervous. But I wasn't saving anything for anyone. I certainly wasn't waiting for marriage, which, at the time, seemed as remote as buying a house, joining the Marines, or dropping out of school and working at a gas station. I wasn't withholding sex; it just hadn't happened to me yet. Apart from some bumbling high school make-out sessions, Michal was my first physical relationship. It just wasn't *fully* physical. We did other things, just not that. A trivial fact, but it becomes important later in the story.

Still, waking up next to her seemed, to me at least, a momentous milestone, comparable to sex. When the morning sun jolted me awake, I sensed a body next to mine, and I thought, *Charlie*. Somehow, I must have drunkenly stumbled into the wrong bed. But I smelled Michal's shampoo, and I remembered. Then she woke up, brushed dark-brown hairs from her eyes, squinted at me, and smiled slyly, like she'd just gotten away with something, stolen some candy, cheated on an exam, or ran a red light. *Two sneaky virgins*, I thought, *in the same twin bed*.

For breakfast, we split a stale croissant, nibbled at leftover birthday cake, and drank Elite instant coffee. Normally, Michal filled in all the silences between us with memories or questions about American culture, or she recited poems and song lyrics or told corny jokes. Her native shyness evaporated around me, and she turned chatterbox. But that morning, she sipped her coffee, moved her fork around her plate, played with the cake, and looked out the window toward the Lerner apartment. *She's either comfortable enough with me now to stop the nervous chatter*, I thought. *Or she's uneasy about me spending the night*. Every few minutes, she'd turn from the window, tilt her head, and look at me. But her gaze never lasted more than a second.

I thought of asking her about the evening: *Was it okay that I slept with her? Should I never do it again? Should we do it every night for the rest of our lives*? But I didn't want to jinx the moment and get the wrong answer. So I brought up a topic I knew interested her.

"So, I'll see you tonight?"

"Tonight? Uh, yeah, sure." She seemed surprised.

"No, I wasn't asking. I meant I'll see you at the Lerner's tonight. For dinner."

She shook her head and opened her eyes widely. She was fully awake. "The Lerners?"

"Dinner tonight. Eight o'clock. After Shabbat. Should I stop by here first, or do you want to meet there?"

"Judah, I don't know what you're talking about. I wasn't invited to dinner at the Lerners." There was a high-pitched snap in her voice, unfamiliar to me and ominous. She was irritated.

"Sorry," I said. "I just assumed." Chaim had caught me in the hallway the day before and told me how much he and Zehava had enjoyed getting to know me. He said they'd like to "do it again." I figured that meant with Michal.

"You're going?" she said, leaning toward me. "You're going to dinner? Without me?"

"I didn't think I could say no."

She studied her cake crumbs. "No," she said.

I wasn't sure what that meant. Is she agreeing I couldn't say no? Or forbidding me from going? Is this our first fight? But what are we fighting about? "Look," I said. "I don't have to—"

"No," she said. "Of course, you couldn't say no. Of course, you'll go. I can tell they like you. And they're so fascinating." She played with the hairs around her right ear, a habit that reminded me of yeshiva boys fiddling with their side curls. "I just don't think. You know, you and me. I'm not sure."

"I shouldn't tell them about us? That we're a couple?"

"I just think we should wait. You know, they'll say something to my parents. It's not time." She smiled at me. "Not yet."

I nodded. I remembered how Michal would quickly release my hand whenever we ran into someone she knew. We avoided campus restaurants, even my favorite cheese toast place. She felt most comfortable with me—she was most flirtatious and warm—far from Mt. Scopus, in crowded places downtown, or in the shuk, filled with strangers. She's hiding me, I thought. I wondered why.

"Not yet," I agreed.

She smiled.

◆ ◆ ◆

"I admit it—that's strange. The secrecy. Dropping your hand. But it's only been one month," Charlie told me that afternoon (actually, it had been fifty-nine days). We lived together, but between his diligence as a regular program student studying with the natives and my time with Michal, I hadn't spoken with him in days. I was sitting on my bed watching him pack for the weekend. A distant Russian cousin had invited him to spend a few days with his family in Ashkelon. I'd told him about my morning with Michal. "That's just the way girls are," he said confidently, like a lecturer on an obscure topic that only he had mastered. "She doesn't trust that it's real, so she's not ready to announce it to the world. But, I mean, you slept together, right? She's clearly committed."

"Hmm," I said. I didn't mention the sex part; that is, the lack of it. Charlie reached under the bed to grab his Uzi. After four months, I still hadn't quite gotten used to an armed roommate, and he read the alarmed look on my face.

"In case I get called. It could happen anytime these days." He ran his finger along the shaft, checking for dust, then shoved the weapon into his bag. "Okay, here's my suggestion. Tell the Lerners."

"What? I told her I wouldn't."

"Yeah, well, tell her it slipped out. You didn't mean to, but, you know, it's hard to keep secrets. Or better yet, don't tell her you told them. Tell them not to tell her."

More secrets, I thought. "I don't get it. Why should I tell them?"

"If there's something off about Michal, they'll tell you."

"Off?"

He shrugged. "It's probably nothing. But, you know, who is she? For Israelis, she's American, and for Americans, she's Israeli. I've asked around. I don't know anyone who really knows her. Anyway, you seem insecure about this girl. She drops your hand in public. You're her little secret. So you should check her out. Is she for real? Don't you want to know?"

"What do you mean 'for real'?"

He hefted his duffel bag on his shoulder. "She's hiding you. Makes me curious. Aren't you? What else is she hiding?"

♦♦♦

I didn't bring up the subject of Michal with the Lerners. But mostly because in the whirlwind of heady conversation topics—Zionism, theodicy, theories of history, consciousness, idolatry, forgiveness, radicalism, massacres, Auschwitz—a two-month, nonsexual relationship seemed ridiculously trivial.

The atmosphere was different this time. Instead of a neatly set table—fine china, silver candlesticks, a gleaming array of wine goblets—we sat in the living room with paper plates on our laps. Oddly, Chaim and I shared the love seat like a cozy couple. Zehava sat across from us in the stuffed armchair, watching us closely like a concerned parent. No brisket or fresh challah this time. Instead, the meal was leftover roasted chicken, day-old pita, and spreads that Zehava had picked up at Mahane Yehuda before Shabbat: purple cabbage, eggplant salad, crushed tomatoes with peppers and onions, coleslaw, chopped carrots with raisins, and, of course, hummus and tahini. And beer. Chaim displayed seven bottles, each a different brand. "Always," Chaim told me, opening a Heineken and handing it to me. He took an Israeli brand—Goldstar. "After Shabbes. Even before the war, my father and I had a beer or two to welcome in the new week." By the end of the evening, there were only two beers left. Zehava abstained, and I only had two. Chaim liked beer.

For the first hour or so, Zehava and I listened while Chaim told several stories about his time as a slave laborer in Buna, the Auschwitz rubber factory. He told us about a time a fellow prisoner managed to smuggle in a mealy apple. Four of them hid behind a machine—risking a beating or their lives—and divided the precious fruit into four parts. "I remembered God," Chaim marveled, "in the juice and pulp of that scrawny apple." He told us about another time the same four—Chaim's closest Auschwitz companions; he was the only one to survive—dragged a repurposed Mercedes bus engine up the stairs to a civilian supervisor's office and were met at the door by the man's young female secretary. It was their first time seeing a woman in nearly a year. "I was aware of two things. One, her ankle, yes? Of course, I could only look down, so that's what I saw of her body. She was not wearing socks, hose, or any covering. This was a young woman's ankle, and it was completely naked. Was this erotic? Of course not; we didn't have the capacity to feel aroused, you understand. But it was beauty. The other thing I noticed was our smell. We were filthy prisoners. We smelled like, yes, we smelled like corpses. Probably worse. Normally, you didn't notice. It was the air, the smoke, the shit, our bodies—and it was the odor of our lives. But suddenly, staring at that ankle, yes, I noticed. Not so much our stench but how we must have smelled to her. This young woman, with her feet of pure beauty." He smiled, as he always did after telling an Auschwitz story. "People think it was nonstop horror," he said. He ripped off a large piece of pita and chewed on it without dipping it in any of the spreads. "And, yes, of course, horror. Impossible to exaggerate, so I don't even tell the most horrific stories. But there was that ankle. That slice of apple. Moments of reprieve."

"Does it help to talk about it?" I asked.

"Help?" He looked genuinely confused. Help. What a weak, incompetent word in the vocabulary of Auschwitz.

"I'm sorry. I just meant . . ."

"I know what you meant, Judah," he said with warmth. "Me, it helps a little to tell stories. Her"—he nodded at his wife across from us. She was looking down, as if studying Chaim's ankle—"not so much. Come. Havdalah."

We conducted the ceremony of farewell to Shabbat. Chaim lifted the kiddush cup and sang the words in a surprisingly pleasing baritone; I held the braided candle, careful not to drip wax on the Persian carpet. Zehava stood silent, motionless, not even shining her fingernails off the candlelight, a key part of the ritual. I assumed she'd lost any religious faith she'd ever had, but when Chaim came to the last stanza and then the famous paean to Elijah the prophet, she suddenly sang along with gusto, harmonizing off my much weaker singing.

After we sat down and Chaim pushed another beer on me, helping himself to his third, I asked them if they were religious.

Chaim chuckled and looked at Zehava. "What is religious?"

I didn't have an answer to that, but I desperately scrounged my twenty-year-old brain for some words. Zehava rescued me by laughing.

"It's okay, Judah," she said. "This is his new obsession. Religion. He spends all his time nowadays with black hats. The ultra-Orthodox. I expect him to come home any time now with a fur-lined shtreimel and kapote." She looked at him. "And to never touch a female again."

Chaim chuckled, then took a long pull from his Goldstar. "If God wills it. But, no, Judah. It's research. I think I can persuade them of something I've been thinking about. About God. Torah. Israel."

"Persuade them?" I asked.

Zehava stood and took our plates and the empty beer bottles. "You'll excuse me," she said. "I've heard this a few times already." Chaim leaned back on the couch and set his beer on the rug. He was still sitting next to me, but he chose to look forward as if addressing an audience. "You see, Judah, it's about blame. Tell me, who do we blame for the Shoah?"

I thought of his class. "God?"

He laughed and turned sideways, as if he'd just noticed me, and I amused him. "Well, okay, yes, that would make some sense. But we are not talking in a theology class. This is real life, yes? Think. Secular Jews don't blame God; they don't believe in him. And the religious? How could they blame God? They *believe* in him. So maybe not God, yes? So, who do we blame?"

"The Germans?"

"Ah, yes, that, of course, is the correct answer. But forgive me. You give this entirely proper answer, a legally correct answer because you're American. And you're young, almost two generations removed from Auschwitz. You see, Judah, the Shoah is not personal for you, yes? It doesn't infect you. Revenge doesn't sing to you. This whole topic—blame, accountability—it's only interesting to you from the legal point of view, no? So, Germans, yes, yes. And now we have a correct response. Nuremberg, yes? Trials, jail sentences, even executions. And reparations. Justice. And, yes, we should say it, a Jewish state, Israel itself, as compensation. This suits your simple—I mean this as a compliment—your simple, rational sense of justice. The stories you tell yourself. Good defeats evil, and then . . . justice."

I wondered how long he would go on. In the classroom, he often rambled for twenty minutes straight or more, but the Israeli students could always be counted on to interrupt him when they got too bored or to get up and leave when class time ended. But here in his cozy living room, redolent of Havdalah wax, fueled on beer, ideas, and memories, I could imagine him going on all night. I remembered a Holocaust survivor who lived around the corner from me in Cleveland Heights. She was a legend in the neighborhood, the absolute favorite for Halloween trick-or-treaters, and a popular volunteer at the library. Teachers from my high school would bring her in to regale us with her horror stories. She'd speak nonstop from bell to bell with always the same story: her mother, who she never saw again, urging her and her younger sister out the window to escape the roundup, sewing mattresses in Chelmno on less than a thousand calories a day, meeting Anne and Margot Frank at Bergen Belsen, and a wild escape run into the forest with the help of Jewish partisans during the end-of-war death marches. Once, my father dragged me along for a home visit after her cancer surgery. Without prompting—without even a greeting—she told the same stories and then sang the partisan song, then told the stories again and burst into song. It seemed to go on for hours. I wondered if this was typical of Holocaust survivors—a desperate search for an audience, a purging, or a venting of toxins into the air.

Sleepiness inserted itself into my eyes as he spoke, but I didn't have the nerve to interrupt. Anyway, parts of him fascinated me. He was the friendliest, warmest teacher I'd ever known, and he seemed genuinely fond of me. But with his incongruous smiles and impish giggles, offered during the worst recounting of torture and tragedy, he generated a weird suspense. Would the kindly professor façade melt away? Would he fall apart? Would I?

He continued with his disquisition on blame. "In Israel, we took blame in a different direction. We came up with our own elegant, convenient solution to the question of blame. We blamed each other." He tilted the beer bottle back and drained it down his throat. Then, he opened a new one—Maccabi, another Israeli brand. I noticed Zehava tiptoeing into the room, rejoining us in her armchair. For the first time, I spotted wrinkles on her forehead. She looked even more tired than me.

"The *haredim*—the ultra-Orthodox, you call them—blamed the secular Zionists. This was God's punishment, yes, for defying His will and returning from Exile before the coming of the Messiah. 'Pushing the fence,' they call it. The Germans were merely instruments of God's will, the tool God used for revenge against our cosmic impatience. How a loving, just God would orchestrate a punishment that involves throwing innocent babies into the crematoria, well, they never quite explain how this could be so. Anyway, for them, for now, theology is not the point. Not really. The point was, *is*, a target for their fiery anger. Yes? These heretical Zionists, they say. *They* provoked God. We should not look to blame our sorrows on outside enemies. The fault is in the family. Fellow Jews. Yes?

"And who do the secular Zionists blame? Of course, they blame the ultra-Orthodox! They stare at the black coats, the long beards, the wigs, the strollers packed with weeping children, the flapping *tsitsit*, and they point their secular Zionist fingers in blame and disgust. Honestly, the nausea they feel in their stomachs when they see these black hats is almost as severe as Hitler's nausea in Vienna when he first encounters the Jew. Because when they see the kapote and the *shtreimil* and the sheitel and the kittel and the gigantic tallis and the *tsitit*, they see the Jewish anti-Zionists who slowed down the Zionist project long enough for Hitler to murder one million children. If, they say, these passive fanatics had embraced the Zionist cause instead of spitting on it, rejecting it, yes, if they all would have moved to Palestine when they had the chance, with their dozens of babies in each family, we would have had a state in the 1930s, and we would have saved those murdered children."

Zehava sighed. Chaim looked at her and smiled. He was suddenly quiet, and he wasn't drinking. Zehava turned to me. Were they waiting for my comment? "Okay," I said. It was all I had.

"Make sense to you, yes?" Chaim said.

"Well, no," I admitted.

He clapped his hands. It was a sharp pistol sound. "Of course, it doesn't make sense," he snapped. It was the first time I'd heard him angry. I searched for the impish grin, the warm laugh, but they'd been expelled. *Is he angry at me?* "The point, Judah, yes, the point itself is that neither claim makes sense. This blaming the other family member, blaming the victim, makes no logical sense. Especially to an American. There are a thousand holes in each bill of indictment, and we don't have the time or energy to point out each one, yes? Anyway, you see it, intuitively, you said it yourself. It makes no sense. Logically. But emotionally? Or let me say it more precisely, yes, in the realm of myth, of the mystical unconscious, from the point of view of narrative, of how we tell our primal stories. Ah, there, it makes perfect sense."

I nodded. It still made no sense to me. I wondered if he was finally finished.

"This is our crisis, Judah. The crisis no one but me and few others see. We will never flourish as a nation if we continue to blame each other for the worst catastrophe of all time."

"Chaim," Zehava said. "I think we should let Judah go. You see, he's tired, and it's a long walk back to Mt. Scopus, right, Judah?"

I nodded again, somehow unable to speak. In fact, I wasn't taking the long walk back to the dorm that night. I'd be walking less than half a block to Michal's place. We'd agreed I'd spend the night again. She'd given me her spare key. But I was tired, and Chaim's monologue left me uneasy and oddly guilty.

"Of course," Chaim said. "Just one more point, Judah, if you'll permit me. And an invitation. You see, this is my project. This is why I spend so much time with the *haredim* these days. It's not merely because I admire their senseless tenacity—though I do. I have a plan for a grand reconciliation between secular and religious in this country. It's too late to go into details, yes? It has to do with theology. Judah, the fact is, I'm getting older. My hip—the pain may never go away. My cursed knee. My thoughts have become suddenly scattered. I need assistance. I need a student aid for this work, yes?"

He waited. "Yes," I managed to answer.

"I've decided this student is you." He smiled, the gentle professor, the mischievous imp. Zehava, I noticed, wasn't smiling.

"I'm not sure," I said. "My other classes. You understand." I thought madly for other excuses. He probably knew that my other classes required almost no work in my program.

He put up his hand. "Of course, you'll think about it. And then you'll tell me, yes? But one favor, if you please. Come with me tomorrow. Every Sunday morning, a group of religious men study the Zohar in the tunnel on the men's side of the Kotel. A great haredi rabbi teaches the class. I study with them. They invited me. Please, Judah, tomorrow, you'll accompany me. You'll meet the haredi of the haredi, the black of the black, as we say. You'll start to understand how they think, yes? You'll learn something real and true about this country. And, yes, you'll carry my books, perhaps take notes, and help me navigate my diseased hip and wretched knee through the cobblestone. Seven a.m., Judah, at the tunnel entrance." He leaned back and studied me, head to toe. "Maybe some different shoes, yes?" I glanced at my white Adidas, scuffed and dirty. I was afraid to tell him that, except for my sandals, they were all I brought with me to Israel. He looked at my hair, tilted his face, and guessed my hat size. "I'll bring you a big yarmulke."

Then, as if all had been decided, the purpose of the evening successfully fulfilled, Zehava and Chaim stood, Zehava with athletic grace, Chaim grunting and pushing down hard on the armrest. They moved so abruptly. I remained seated for a few seconds, watching them look down and smile at me like parents beaming at their bright four-year-old. Then, I scrambled to my feet. Chaim took my hand, and Zehava kissed my cheek.

They walked me to the door. Zehava opened it. I was just about to step through when I caught a glimpse of a family photo on a side table by the entrance. A young Chaim and Zehava stood smiling on both sides of an eight- or nine-year-old boy with wild, wet dark-brown hair. He glared at the camera through thick-lensed glasses, smiling like a nervous chimp. They were posed in the sand, the blue ocean just a few feet behind them. Zehava looked surprisingly attractive in a bright yellow one-piece bathing suit. Curly reddish-blond hair flowed past her shoulders. Chaim's face, smiling and sunburned, was the picture of sunny satisfaction.

Netanya, I guessed, though it could have been some beach anywhere, even California.

"How is Yoav?" I asked.

Chaim and Zehava looked at each other, waiting for the other to answer. Zehava finally turned to me. "The truth is, it's been difficult."

"The army is not an easy place for our Yoav," Chaim said. "He handles communication for his unit. In the rear but always part of the battle."

I nodded, trying to think of a sympathetic response that wouldn't provoke another lecture. "I'm sure," I said, as if I were an experienced infantryman myself.

"It's this Lebanon adventure," Zehava said.

"Zehava," Chaim said quickly. She glared at him. Something passed between them. But it would have to play out without me. I mumbled another quick goodbye and left.

Michal was sleeping when I arrived at her apartment. I thought about walking back to my dorm room. But I remembered my 7 a.m. date with Chaim. Michal's place was much closer to the Old City. Michal's arms and legs were sprawled out, covering the twin bed. So, I curled up on the couch and fell asleep right away.

♦ ♦ ♦

There was a chill in the air first thing in the morning at the Western Wall. After a hot summer and a bone-dry autumn, winter was finally, clearly announcing itself, though I was strangely comfortable jacket-less and with sandals. I misjudged the walk, so I was there greeting the sun at 6:45 a.m. Five minutes later, Chaim limped toward me with a black coat, white shirt, blue tie, and professorial impish grin. He carried a multicolored Arab-style head covering in one hand and a pile of books in the other, but no cane. He plopped the yarmulke on my head, then handed me the books. "You are so kind," he said.

He led me through the stone archway into the tunneled section of the Kotel. The chamber was already half-filled with black-hatted, black-coated men swaying, shuckling, chanting, and mumbling. Many stood flush with the wall itself, touching the stones with their fingertips or foreheads. Chaim led me to the narrow, far end of the tunnel. We turned into a small chamber about the size of my childhood bedroom. One bare lightbulb hung from the ceiling. The floor was unvarnished concrete. I thought of cobwebs, mice, dungeons, but the room was comfortable enough. A dozen or so folding chairs were arrayed in a circle, half of them occupied by middle-aged men in dark business suits and large black yarmulkes. Three of them read Hebrew newspapers; the rest chatted softly. They all nodded silently at Chaim and looked at me, puzzled. Chaim pointed to two empty chairs, and we sat. He leaned forward and whispered in my ear, "The deputy defense minister." He nodded at a man across the circle. "And over there, a former finance minister. And there, the director general of the foreign ministry, yes? Next to him, the CEO of Bank Leumi." Despite the room's dampness, we were evidently in the VIP section. At exactly seven o'clock, an ancient-looking man with a long black coat, black hat, and full white beard shuffled slowly into the room, flanked by two younger haredim, who gripped his elbows, helping him walk. The assistants also carried thick piles of books. As soon as they all sat, books on their laps, the newspapers were put aside, and the room was as quiet as an abandoned church. The teacher leaned forward, closed his eyes, took two long, deep breaths, and began.

It took me several minutes to realize that the class consisted of short readings in Aramaic, followed by explanations, discussions, arguments, questions, digressions, and jokes, all in Hebrew. I knew exactly zero Aramaic, and despite having lived in Israel for three months, I'd only mastered enough Hebrew to order in restaurants or ask directions. I caught a few Hebrew words—mi, mah, and lamah, the words for "who," "what," and "why"—and several proclamations of mah pitom, Hebrew slang for "what on earth are you talking about?" I also heard a few muttered exclamations of "yah ben zona," Hebrew for "you son of a bitch," a popular epithet that I'd only heard before directed at soccer referees. For the first ten minutes, Chaim sat silently, staring intently at the page in one of his large leather-bound volumes as if it held the secret of immortality. But suddenly, he looked up, smiled, wiped his glasses, took a breath, and asked a short, two, maybe three-word question. The man from the finance ministry whispered, "Yah ben zonah" loud enough for everyone to hear. The deputy defense minister laughed hard, cackling like the Wicked Witch at Chaim, not with him. The white-bearded teacher gently put down his book and rested his face in his open hands. For the next half hour, loud guttural Hebrew filled the room, much of it directed at Chaim. He gave as good as he got. He shouted like a drill sergeant, sang his objections like a yeshiva bucher, and rolled his Rs like a Yemenite. Finally, the teacher seemed to snap awake. He pounded his book twice and yelled, "Sha!" Then, he turned to the cave ceiling—or maybe the heavens—and mumbled what I assumed was a prayer. Then, everyone stood up, shook hands genially, smiled warmly, and departed quickly as if no intellectual combat had occurred.

As Chaim gathered his sacred volumes and handed them to me to carry, I asked what the argument had been about.

"Ah, not an argument, yes? A disputation. We call it a makhloket. A disagreement for the sake of heaven. You see, we were studying a section from the Zohar about God's names. You would like to see, no?" He snatched the top book off the pile and flipped through the pages.

"I can't read Aramaic," I told him. "Or Hebrew," I added. And, in case there was any misunderstanding about the extent of my inabilities, I said, "I can't really speak or understand it, either."

He shrugged and tilted his head as if my ignorance were an interesting curiosity, not something that would disqualify me from working for him. "Well," he said. "Let me explain. You see, the rabbis in the Zohar are playing with this verse: 'Look at the sky; who created these?' The Hebrew is *Mi barah eleh*—you see, the Hebrew word '*Mi*" means 'who.' But this is their game. They claim that *Mi*—that is 'who'—is a name of God. 'Who created these?' then is not a question. It's a statement. God, whose other name is 'Who,' created the universe. God's name is a question. To invoke God's name is to ask a question, to search for an answer. Spirituality is inquiry. This is fascinating, yes?"

Or it's funny, I thought, *like the Abbot and Costello sketch.* Who's on first? Exactly, replied the ever-baffled Abbot.

"And the passage continues," Chaim said, moving his finger a few lines down the page. "Now the rabbis discuss grief, particularly the devastating national grief of losing the war to Rome, the total destruction. How did they reach this topic? To show us another name of God. More wordplay. Here's the verse from Isaiah: 'You've lost it all. What can comfort you?' Of course, you and I read this as a rhetorical question. 'What can comfort you' means no one can comfort you. You've reached a level of suffering beyond help. What can comfort you? Nothing! That's what the verse means. Yes?"

Usually, his "yes" or "no" interjections were conversational tics. They didn't call for responses. But this time, he seemed to require an answer. "Yes," I said. It seemed the easiest thing to say.

"Yes! But those tricksters, the rabbis of the Zohar, they say that the Hebrew word *'mah'*—meaning 'what'—is another name for God. Again, God's name is a question—just a different question this time, yes? We have questions about the stars; our question is 'Who?' We have different questions about suffering; our question is 'What?' Asking these questions brings us closer to God, and thinking of God raises these questions, no?"

He'd sort of lost me, but I didn't want to admit it, and I definitely didn't want him to stop. I nodded. He must have been satisfied because he continued.

"Rabbi Kaplowitz." He gestured to the white-bearded teacher who was still seated at his place in the circle, sipping tea. His two young *haredi* companions stood on either side, like a mini Jewish Praetorian Guard. "He taught me something marvelous today. That the word *'Mi'*—that is 'Who'—is the aspect of God that is remote from human experience. We can sense him slightly by staring at stars or contemplating nature, yes? But otherwise, this aspect is distant. But '*Mah*'—'What'—is the aspect of God that is close to our hearts and souls. We find this God not in the stars but by looking inward, exploring the divinity that everyone enjoys. And here's the teaching, which, I must say, I never heard before. And please, Judah, don't get lost in the wordplay or the ingenious manipulation of scripture. The lesson is very simple. If you're suffering, God will help you. But it's that part of God that is already within you that rises to the rescue. A part of yourself, the divine part, untouched by pain, that is the seed of healing. This divine healing energy is there. Its name is "*Mah*"—"What." You just must keep asking questions. By engaging in this inquiry, you discover the God within yourself. And that begins the healing. This is a beautiful notion, yes? Not so different from modern therapeutic theories, no?"

We'd progressed much farther than Abbot and Costello. I assumed he was thinking of the Shoah and his own suffering, which made the lesson immediately and poignantly relevant to him. Unfortunately, at the time, I didn't have enough experience with sorrow to truly understand Rabbi Kaplowitz's teaching. It would come later. "That was the whole discussion?" I asked. "It sounded like you were arguing."

He chuckled. "Yes, well, that was my fault. I added a touch of heresy to the proceedings. They're used to it by now, but somehow, they retain the capacity for shock. Though, personally, I think it's playacting. They have to pretend to be offended. But they always invite me back."

I thought of the swear words, the flushed faces, the clenched fists. It didn't seem like playacting. "What did you say?"

"I simply asked a question. I said if two of God's names are 'What' and 'Who,' what about that other common interrogative? 'Why.' Shouldn't 'Why' also be one of God's names? Meaning when we approach God, we must always ask, 'Why?'"

I thought for a second. "'Here there is no why,'" I said, quoting Lerner at my first meal with him. The sentence the Nazi guard hurled at Chaim defined, for him, the evil nihilism of Auschwitz.

"Ah, you remember. You're so kind."

"Asking why is heretical?"

"Not necessarily. But demanding 'why' of God. Seeing the very act of asking why as the essence of the human relationship with God? Yes, this makes them uncomfortable. Or maybe not. Like I said, it's likely they are playing their parts in a *makhloket*—a disputation for the sake of heaven. After all, these are my friends, yes? I've been studying with them for almost two years."

I felt a cool breeze caress my face. The wind outside the tunnel must have picked up. *Autumn*, I thought. Later and milder than in Cleveland and Chicago, but still inevitable. I waited for Chaim to lead the way, then turned to follow while he limped, my arms sagging with books. I stopped cold when I felt a hand tightly gripping my forearm. It was Rabbi Kaplowitz. I noticed how short he was. He barely reached my chin. He looked up at me and held my gaze for several seconds without speaking. His damp eyes suggested tears, rheumatism, or hay fever. I would have guessed from his wrinkles and beard that he was eighty-five or ninety, but the steel grip of his bony fingers made me think twice. He smiled warmly. "You are the student of Dr. Lerner," he said with just a slight accent.

"I'm *a* student," I said. The pinch of his fingers began to hurt. Could I pull away without insulting him? His two companions flanked him on either side. They regarded me closely, suspiciously, as if I were a terrorist unless proven otherwise.

He clicked his tongue—an Israeli gesture meaning sharp disagreement. "You are *the* student. You are the student he brings to our little session. He has great plans for you."

I looked for Chaim and saw that he had already reached the mouth of the cave and was limping forward. He wasn't slowing down for me. But the old rabbi still gripped my arm.

"You are fortunate," he said. "Fortunate to have such a teacher." His companions both frowned. They seemed to disapprove of their rabbi's statement. Or maybe it was just the fact of him speaking to me that they disliked.

"I agree," I said.

"He is a good man. A mensch."

"Yes," I said.

He reached for the top of my head so he could pull my face down. I thought he was going to bless me. But he whispered in my ear, "Be careful."

I didn't understand. I shook my head.

"Be careful," he repeated and pushed me away. "Your teacher is waiting for you."

◆ ◆ ◆

That night, I struggled to explain to Michal how the Zohar class in the cave moved me. "I couldn't understand a word," I said. "Or, maybe, one word, here and there. The swear words. I mean, it could have been Russian. Or Latin. But I was captivated. It was like watching a symphony from another planet. I didn't want it to end."

We were drinking coffee in Michal's kitchen. Like many Israelis, she drank coffee at night before bed and still slept like a baby. I'd be up all night. For the first time since I'd been hanging out in Michal's flat, I wondered when she'd put the heat on. I shivered, then cupped my hands around my still-warm coffee mug. I shook my head. "In the end, I can't really describe it; it became adversarial. Chaim was his usual jovial self, smiling, chuckling. But the other men in the circle—especially the non-haredi, the guys in business suits, the VIPs—looked like they wanted to kill him. Chaim tried to explain it to me. It was some argument about wordplay—how to understand God's names." I shrugged, then took a tiny sip of coffee. I didn't want to drink it; I only wanted it as a source of heat.

"Well, of course, they hated him," Michal said. She sounded impatient with me. That was unusual, at least at that stage of our still-young relationship. I looked at her, surprised. "Think of what he's teaching in our class," she continued. "What he writes about."

"Theodicy," I said. I thought for a moment. "Job. Questioning God."

"Yeah, but what's his solution?"

I remembered. Lerner's was the only class where I paid attention. "The weak God. Not all-powerful. Wants to help but really can't. Okay, I can see how that would piss off the black hats. But the guys in business suits? The government guys? Hate-filled looks because of theology?"

"Sure, it's possible. Just because educated Americans don't take God seriously doesn't mean others don't. Religion is a big deal here, even if you don't wear a shtreimel. A whole new definition of God. How do you think they'd react? And, Chaim, you know. He's a celebrity in Israel. He's our Eli Wiesel. People listen to him, so politicians and rabbis care about what he says. And not just his theology. I'm guessing there was another reason those government guys got so angry. It's the war."

In my junior year of galivanting about the country and my desperate, budding romance, it was often easy to forget that, in fact, Israel was at war. A great deal of its army was stationed beyond the border in Lebanon. Thousands of boys my age fought battles every day with Lebanese militias and Palestinian terrorist groups. But the closest I'd come to combat was watching Charlie clean his gun. "What about the war?" I asked. I remembered him defending the Lebanon operation from Zehava's attacks. "They hate him because he supports the government?"

"What?" Michal asked. She moved aside her coffee cup so she could look me in the eye. Her face whitened, like she was developing leprosy. Had she always been this pale? "Boy," she said, disgusted. "You really don't know anything."

I thought of getting up without a word and hiking back to Mt. Scopus on my own. How am I supposed to respond? Yes, I do know some things? But actually, I didn't. Not really.

Michal reached across the table for a newspaper. She flipped to the second page and shoved the article under my nose. "Look!" she said, pointing at a bold Hebrew headline. I looked up at her and shook my head. Was she going to make me say it? The only things I could understand on the page were the pictures: a leopard in a zoo, a muezzin and a mosque, and, oddly, a topless young woman holding a rubber duck. "Oh, right," Michal said. "No Hebrew. I'll read it to you." She zoomed through the Hebrew in the most rapid reading I had ever heard, then translated to English. Chaim was preparing a statement condemning the Lebanon War and every decision the government had made leading up to the conflict. Evidently, the purpose of the statement was to influence public opinion. Chaim Lerner, the saintly Holocaust survivor, the beloved public intellectual and theologian, who up until then had stayed out of politics, was taking a stand.

"I don't get it," I said. "Twice, at the dinners, I heard him call out Zehava because she criticized the war. Just last night, she called it an adventure, and he shushed her."

"Zehava supports the war," Michal said. She crumbled the newspaper and set it aside. "Not the government, per se—she's in the opposition. But she supports the aims and even the execution of the invasion."

I shook my head. "I don't understand."

She rubbed her eyes and then sat still, her chin resting on the palm of her hand. "I guess now's the time to tell you," she said. "You're getting close to him. I can see that. You're fond of them. Great. But you need to know this. Nothing about Chaim and Zehava is what it seems. Nothing."

"What do you mean?"

She reached behind her back and shut off the light. She got up slowly and walked to the bedroom.

Are we fighting? What are we fighting about? I knew less about quarreling couples than I knew about Israeli politics. Am I supposed to follow her into the bedroom? I did.

She turned around but made no motion to stop me. "Nothing is what it seems with them," she repeated. "Nothing."

♦ ♦ ♦

The next morning, she woke up cheerful and loving. She held my hand as we made breakfast together and called me motek—sweetie—several times. Whatever had irritated her the previous evening, she was over it. I considered saying the three words—I love you—but I didn't want to push my luck.

It was Monday, and we both had a full load of classes. But she urged me to skip. She wanted to take me to her favorite store in the Old City. It didn't take much convincing. To my consternation, we biked to the Arab market. We petaled through traffic, zigging and zagging past tiny, white Renaults, huge buses, and delivery trucks. Michal answered each car horn with her middle finger, sending me into a panic whenever she lifted her hand off the handlebars. What a weird way to die in Israel, I thought. Not by terrorism, not by war. Smashed by a truck while riding a bike with my first girlfriend. At least my parents would be impressed that she was Jewish.

We glided through the Jaffa Gate, and Michal squeezed the breaks. I quickly climbed off and hopped three feet away so she'd know I'd had enough. She laughed. "Even I know enough not to ride through the market," she said. We walked the bike through the crowded alleyway. The first set of stores were all for tourists, selling yarmulkes and crosses, backgammon sets, mini drums, and carpets. But as we traveled deeper into the market, past the cafés and bakeries, we reached a few practical stores for residents—grocery stores, barbers, shoe repairs, leather goods, and keffiyeh shops. I trusted Michal's every zig and zag. I would have been hopelessly lost after the fifth turn, but she clearly knew where she was going. It took us less than ten minutes of fast walking.

"Rafik," she called out when we stopped in front of the largest store I'd seen in the shuk. The tables in front held rows and rows of silver tea sets, gold Turkish coffee pots, and water pipes. Beyond the water pipes, I could see modern clothing: jeans, polo shirts, sweaters. Beyond that, chess, checkers, and backgammon. A department store, the Macy's of the Arab Market.

A tall, skinny man with jet-black hair and a mustache rushed to greet us. He embraced Michal like a long-lost daughter. They jabbered for a few minutes in Arabic; then, she pointed to me. He laughed, clapped his hands, then kissed me on both cheeks long enough for me to feel his day-old whiskers. "You're lucky, man," he told me. I couldn't disagree.

He took us to his office, a store corner with huge red, gold, and blue Persian carpets stacked on top of each other. We sat on large cushions. He lit a human-sized water pipe, took a long drag, and handed it to Michal. She giggled and put it to her mouth. It seemed like she didn't inhale, but I couldn't tell. She handed it to me. "What's in here?" I asked. They laughed. I inhaled deeply, coughed, then inhaled again. Tobacco, I thought. Probably just tobacco.

After smoking a few rounds, Rafik took us to the back of the store. The shelves were filled with robes, pants, dresses, and veils, all in thick, dark red fabrics. Michal surprised me by cooing with delight and choosing two robes and a dress. "I collect this stuff," she told me. Rafik nodded, expressed his approval in Arabic, gestured to us, and pointed to a row of ankle-length, long-sleeved dresses with bright colors—green, blue, yellow, gold, orange, turquoise—smashed together in a wild, festive display. Oddly, they smelled like animal flesh, as if made of donkey hide and not cotton. "Bedouin wedding dresses," Michal whispered to me, though there was no reason to whisper. It was like she was in church. "Aren't they incredibly beautiful?" I wondered if she was joking. They were impressive. A little scary. Disorienting. Beautiful? Maybe.

"One day for you," Rafik said.

Michal laughed. Rafik looked at me and winked. "Maybe soon?"

Michal took my arm. "Who knows?" she said. "Maybe soon."

CHAPTER 7

July 2005

After two quick showers, Michal took us to an outdoor café on the Ben Yehuda mall. She waited until I agreed to let Hannah wander on her own through downtown Jerusalem before laying into me. First, as a kind of warm-up, she scolded my parenting skills. "You let your teenage daughter roam freely in a foreign country?"

After a warm morning, the noonday sun hung in the air. Heat was settling in. I asked our waitress for more water, and she quickly fetched us a large bottle. "Service has gotten a lot better in the country," I said, filling both our glasses. "In 1983, I would have had to really work to get the waitress to pay attention to me. And even then, she wouldn't have brought us a whole bottle. Or put ice in it."

"You've heard of the intifada?" she said, quickly changing the subject. "Suicide bombers, especially downtown? You let your daughter loose?"

I looked around. The cobblestone mall was packed with rushing pedestrians, street musicians, jewelry hawkers, café diners, tourists, and shoppers. Even dogs on leashes, something I didn't remember from last time. The crowd included several gangs of teenagers who marched down the street, laughing and singing, clearly unafraid. I'd read just that morning that violence from the Second Intifada had leveled off. At least for now. "Looks pretty safe to me."

"And if she gets lost?"

I studied Michal. The longer we sat together, alone, without Hannah, the easier it was to imagine that I'd commandeered a time machine, traveled back twenty-two years to my junior year of college. Back as a visitor on a tourist visa, not as a permanent resident. My life after Michal couldn't be erased. At least not that easily. "She has a phone. We got them at the airport. You arranged it. Remember?" I drained my water glass and poured another. I didn't remember Jerusalem getting quite this hot. But maybe I'd become more sensitive. "Do you want to tell me why you're angry at me?"

She waited, watched the crowds. Then turned to me. "What are you doing here?"

"I'm pretty sure I explained it."

"Chaim? You want to write about Chaim? Read his books. A lot of his lectures are on YouTube. Critique his works. Or celebrate his ideas. You don't need to fly across the globe for this, to bother his family. Or drag your daughter to Israel."

"You know it's not just about his ideas."

"His suicide? Really? That's your angle?"

"Maybe it wasn't suicide."

She slapped the table. I remembered her temper, pursed lips, furious, wide-open eyes, and sudden Israeli accent. Slapping tables, or whatever else was available. She'd only gotten this angry once, maybe twice, during my junior year. But it was memorable. "Are you serious? That's why you're here? You're a conspiracy theorist now? What next, the Kennedy assassination? You think maybe Jim Morrison is alive and lives in Tel Aviv?"

Actually, I had written pieces on the Kennedy assassination, and I'd expressed my suspicions about Jim Morrison's quick cremation on my blog. "It's my job, Michal. You may have noticed that print journalism isn't exactly thriving. I got an advance for this project: look into Chaim Lerner's mysterious death. I need the work."

"Mysterious death? For God's sake. Mysterious to who? To Hannah? Do you know what opening this can of worms will do to Zehava? You want to break her heart again? And think about her position. You've followed her career? She's a very important lady here. Too busy for this nonsense."

Of course, I knew that Zehava had become the leading figure in Israel's political opposition. Her eloquence and activism during the Second Intifada had propelled her to the elite of Israel's political class. Many respectable pundits predicted she'd become the next prime minister, the first woman since Golda Meir. "I imagine Zehava can take care of herself. Besides, she doesn't seem opposed to my project. She invited me to dinner."

"You're a reporter! Of course, she invited you for dinner. She's seducing you; she seduces every journalist. It doesn't mean she wants to relive her husband's suicide—the worst moment of her life." She took a quick sip of water. Then, she looked around the café. She must have feared that she was speaking too loudly because the next question came out almost as a whisper. "And what about Yoav?"

I waited. Had I heard correctly? I replayed the question in my mind. "What about Yoav?" I asked.

"It's a scab, Judah. An ugly scar. Yoav's never gotten over it. I know you think it's twenty-two years ago, so now for you, it's a historical curiosity, a fun mystery, like who really killed Kennedy. But we're still living with it. Anyway, it's not a mystery! He killed himself."

"Maybe," I said. "I'm not so sure. I hear there's some new evidence."

"What are you talking about? New evidence? Don't you think the family would know if there was really new evidence? What new evidence?"

This wasn't the time to go over my file. I needed a night's sleep, and Hannah would be back any minute. So, I stuck to my primary question. "Why didn't he leave a note?"

"Are you fucking serious? The note question? You're still asking about that? We know the answer. Most suicides don't leave notes. They're too fucking depressed."

"Chaim wasn't most people. He was a writer. He dedicated his life to articulating evil and suffering with his unique set of words."

"Oh, that's lunacy. That's your hero-worship. He didn't leave a note because . . ."

She stopped suddenly because Hannah appeared, smiling, humming, and drinking something from a large paper cup. She plopped down next to Michal. "I love Jerusalem," she said. "This is the best coffee I've ever drunk."

Does she have a lot of experience drinking coffee? At least it isn't beer. "Where did you go?" I asked.

She hesitated. I noticed Michal was staring at her intently, waiting for her answer. "Sbarros," she said.

Michal gasped, then shot me a deadly look. "There is no more Sbarros," she said.

"I mean where it used to be," Hannah said, a touch defensive. She turned to me. "It's my school project," she said. "I told you I had to do some research while I was here."

I didn't understand. "Your school project is about Israeli pizza restaurants?"

"Judah," Michal said. "Sbarro's was blown up by a suicide bomber. Almost two years ago. Twenty people murdered."

Hannah nodded. "That's my project," she said. "Suicide bombers."

"Oh my fucking God," Michal said, talking to Hannah but staring accusingly at me.

"I also bought some sandals," Hannah said. She pointed to her chest. "And a new shirt."

◆ ◆ ◆

Zehava answered the doorbell less than one second after I pressed it. She smiled and embraced me warmly, with a hint of desperation, like I was a son home from the war. I smelled clover, and the scent immediately transported me back twenty-two years to the last time I'd hugged her, not long before Chaim died. She grabbed my shoulders and pushed me back, lifting her head, taking me in.

"Amazing," she said. "You haven't changed at all."

The statement was so obviously untrue, I didn't know how to respond. My hair was now almost entirely gray. I wore contact lenses, not glasses. I sported a healthy paunch and had added twenty pounds. Back then, the first word people used to describe my physical appearance was lanky. Nobody called me lanky now. Zehava, on the other hand, did look very much the same. Partly, that was because she always looked to me like a matriarch—strong and spirited and protective—old enough to care for a flock of children but otherwise of indeterminate age.

Also, her hair was still the same exact shade of brown, though that was easily explained. Still, if I hadn't known better, I would have guessed fifty or maybe fifty-five. But doing the math, I knew she was at least seventy. She didn't look it.

She hugged Hannah with nearly the same ardor that she'd given me. "Judah, your daughter is a young lady," she said. "I was expecting a child." She gripped Hannah's shoulders the same way she'd grabbed me, then looked her up and down. "I love your sandals," she said. "And what a beautiful shirt. And your hair, oh my. Hannah, I love everything about you."

Hannah seemed absolutely stumped by Zehava's display of affection. Normally never at a loss for words, she stood paralyzed in the doorway, looking at me. "I love you too," she finally said, turning to Zehava, and we all laughed. We followed Zehava into the living room. I was astonished that the apartment was exactly how I remembered it. Same love seat and stuffed armchairs, same dining room chairs and tables, same Persian rug, perhaps a shade or two duller. I even spotted Chaim's desk next to the kitchen, cluttered, as it was back then, with thick, leather-bound sacred volumes, paperback novels, scattered pens, and loose papers. Zehava clearly preserved everything. The whole flat stood as a sacred altar dedicated to the memory of Chaim Lerner. Even the balcony furniture hadn't changed.

If Zehava smothered us with warmth, Yoav chilled me to the bone. He carefully studied my every move, as if he were a security guard and I was a likely suicide bomber. He winced whenever Hannah spoke, as if she were banging hard on an untuned piano or emitting an unpleasant odor. Michal completely ignored me. But she peppered Hannah with questions, inquiring about American high schools, Jewish boys, popular music, girls' soccer, celebrity gossip, college applications, clothes, and books. She had a weird intuitive sense of what was interesting to American teenagers.

For me, this wasn't a night for research or interrogation. That would come later. This was a night to become reacquainted, to win Zehava's trust, and maybe even Michal's, so my official interviews with them could bear fruit. Anyway, I was hitting a wall after my endless flight, sleeplessness, and jet lag. My head was in constant danger of falling on my plate. I wouldn't have been able to interview my own mother.

So, Hannah became the star of the evening. During the main course—lamb kebabs, shakshuka, hummus, pita, and salads—she regaled us all with stories from her soccer team. Reading the crowd, she called it "football," which confused only me. I kept picturing her as a linebacker covered with pads. She described each of the ten goals she'd scored in the spring season, exaggerating only slightly. As Zehava served the baklava and vanilla halvah—two deserts I despised—Hannah moved on from "football" and recounted her featured role as Yenta in our JCC production of Fiddler on the Roof. She sang a few bars of "Anatevka," the final number. Zehava sang along; Michal beamed; Yoav glared. Sipping espresso—I was too tired to stop her from ingesting the caffeine—she started to describe the topics from her favorite class, Speech and Debate. But she suddenly fell silent and looked at me. I tried a subtle head shake, then realized the fruitlessness of hidden gestures in such a small group. Instead, I stood and thanked Zehava for a beautiful evening. No one else stood, not even Hannah.

"Tell us about your debate class, Hannah," Michal said. I sat.

Hannah shrugged. "Israel and Palestine was the whole topic the second half of the semester."

"Israel and Palestine," Michal said. "You mean Israel and the territories? Israel and the West Bank? As of today, there is no Palestine, if I'm not mistaken."

Hannah was unshaken. "Well, yeah, okay. Whatever. It was about the Occupation. That's how I got interested in suicide bombings."

"I see," Michal said. Yoav noisily helped himself to more halvah. Zehava kept up a smile at Hannah but looked worried. I yawned. I wanted to escape and get myself and Hannah to bed, but fatigue rendered me useless. "Tell us about suicide bombings," Michal said.

Hannah spoke for a good five minutes about fanaticism, conditions in the Gaza Strip and West Bank, Islamic teachings, economic incentives, and madness. It seemed smart and unobjectionable. Even Yoav paid attention, nodding occasionally. But then she spoke about suicide in general—differing motivations, depression, trauma, hopelessness, chronic pain. She mentioned her mother. I was moved and proud. She seemed to be winding down after dedicating a few words to suicide notes when Yoav interrupted.

"And this is related to my father?" he said. He spoke softly, with a quiet fury.

Hannah looked at him. She had the presence of mind and maturity to say nothing.

"You are comparing my father—your mother!—to a suicide bomber? You think there is a similarity? Tell me, do you know how many innocent Israelis these suicide bombers have murdered? How many children they've blown to bits, yes? My father was a humanitarian! You dare compare him to these wild animals?"

"Yoav," Zehava snapped. "She's a young girl. Fifteen!" Then she barked a few words in Hebrew, a language that confounded me even more after twenty-two years.

"Fine!" Yoav replied. "I'll talk to the father. I think he's old enough, yes?" He turned to me like a prosecuting attorney facing a wicked defendant. "Why are you here?"

I so wish I wasn't, I thought to say. *I wish I wasn't here in this room. I wish I was in a bed, any bed, anywhere.*

"Is it my father's reputation you want to destroy?" Yoav continued. He opened his gray eyes so wide that I felt like Jonah contemplating the whale. "Or my mother's? Or do you simply enjoy inflicting emotional pain? And using your daughter as a shield."

Zehava and Michal yelled at Yoav in Hebrew, and he volleyed back with his own guttural exclamations. Hannah observed from her seat, wide-eyed, more fascinated than frightened. I woke up enough to stand up and apologize. "You're right, Yoav," I said.

Like engines sputtering to a halt, it took them a minute or so to spit out their final arguments, but then they looked up at me and listened. "This was an inappropriate topic for this evening," I said. "We apologize. Right, Hannah?"

Again, making me proud, she nodded quickly. "Oh, yeah. Definitely. Apologize! I'm just a kid. So sorry."

We took our leave. I confirmed my appointments with Yoav and Zehava. At the door, Yoav thrust out his hand, and I took it. He squeezed limply, as if shaking my hand didn't merit any extra energy. Michal shocked me by kissing me on the cheek. Zehava hugged us both. We were still descending the steps, not yet outside, when Hannah whispered, "Asshole." I wanted to reprimand her language, but instead, I laughed. I couldn't help myself.

At our two-bedroom vacation shack, a quick walk from the Lerner's, I had one more task to fulfill before falling into bed. I called Charlie. He welcomed me to Israel, asked about Hannah, and wondered how I was holding up with all the suicide talk.

"I'm exhausted," I told him.

"Of course."

"Any news?" I asked.

"Oh, yeah," he said. "Lots of news. Just waiting for you to arrive. Ready to get to work?"

I took a breath. I thought about Yoav's question. Why am I here? "I'm ready," I said.

CHAPTER 8

1994-1995

The diagnosis didn't surprise me, but it seemed to astonish Mary. I'd noticed the hard nodule in her breast months before—oddly, on our wedding anniversary. I'd been nagging her since that night to get it checked out, but like many doctors, she ignored her own symptoms. Finally, I got her partner, our family doc—Mary's college roommate—to ambush her one night after work. Palpations, blood tests, biopsy—an all-in-one excruciatingly slow week—and finally, the inevitable verdict—cancer. Mary had them run every test again. Same result.

We weren't particularly frightened at first. I should say I wasn't particularly frightened; Mary refused to discuss anything about the disease other than coordinating child care so she could make oncology appointments. Breast cancer was eminently treatable. We both knew several young women who'd beaten it.

Even after we found out that she'd need a radical mastectomy (both breasts) and chemo, we (I?) figured recovery would just take a little longer.

The months after her surgery were perhaps the most fun we had as a couple. With med school, internships, and then the baby, Mary was always too busy to travel more than a long weekend once or twice a year. But, now well established in our careers, she took the time off from her practice after her final round of chemo and came with me on my reporting trips to the World Cup in Barcelona, the Super Bowl in Dallas, a Bob Dylan concert in Paris, and a three-day interview with Salman Rushdie in Bombay. Mary toured while I worked. If her usual frenetic energy waned a tiny bit, only I noticed. She paused a few times, climbing the stairs to Montmartre. So what? I also needed the rest. She requested we take the Underground back to the hotel from Peace Square in Bombay instead of the two-mile walk. I happily agreed. She'd slowed down to my speed, to a more human pace.

We also vacationed—snorkeling in Cozumel and skiing in Vail. My sister Ilana took Hannah each time. We nearly exhausted our savings, but we figured Mary would be back at work soon enough. Toward the end of that year, a week before a scheduled round of scans, Mary suggested we visit Israel. I'd told her some of the story, not all of it. "You haven't been back since your junior year, have you? You have some friends there, right? I've never been. What are we waiting for?"

"Friends?" I said.

"I see the phone bills."

"Oh, right." I looked at her. She was at the punk rock stage of hair regrowth. It was coming in harsh, black, and spiky. She'd gained back a little weight. Her face was baby-smooth, smiling, and worry-free. She'd never expressed any interest before in traveling to Israel, never seemed curious about Judaism in general. Why would she? After fleeing Israel my junior year, I avoided the subject of Israel and Judaism as much as any American Jew living in New York could. Like most long-term couples, Mary and I had inventoried our previous lovers, so she knew something about Michal. But I never said a word about that Jerusalem balcony, Zehava, Yoav, or Chaim. "Let's wait on Israel," I said. "We've got plenty of time."

The fun stopped after the recurrence and the second round of chemo. This time, Mary's medical knowledge worked against our mood. She knew the odds and never hesitated to inform me. Her doctors were almost all friends or colleagues, often both. I accompanied her to every appointment. Mary would sit on the doctor's cot in a hospital gown, surrounded by her specialist friends in white doctor robes. I'd sit in the corner and listen to them speak physician talk. The only words I could pick up were bad news—recurrence, malignancy, staging, metastasis. Mary would join in on the learned discussions. It was as if they were sharing a panel at a conference or consulting dispassionately on an interesting VIP patient. On the cab rides home, she'd sit quietly, jotting notes in her notebook. I'd sometimes hear her on the phone speaking clinically about her case with her first cousin, a dermatologist, or her aunt, the gynecologist. But she hated talking to me about her illness. She shared more with Ilana than with me.

When things got worse, Ilana moved in to help with housework and child care. I say worse, but that was from my perspective as the husband of a hyperactive high-achieving wife. She still went to work every day. Every night, we watched TV together as a family. She ate as much ice cream as Hannah. Her hair grew back. It was shoulder-length and curly like before, only now with streaks of gray. Her doctor's gown hid much of her weight loss, and at home, she wore bulky sweaters and sweatpants. She enrolled in a clinical trial. We were still fighting.

But she'd given up. First on me. No more dates, no more sex, no more talking, really, unless she needed me to pick up something at the pharmacy or remind me to take out the trash. I understood. Real talking—genuine communication—would have meant broaching the subject of her death, the only topic that really mattered in those days. Neither of us was mature enough for that discussion. We gave up.

Sadder, perhaps saddest of all, she gave up on Hannah. Ilana or I read her a story at night. Mary explained to Hannah that she was too tired, and Hannah, for whatever reason, accepted the excuse without question. Ilana also cooked her scrambled eggs, watched Barney with her every morning, picked her up at school even on Mary's day off, and walked her to ballet and piano lessons. On Saturdays, she took her to synagogue. The old Mary—a committed atheist with an occasional taste for the music of Christian worship—would have protested. But now she registered no complaint and used Saturday mornings as a time to nap.

Despairing. Hopeless. Depressed. These weren't exactly the words I'd use now to describe Mary during that period. I would have described her in many different ways. She was preserving her energy. She was thinking things through. She was practicing radical focus—so she could work normally, rest when she needed it, and then continue to research her disease. She was sick during those sick months but also alive and mobile and active: a doctor to her patients and a mother, if diminished, to her daughter. I didn't study mortality charts, but I thought we had plenty of time. I only knew for sure that she'd entered the darkest tunnel when Hannah showed me her body, swaying on the steps.

◆◆◆

I didn't find a note. At first, the fact didn't disturb me. It was, at least on the surface, obvious why she'd done it. Unlike Chaim, Mary didn't have a poet's soul, a calling for the artistic placement of words, for eloquent theorizing. If something didn't need further explanation, why bother? It was only five years later that I considered the question. I was putting Hannah to bed. I knew this particular ritual—reading, cuddling, kissing—was coming to an end. She was growing up. Already, she now read to me. And, since she could read much more quickly to herself and was often anxious to finish whatever Harry Potter book she was reading on her own, she only chose books she'd already read to recite to me, and she didn't bother to hide her boredom. Also, after a few weeks of moving two or three inches away from each other, we now weren't cuddling at all. She was ten years old, after all. Double digits. A few years from being a teenager. She put down the book—an old Judy Blume title—and, for the first time in weeks, touched my fingers with hers. "Daddy," she said. Also a reversion. She'd substituted "Dad" for "Daddy" months before. "Why do you think Mommy . . ?"

She stopped. Here it comes. She'd never asked. Why did she do it? Why did she leave us? There was still time. Why?

But she didn't ask the obvious question. Which I was ready to answer. I'd been ready for years. She asked the question I couldn't really answer, not fully enough to satisfy myself.

"Why didn't she leave you a recording of her voice?" she asked.

A recording. Yes, that made sense. Hannah wouldn't miss a handwritten note. After all, when her mother died, she could barely read. But why not a recording? Or a video? The question made much more sense than my own ponderings about a written note. "Why?" I repeated softly. Hannah's hair was unlike her mother's. She'd been born a curly redhead. Everyone told us it would change. It did. As sure as a caterpillar becomes a butterfly, she became a blond with smooth, straight hair. I watched her move long, silky strands out of her eyes so she could stare at me directly, and I saw her clearly as an adult, in her twenties, still pondering the complexities of her mother's life and death. "Just to say goodbye with her voice," she said. "You know."

But I didn't know.

"Why?" she repeated.

Could I just refuse to answer? Plead the fifth. Could I grab the Judy Blume book and start reciting? Could I change the subject, ask about boys or soccer or ballet? I touched her hair. "I don't know why," I said.

"Yeah, but what do you think?"

Suddenly, the words popped into my head from another place, like prophecy or poetry. In some ways, this was *the* note. Not her's specifically, but available to anyone. I brought Hannah close. She burrowed her head under my arm. We cuddled. For the last time? "Sometimes," I told my daughter, "there is no why."

Part 2

CHAPTER 9

December 1982-April 1983

When Chaim hired me as his "research" assistant, I figured I wouldn't be doing much research. Chaim was a theologian, and I didn't have the first idea how to research theology. I assumed the job meant fetching Turkish coffee, mint tea, pita, and hummus, handing him his cane, reminding him to take his medicine, and lugging the ten or so leather-bound heavy Jewish volumes he required for every meeting, lecture, and seminar. And it was all that. I also kept his personal calendar, which meant two things: the dinners Zehava arranged with his many friends, family, and fans and his doctor appointments—his cardiologist, pulmonologist, allergist, orthopedist, gastroenterologist, hypnotist (for pain), and otolaryngologist. There were at least two of those every week.

I didn't expect that he would ask me to help edit his manuscript. I was twenty years old and not what any of my other teachers would have called a reader. Chaim had probably written more books than I had read. The only texts I studied with singular dedication were the Cleveland Plain Dealer sports pages and the back covers of rock albums. But that was precisely why Chaim asked me for help with editing. "I don't want to sound like a professor, God forbid. Or like a theologian, yes? I want no whiff of Latin or church or *shull* in this book. I want to sound like the sports reporters that you love, that you, Judah, aspire to become, no? I'm not a professor in this book talking down to my students. I'm a friend, sharing my enthusiasm. With rigor, certainly, intelligence, evidence, all that, yes. From an academic point of view, I know what I'm talking about. But when it comes to Job, Satan, Moses, God, I'm what you Americans from Cleveland call a true fan. A God fan. A fan of theology. And I want readers to become fans, so then I can share my ideas with a compelling style, a style they're accustomed to from their newspaper. You'll help with this, yes?"

A friend sharing his enthusiasm with rigor, intelligence, and evidence. A fan communicating with other fans. It sounded like a good recipe for a sportswriter. I didn't know it at the time, but in the years ahead, Chaim's style prescription became my professional compass. He made my career, first in sports and then in entertainment.

I made surprisingly few suggestions about the manuscript. Chaim already had a flowing, breezy style in English, impressive for anyone but especially for someone born and educated in Poland and living in Israel, a scholar whose first three languages were Yiddish, Polish, and Hebrew. He would have made a great Cleveland sportswriter. Mostly, I dumbed down the fancy words. "Excessive" became "more." "Artful" became "nice." "Solipsistic" became "big-headed." I did most of the work in

Michal's bedroom, so she helped with the dumbing down. She eliminated all semicolons, turning them into periods, cutting up long sentences into two or three or even four short ones. She snuck in a few sports metaphors. God became a quarterback. Job's friends played defense. Satan scored two goals in Job's first chapter. I made sure she changed football to soccer. Chaim was aiming at an American audience.

Michal took a cackling delight in attacking Chaim's prose. "Cocky asshole," she said one day, scratching out several lines with her red pen. That surprised me. She'd chosen two words I would never have used to describe Chaim. For a world-renowned scholar, he struck me as remarkably humble and down-to-earth. I'd never heard him boast. He certainly expressed confidence in his ideas, but then he gave them over to two undergraduates for editing. How cocky was that? And "asshole?" Chaim was courteous, kind, thoughtful, dependable. If Chaim was an asshole, I didn't know what the word meant. "You don't know him," Michal snapped.

Chaim remained the only source of conflict between Michal and me. She accused me of hero-worship, of "falling for the old bastard," of, inevitably but ridiculously, "caring more for him than you do me." Her attitude mystified me. She, after all, was the one who insisted I meet him. She'd called him "amazing" and arranged for Zehava to invite me over for dinner. Also, every few days, while working on the manuscript, she'd sigh, underline a few lines, copy them into her diary, and mumble "how beautiful" or "gorgeous." She did so that very day. Twenty minutes after calling him an asshole, she smiled beatifically at one of Chaim's paragraphs, whispered, "Amazing," and grabbed her red diary so she could transcribe it.

"See, you admire him also," I said.

"It's different with me." She tossed aside her diary and focused on the manuscript. She crossed out two lines.

"How?"

She flipped a few pages, then scribbled something in the margins. "It's complicated," she said.

◆◆◆

The published manuscript—*Our Imperfect God*, not my idea for the title—quickly became a bestseller, both in the United States and Israel. I had nothing to do with his original ideas or self-help advice, and I certainly couldn't claim any credit for the impressive sales numbers. So I was astonished that he listed me second in the acknowledgments, before Zehava and Yoav. I was also surprised that his first acknowledgment was to Michal. "My most careful reader," he wrote.

Two weeks after publication, I was in his study packing books for a lecture he was giving that night in Pisgat David, a settlement just past the 1967 border about a twenty-minute drive from Jerusalem. Chaim was looking over his notes. He'd asked me to drive, but I was nervous enough about navigating past Israeli drivers. I certainly didn't want to steer his car through the West Bank. I ordered a *sherut*, an Israeli taxi. "I'm surprised that this is your book tour," I said. I shoved his thick volumes into my backpack and helped Chaim down the stairs, where we waited for our ride. "I would think your editors would want you to start in Tel Aviv. And then the US. New York, Chicago. That's who's buying the book, right? That's why you wrote it in English, like an American sportswriter."

"Oh, they do want me to tour America. They have no interest in Israeli readers."

"We're going to America?" I asked. I didn't know how I felt about that. I'd committed to a full year in Israel. Visiting America in the middle seemed like cheating. And what about Michal? On the other hand, I couldn't imagine that he'd go without me.

He must have heard the concern in my voice because he quickly chuckled. "Oh, don't worry, Judah. I turned down the American book tour. The book is selling well, yes? Even without my brilliant lectures." He winked at me. "The people of Chicago will survive without me, yes? It's my hip, you see?"

I nodded. He never complained about the pain, but I couldn't miss the wincing groan whenever he got out of his chair. "Who knows how much time I have left, Judah."

I was surprised. He was in his midsixties. He had decades left, I figured. Of course, I was wrong. He had less than a month.

"Now that I've published the book, I will commit my diminishing energies to one project alone."

"The *haredim*," I said. I remembered his aspiration for a grand reconciliation between Israel's feuding tribes. His fears of a civil war.

"*Haredim*. Exactly. And," he said as an Arab taxi pulled up to the curb. He held my outstretched arm and climbed slowly into the vehicle. I hopped in next to him and shut the door. "And," he continued, "the West Bank religious settlers"—he pointed with his cane toward the Judean Hills—"that's who I will be speaking with about my book." He smiled as if he were enjoying an inside joke. "All the people I hate," he said. "And those who hate me."

When Chaim told me we'd be traveling to a West Bank settlement, I assumed tents, patrolling soldiers, prefab structures surrounded by guard towers, and several feet of barbed wire. But the only structure marking Pisgat David's border was a "Welcome to Pisgat David" sign in Hebrew and English, with each letter in bold, bright colors—orange, purple, red, blue, and hand-drawn lilies surrounding the writing. As we pulled into town and headed down the main street, I was surprised to see large, two-story, red-roofed homes with driveways, garages, and green lawns, front and back. At this point in my Israel sojourn, I'd only really explored Jerusalem and the bar scenes in Tel Aviv and Haifa. I assumed everyone in Israel lived in apartments, that houses with yards were an American extravagance. But Pisgat David looked more like Shaker Heights, Ohio, than Jerusalem or Tel Aviv. I even saw kids in the street tossing around an American football.

Chaim spoke in a large movie theater, bigger than any I'd ever seen. I estimated 1,000 dark red velvet seats, and every one of them was filled. He lectured in Hebrew, so I didn't understand most of it. But the response was unmistakable. The crowd laughed uproariously for the first ten minutes, with Chaim offering punch line after punch line. Was this post-Holocaust stand-up? Or Borscht Belt–style storytelling? Either way, I was relieved. Chaim was clearly winning over the audience. But then, suddenly, there was near silence. Chaim's voice dropped to a whisper. But he held their attention. Everyone around me watched intently, leaning forward to catch every word. I spotted several tears flowing down various cheeks. *Okay*, I thought. *Now the sentimental stories.* The book was full of them. I'd dumbed them down personally to intensify their naïve poignancy.

But then, after one particularly short sentence and a shy smile from Chaim, the crowd began to mumble. At first, it was just murmuring among themselves, private conversations in a 1,000-seat hall. Chaim raised his voice and waved his arms, but that only provoked further grumbling. Then, two older men wearing business suits and knit yarmulkes yelled something at the stage. Chaim yelled back, and now everyone was screaming—the audience at Chaim, and Chaim back at them, with nearly equal volume. This went on for at least ten minutes. Finally, Chaim banged his cane on the stage floor ten times, as if he were Moses, silencing his flock with a staff. The hall quieted down, though there was still a steady whisper of protest. Chaim finished his lecture and limped off the stage. Three people applauded—me and the two men who'd first yelled at Chaim directly.

"Come," Chaim said when he reached me, handing me his cane and books to carry. "I hear there are refreshments."

◆ ◆ ◆

"What happened?" I asked. We were standing in the corner of a large reception room. Chaim was munching contentedly on baklava. I wasn't hungry.

Chaim shrugged, then swallowed. "I told them a few jokes. Then, some of my Shoah stories. And then, well, you saw."

"They screamed at you. But why?"

"Why? Well, I told them what I thought. That is why I came here to begin with, yes? I told them that with their actions here, they are dooming us to perpetual war. I said they are corrupting Jewish culture and memory by creating a permanent occupation. I suggested to them that there are parallels between what they are trying to accomplish in the territories and Hitler's ambitions."

"You didn't. Chaim. Really."

He shrugged again, then finished off the baklava. "Perhaps I went too far. But my point was to provoke a dialogue. And you saw. I succeeded."

I scanned the room. Only a dozen or so settlers had stayed for the reception. They were all huddled by the refreshment table, far from us. I didn't perceive much of a dialogue, but maybe yelling back and forth in a crowded theater is what Chaim had in mind.

On the way out, someone grabbed my arm with a tight grip. Chaim, unaware or unconcerned, limped away. I stopped and turned around. It took me a few seconds, but I recognized the man holding my forearm. Dark suit, white shirt, navy blue tie, neatly trimmed black beard. Up close, he looked much younger than I'd thought, likely in his forties, maybe even thirties. He was one of the government officials Chaim had pointed out to me in the *Kotel* tunnel study circle. And now I saw that he was also one of the two other guys besides me who'd applauded politely after Chaim spoke. He was carrying a copy of Chaim's book. After staring at me for a few seconds, he released me. Then, he babbled several sentences in angry Hebrew. He sounded furious, on the verge of a tantrum. I told him, calmly, in English, that I didn't speak Hebrew. I looked toward the exit for Chaim to rescue me, but he was nowhere to be seen. Hopefully, he'd wait. I had no idea how to summon a taxi to a West Bank settlement.

"This is you?" the man said. He opened the book and pointed to the line in the acknowledgments thanking Judah Loeb. I admitted that it was me.

He looked me in the eye. "Stop him. You understand me? Stop him."

American, I thought, though the accent was hard to place. Somewhere between Brooklyn and Warsaw. I shook my head. "I *don't* understand. I just carry his books. Help him walk. I bring him water. I don't . . ."

"Stop him!" he interrupted. He grabbed my arm again, this time pinching it so it hurt. "You stop him. Tell him. Tell him to stop."

I yanked my arm away and jogged to the theater parking lot. Chaim waved to me from the back seat window of a black Mercedes. Would he have left without me if I hadn't just showed up? I climbed in the car. Chaim spoke in Arabic to the driver, and we pulled out of the parking lot. "Nu?" Chaim said. "What did our friend have to say? The deputy defense minister. My impression is that he doesn't speak English, yes? Am I right? Between us, he is also not so literate in Hebrew or in any language. But his English, I understand, is nothing, no?"

"He speaks English just fine." I said.

"Ah," he said. "Well then, what did you speak about?"

"Stopping," I said. "He knew that word for sure. He told me to tell you to stop. He seemed pretty agitated. He kept saying, 'Stop him.'"

Chaim tilted his head, frowned, and studied the dark scene outside his window, gathering his thoughts, as if the deputy minister had introduced a profound idea and Chaim was mulling it over. "Stop," he said and chuckled. "Well, he won't be the last to make this request." Then, he shut his eyes and slept the rest of the ride back to Jerusalem.

It was past midnight when I arrived back at my dorm room on Mt. Scopus. Michal had an early test so we agreed I wouldn't sleep over. I was pleased to see that Charlie was still awake. Since my relationship with Michal had heated up, I saw less and less of my roommate. I felt the absence since, apart from Michal—and that was a romance—or Chaim—and that was, well, I'm not sure what—Charlie was my only friend in Israel. I didn't have the emotional energy, or really the time for anyone else. That night, he told me about his criminology paper, a study of Israel serial killers.

"They give you credit for that here?" I said. "Studying serial killers? In America, you just watch movies about them. It's popular entertainment. But wait a minute. Israel has serial killers? The dream of 2,000 years, but with serial killers?"

"You'd be surprised. I'm going to make this my graduate thesis. This will be my career when I'm finished. Here, in Israel."

"Serial killers?"

"Well, not only serial killers. Murders. Homicide. I want to be an Israeli cop."

I'm not sure why, but the idea seemed especially apt to me. On one hand, Charlie was aerobically friendly. He chatted up any stranger we'd meet on the street—homeless beggars, harried commuters, newspaper hawkers, the guys at the nut shop. He seemed too kind and empathetic to dedicate his life to catching crooks. On the other hand, he'd make a great interrogator. He'd get anyone he questioned to trust him. "You know," I said, "I'm surprised there aren't more murders in Israel. Everyone gets a gun at some point." I pointed under the bed. "In America, someone would steal that thing and shoot up the dorm."

"Yeah, guns aren't toys here. We get the speech all the time. Especially in Lebanon. The gun is sacred. Only use it if it's absolutely necessary."

I marveled at the difference between me and Charlie. I could never imagine myself in a situation where I'd have to make a decision about whether or not to fire a gun. I couldn't imagine holding one in my arms, even Charlie's unloaded one, two feet away.

"Speaking of soldiers and guns," Charlie said. "Have you met Yoav yet, Lerner's son?"

"No. Why?"

"His case has gotten kind of famous. Especially if you serve in Lebanon."

"His case?"

"I guess it hasn't been in the English papers. Or you missed it. The word is he had kind of a breakdown. He took his gun and just started shooting at ten-year-old kids. In Southern Lebanon—the Israeli zone, near the border. Word is he's a fucking poor shot, but by some reverse miracle, he hit them both."

"He just shot them? For no reason?"

"Well, he could have made up plenty of reasons. Those ten-year-olds sometimes have bombs in their backpacks, or they hide pistols in their pockets. Or they throw rocks. But that's not his claim. He says now that he doesn't even remember it. Maybe that's what his lawyer told him to say. Probably, he just snapped. It happens."

"But where is he now? In jail?"

"Most likely not exactly jail. At this point, it's just rumors. I hear he's in a military hospital in Haifa. Maybe the mental ward? The army will have to decide what to do with him. Prosecute him? Treat him? Let him go?" He shrugged. "It's a shitty war."

I thought of Chaim and Zehava, how the tension in the room thickened to the point of asphyxiation whenever I asked about Yoav. What an ordeal for them. I wondered if Michal knew. I remembered her telling me they grew up together—same middle school and high school, same scouts youth group, same age, living right across the street from each other. From the way Michal stiffened whenever his name came up, I suspected an old romance. Maybe they were high school sweethearts.

I asked Charlie if he'd ever shot at ten-year-old kids. He winked at me. "Not yet," he said.

♦♦♦

Chaim's next book talk was two nights later. This time, the audience was modern Orthodox rabbis from North America, on convention in Jerusalem. He spoke at the Rav Kook Institute, a block-long seven-story building just a ten-minute drive from Chaim's apartment. Chaim seemed acquainted with many of the younger rabbis, who dressed informally in polo shirts and jeans and small knit yarmulkes, some in vibrant colors, like they were designed by The Grateful Dead. Apparently, many had been Chaim's student. He grinned and pumped dozens of hands and slapped one back after another as we walked into the building. He reminded me of a small-town politician, backslapping, grinning, joking. As we climbed the steps to the wide stage, he grabbed my arm and tightened his grip on his cane. I noticed his limp had grown more pronounced. I could see him struggling not to wince or cry out.

This time, he spoke in English. Just like in Pisgat David, he started with a few jokes. The first two contained punch lines in Yiddish, so I didn't understand at all. Still, I couldn't miss the strong laughter and applause. Then, he told one about a samurai and a mohel, the rabbi who performs a baby's circumcision. The crowd roared. I didn't get it, though I suppose just the word mohel is humorous in almost any context. Then, he told a long story about a sukkah—a ritual booth where observant Jews sleep and eat for the eight days of the Festival of Sukkot. He lost me halfway through the meandering tale, but the crowd laughed even harder than the first joke. Weirdly, I laughed along. After the jokes, he asserted his "unlimited admiration" for the work of Modern Orthodox rabbis in America. He suggested that if history had worked out a little differently, he likely would have become Modern Orthodox, and almost certainly a rabbi. The living theologians he most admired were Modern Orthodox. The crowd nodded and listened intently as Chaim praised them. Then, he told a few Holocaust stories (after a drink or two, with only Zehava and me in the room, he referred to this part of his speeches as the *Shoah* business). The stories were sad, inspiring, sentimental, sacred, sometimes brutal. Parents died to save children. A rabbi survived a hundred-mile death march in the snow because a spectral image of his murdered son appeared and guided him. A brutal, endlessly cruel kapo became a sobbing wreck after hearing a child chant the *Kol Nidrei* prayer on *Yom Kippur*. A mother in Auschwitz managed secretly to give birth to a baby. Just before the newborn son died of malnutrition, she found a knife and circumcised him. Then, she killed a guard with the same knife and threw herself at the electric barbed wire. These stories never failed to bring at least half the crowd to tears. This time, it looked like every rabbi in the crowd was weeping.

Unfortunately, the jokes and the stories were just his warmup. "Now I must tell you, my good friends," he said, shifting the volume and tone of his voice, so he suddenly sounded like a sergeant barking out an order or a kapo screaming at a prisoner or Moses reciting the commandments, "everything you now are doing is wrong. Every action you are currently taking will destroy our people." He started with how Modern Orthodox rabbis shunned their non-Orthodox colleagues: Reform, Conservative, and Reconstructionist rabbis. "You place them in *herem*, excommunication. You boycott their synagogues, their rabbinical associations. You refuse to participate in vital community discussions if they are present. You behave as if all disputes, for heaven's sake, have been resolved in your favor. Forgive me, but you are more polite and collegial and cooperative with priests and ministers, leaders of a religion which has inspired the murder of our people."

No, I thought. *Don't do it. Not another Nazi comparison.* Strangely, though, he hadn't yet lost the crowd. Most of the men—it was all men—leaned forward, as if he really was a prophet. "Just like Goebbels' best propaganda, you viciously insult them," Chaim continued. "Well then, how do you expect them to feel? Of course, they resent you. Hate you. But that's okay. I can live with that. You are rude, they are hurt. They insult you, you are hurt. You're big boys. You can take care of yourselves. Or not. This petty feuding among our spiritual leaders is distasteful, but it is trivial. But, friends, consider the followers of these rabbis, whom you openly denounce as heretics. You somehow forget that this is 90 percent or more of North American Jews. I couldn't care less about the feelings of the rabbis, or your feelings, your misguided arrogance and resentment. But by delegitimizing their rabbis, you insult and alienate the great, great majority of Jews in your communities. You incite. You provoke. You inflame. At a time when we should unite around the project of rebuilding, you feud. You divide. It's exactly how we allowed the Nazis to burn our bodies. It's why we lost the Temple."

The grumbling started with the word "Temple." But it was more subdued than in Pisgat David. No one shouted at Chaim or shook their fist. They mumbled among themselves. Because he never lost his smile or jocular tone, some wondered if he was still joking. They stretched forward, like rubberneckers watching a car wreck while Chaim cheerfully accused them of collaborating in the destruction of American Judaism. I wondered for the first time if Chaim was something other than a charming troll, a brilliant, mischievous prophet. *Maybe*, I thought, *he's lost his mind. Literally lost it, in a confounding haze and maze of genius intellect and death camp trauma.*

"But your arrogant, aggressive divisiveness is not your worst sin," Chaim continued, drawing out the final sibilant, like a hissing snake. *Sssss*. "Much worse is your theology. Because here, you are not just sinning against your fellow Jew. No. You sin against God. I'm referring, of course, to your paltry, irrational, cowardly, insulting responses to the Shoah." This was Chaim, selling his book. Abuse anyone who held contrary beliefs, but with warmth and a glowing smile so it took you awhile to realize he was serious. In this cheerful manner, Chaim lambasted Orthodox theology. "Some of you preach that the Jews sinned. What sin? Well, you speculate, daring to look into God's mind, and you say, aha! Reform Judaism. It was, after all, German rabbis who invented it, so God used the Germans as His instrument of punishment. Isn't God clever? My dear rabbis, in the entire history of human thought, from Job to Wittgenstein, has there ever been a more ridiculous and disgraceful idea? God burns babies alive because a few rabbis in Germany came up with a slightly different way of practicing Judaism? Most of you, I know, abhor this idea. But you've all heard it whispered among yourselves in your conventions and colloquiums and conferences. Your professors whispered it to you, if not in the classroom, then the hallway."

Now the catcalls commenced, mostly quiet protests of "No" and "Not true." Chaim easily powered ahead. "Yes, okay, friends. So, yes, you object to this abominable theology. Not loudly enough for my taste, but you object, at least now, yes? But, friends, what is your answer? Six million slaughtered. Why? Okay, so it's not Reform Judaism, God forbid. But, then, why? And you answer— I've heard you—I've read hundreds of your books and articles. You say, yes, there was a sin. A sin that deserved punishment, yes? I ask, then, what sin? And you answer, foolishly, recklessly, with great ignorance and abject cowardice, that it's a grand mystery. God has reasons, but his thoughts are not our thoughts; his ways are not our ways. Friends. Friends. Let's first ignore the moral vacuum you impose on God with this idea—the idea that God burns babies as punishment for a sin *we didn't even know we committed*. That you turn God into an inept tyrant. We'll ignore this, for now. Let's stick, for the moment, to logic. We are, after all, moderns, yes, the Modern Orthodox? God punishes, you say, but won't reveal the sin? How, then, in the name of God, can the sinner ever change his ways? The youngest, most ignorant parent knows the folly of this theology. Punish your child, but don't say why? Foolishness. Every dog owner understands you punish to change behavior. If the sinful behavior is a mystery, then the punishment is a cruel absurdity.

"But this is not most of you, I know. Maybe you consider the first answer; maybe the second answer occurs to you. But, yes, we are moderns, and logic alone collapses these answers. So, you shrug your shoulders. You pretend that you are humble and brave and wise. And you claim, with the credibility your *semichah* grants you, that it's all a *mystery*. Everything. The cosmos. You. Me. Existence. God. Yes, a mystery. You absolutely hide in the word. It is your sheltering rock. So no one will find you. Yes, sometimes you even use this strange word: 'hiddeness.' You claim that God is hiding His face. But, really, friends, you are hiding, yes? You hide from your seekers. We don't know why the world is as it is, you preach. That is your response to the holy seekers who demand answers to the ultimate questions. 'Why?' they demand. And you honor me with the quote from the kapo in my book. 'Here there is no why,' you teach your students. But for you, 'here' is not Auschwitz. 'Here' is our world. Which is to say, our world is Auschwitz. This is the comfort you offer your flock. You transform the entire universe into the *lager*, the death camp, yes? And you tell your Jews. Live. Live. Live. Live in this horror world."

A dozen or so muttering rabbis pushed toward the exits, but the hall still seemed packed. The catcalls ceased with Chaim's spitting out the word Auschwitz. Everyone now listened, but probably more for the spectacle than any wisdom they might glean. For the next ten minutes, Chaim laid out his theory, his theology. Which was, simply, that God was not all-powerful. God wanted to help but couldn't. It wasn't a complicated idea. A sportswriter could explain it. It was simply and merely heretical. But for Chaim, it solved every problem.

A few brave rabbis applauded politely after the speech. The rest hurried out of the hall. Chaim, refusing my help, limped off the stage and collapsed into a front-row chair. He placed his finger over his mouth, either shushing me or contemplating the universe. He waited until the room emptied and then nodded at me. I helped him limp toward the exit. His grip on my arm felt suddenly loose, as if he'd lost half his energy. He winced in pain with each step.

The last time I'd checked the auditorium, everyone had gone. But now a short, old, gray-haired, black-hatted *haredi* seemed to have materialized out of thin air. He waited for us at the door. His forehead erupted in wrinkles as he smiled warmly at Chaim. It took me a moment to recognize him. This was the rabbi who taught the *Zohar* class in the *Kotel* tunnel. Eli Kaplowitz. He embraced Chaim and then whispered what sounded like Yiddish into his ears. Then, he kissed him on both cheeks and startled me by also kissing me on both of my cheeks. Then, he hurried off.

I touched my face. "What did he say to you?" I asked.

Chaim chuckled. "He offered a logical question, yes? My theology is that God is not all-powerful, correct?"

I nodded. I'd only heard it about a thousand times.

"Rabbi Kaplowitz warned me. He said if I keep saying God is not all-powerful, God might be forced to show me His power."

I led Chaim to the car, which I'd finally agreed to drive. He struggled to open the door, and I wondered how much longer it would be before we needed to get a wheelchair. I helped him climb into the passenger seat, then waited before I shut the door. "You say he warned you," I said. "But you mean he threatened you. God showing you his power. Chaim, that's a threat."

He laughed. He thought I was joking.

◆◆◆

"I don't understand what he's doing," I told Michal in her apartment. She'd cooked me a late dinner—an omelet with half a loaf of whole wheat bread and Israeli salad. That a girlfriend might cook me a late-night meal and then sit across from me in jogging shorts and a sports bra was a source of total amazement. Love. I never imagined I could experience such happiness. I wondered how long it would last. "He just insults them. Compares them to Nazis. Is this how he expects to sell his book? At Pisgat David, he didn't even have books out to sell."

"I don't think selling books is the point," she said. She smiled sadly.

"What is the point?"

"Making trouble. Stirring things up. Pissing people off. Drawing attention to himself. He's a great thinker. He's also a narcissist. And an asshole."

"Really?" I said. Again, her judgment of Chaim surprised me. "Yes, sure, stirring things up. Sure. But an asshole?"

She shook her head. "You don't know him," she said.

For the past seven months, I'd spent at least three hours a day with him, probably more time than I'd spent with Michal. He'd shared more with me about his life struggles than any adult, including both my parents. I knew him pretty well. But I noticed a peculiar sensitivity emerge whenever Michal and I discussed Chaim. Her ears and cheeks would turn pink, a blush that reminded me of junior high crushes or bitter high school feuds. She'd insult him, sometimes subtly, often sharply, with words like bastard, egomaniac, and, of course, "asshole." I'd grow defensive. We'd quarrel; it was the only source of our quarrels. That night, I didn't want to argue. So I nodded.

"Can we go to bed?" she asked quietly.

Such good fortune, I thought. *Wow*. I followed her into the bedroom.

♦♦♦

Two weeks later, Zehava invited me to brunch on a Saturday morning. Michal was away visiting friends for Shabbat, and Charlie needed to study, so I was happy to accept the invitation. The sun came out that morning—the first time in weeks. It had been a cold and rainy winter. Several snowy days alarmed and delighted the native Jerusalemites. But that early April morning, the weather was warm, more summer than early spring. We sat outside on the Lerner's balcony, the first time I'd sat there. Almond branches with their pink buds extended over the brunch table, as if they might grab a bite to eat. Zehava laid out olives, pickles, mushroom burekas, pita, and, the main course, shakshuka—a tomato, onion, and egg dish that I'd grown to love, partly because even I could cook it. The balcony smelled like strong coffee, fresh bread, and fried onions. It was redolent of my favorite Israeli restaurants, and therefore, ironically, as we'll see, the odor reminded me of my greatest happiness, my times with Michal.

Chaim sipped iced tea and stared into the distance, looking past the balcony railing to the Old City and the *Kotel*. *Ruminating on his next theology*, I figured. Zehava took over the conversation. She lectured me on Israeli politics, who was in, who was out, who was left, who was right, who she considered an ally, and who, in her opinion, would destroy Israel's young democracy if granted the power. I suffered a combination of ignorance, naivete, and indifference when it came to politics, but I listened politely and nodded agreeably at Zehava's opinions. She was as charming and funny as Chaim and, I realized, as she held my gaze with her wide, green eyes and brushed her brown hair from her forehead, as attractive as Michal. Despite her humility, I gathered she was an important figure in the center-left opposition. She described herself as "the original liberal Zionist," passionately dedicated to common sense. Who could argue with that? "I'd vote for you," I said as I helped myself to more shakshuka. She laughed, a little too long, as if the idea of me ever voting in an Israeli election was the funniest thing she'd heard all week. Chaim, still lost in thought, or lost in something, smiled enigmatically, a hypnotized Jewish Mona Lisa, staring at the metal bars on the balcony railing.

The phone rang. Chaim jerked his head toward the inside of the flat and jumped up, dropping his cane. He ran to the phone, the first time I'd seen him move without a limp.

"Must be Yoav," Zehava told me. "He's been trying to get ahold of us all of Shabbat."

"How is he?" I asked, then immediately regretted the question. "Must be incredibly difficult," I offered.

She squinted at me, as if I'd suddenly shifted out of focus. Then, she answered, "Yes, it's been hard. There was an incident. I guess . . . maybe you've heard?"

I nodded.

"We sacrifice so much for this country. Chaim says we give our hearts, but for the mother of a soldier, I think it's the kidneys and the liver. We keep the heart, but it breaks. Do you understand?"

Of course, I didn't understand. I wasn't an Israeli, or a soldier, let alone a mother. I was thinking of a way to articulate my abject ignorance that didn't make me sound like a total fool when Chaim rushed back to the balcony. My first thought when seeing him breathless was *Bad news*. The worst possible news. But then I noticed he was grinning, the widest grin I'd ever seen from him—and he was famous for his smiles. He spit out several quick sentences in Hebrew. Zehava covered her mouth with both hands, leaped out of her seat, and hugged Chaim tightly. They embraced for several seconds. Zehava laughed joyously, and Chaim shut his eyes. Finally, he disentangled himself from Zehava and turned to me.

"Our apologies, Judah. We just received excellent news, yes? The best news. Our son is engaged to be married!"

"Oh," I said. "That's wonderful. Mazel Tov!" I was proud I could offer something in Hebrew. "Who's the lucky bride?" I asked. To this day, I don't know why I asked. Did I suspect I already knew the answer? If so, I was hiding it from myself.

Zehava looked at Chaim, then smiled at me. "Well, we thought maybe you knew," she said. "You two have become such good friends."

I held my breath.

"It's Michal," she said, her shiny, pretty face the picture of joy. "He's marrying Michal."

CHAPTER 10

July 2005

Breath, flowing slowly into my ear. Someone blowing? I drifted back to sleep. Then, a voice, soft but ringing. "Dad. Dad! It's time to get up."

I jerked awake. The room was pitch-black. For a moment, I couldn't remember where I was or who was blowing into my ear. Mary? I sat up, leaned my head against the headboard. *Jerusalem*, I thought. *I'm back in Jerusalem. In my underwear.* I quickly covered myself with a sweaty sheet. I blinked and spotted a shape about five feet away. Hannah. She opened the blackout shades. Light flooded the room and assaulted my eyes. "What time is it?" I barked.

Hannah stood quietly and pointed to my wrist. I looked at my watch: 9 a.m. My first night in Israel and I'd slept twelve straight hours. "What are you doing today?" Hannah asked.

I saw that she'd showered. Her long brown hair still dripped on the carpet. She was dressed in blue shorts and a dark gray tank top, certainly inappropriate for the *haredi* neighborhood that surrounded our rental. I anticipated an argument: I'd demand she change clothes; she'd refuse; we'd fight; she'd win; I'd lose. So I limited myself to good morning.

"What are you doing today?" she repeated. She took her phone out of her pocket and looked at the time. I blinked twice, trying to bring myself awake. Was there coffee in the apartment? Did *haredim* drink coffee?

"What do you mean, what am *I* doing? It's what are *we* doing. Charlie's picking us up at ten-thirty. He's showing us around Jerusalem."

Hannah clicked her tongue twice. It took me a few seconds to remember that was an Israeli way of saying no. Not necessarily rude, though it certainly sounded that way to inexperienced Americans. Hannah had learned it quickly. "I'm not coming with you," she said.

I sighed. Here we go. I geared up for a lovely quarrel. But this time, I would win. Hannah was not wandering around the city on her own, wearing shorts and a tank top. "Of course you are," I said. I cycled through a list of objections. She had no money. She had a terrible sense of direction. She knew zero Hebrew. She had no knowledge of the local public transportation. There was still an intifada.

"I'm meeting with a suicide bomber," she said. "For my history project."

I reached for my jeans on the floor and pulled them on under the sheet. Then, I grabbed a blue polo shirt from my suitcase and threw it on. One problem solved. I was no longer in my underwear. Next, my daughter meeting a suicide bomber. Should I start with the logical fallacy before moving on to the fantastic outrageousness of the whole idea? You can't meet with a suicide bomber because, by definition, they're dead. Or did I simply review the fundamental rules: I'm the father, she's the daughter? While we're traveling together in this foreign country, she listens to me.

"Sorry, that came out wrong," she continued while I was still wondering what to say. "Obviously I'm not meeting some dead guy who's already blown himself up. I'm meeting with a Palestinian who *meant* to blow himself up, but the bomb didn't explode. This was almost ten years ago. He's in jail. I'm interviewing him. For my project."

I stared at my daughter. Was I still dreaming? Did Hannah really expect me to research Israeli prisons, find the failed bomber, and allow Hannah to visit with him? Once again, I had too much to say, so I said nothing.

"Michal's taking me," Hannah said. She looked at her phone again. "In ten minutes."

"Michal."

"In ten minutes. I already ate breakfast. I bought some rolls and cottage cheese and coffee for you. There's a great store up the block. I also got some Israeli bubblegum. And this weird chocolate pudding thing with whipped cream. I got one for you."

"Michal," I said. I wondered where she got the money for the food.

"I took the money out of your jeans," she said, answering the unspoken question, ignoring the obvious one.

"Michal is taking you?"

"Yeah," she said. "I think you'll like the cottage cheese. It's like thirty percent fat. Oh, and I made the coffee. Turkish!"

"Hannah," I said. "You know you can't . . ." The doorbell rang. I tucked in my shirt and stepped toward the door. But it opened before I got there. It was Michal. She was wearing white shorts and a red tank top. Though I knew it wasn't possible, it looked like she was wearing the same sandals from our nine months together. Her toenails were red and neatly trimmed, like before.

"Boker tov, chaverim!" she said and marched into the room. She looked at the couch, the TV, the kitchen table, and nodded, satisfied. "Hannah, motek," she called out. "You're ready?" She looked at me. "Is she wearing sunscreen?"

While I sipped the muddy coffee, Hannah ate another container of 30 percent cottage cheese (it really was, as I remembered, delicious). Michal explained that Hannah had emailed her the night before about her school assignment. Through the night, they'd exchanged half a dozen texts on the topic. "Honestly, I learned some things." Michal said. "And I'm sort of an expert. So I offered to bring her to see Kamal. I worked with him on a documentary. He tried to blow himself up in a crowded restaurant. Lucky for him, for us, the fuse refused to ignite. He's been in jail for ten years. He's one of the government's best sources on the psychology of suicide murderers. I must say, it's an intriguing topic for an American high school student. Especially, well, considering Hannah's background." She turned to me. "Was this your idea?"

"Uh, not quite," I said. I finished my cottage cheese and bit into the roll. Also excellent.

"He just heard about it yesterday," Hannah said. She giggled, then covered her mouth.

Michal studied my face. "So. You didn't know I was coming this morning, did you?"

I shook my head. I didn't even know how Hannah got Michal's email.

She shrugged and grabbed her black canvas purse. "Teenagers," she said. "What can you do? Yallah, Chanele. We don't want to keep our suicide bomber waiting." Hannah slammed the door shut on her way out before I could remind her to put on sunscreen.

◆ ◆ ◆

Charlie showed up two hours later, half an hour late. He wore an Israeli police uniform—navy blue pants and a light-blue shirt, with epaulets and patches along the right sleeve and front pocket. He carried a large brown leather briefcase, thick with folders and loose papers. Other than slightly longer hair, he looked like the young soldier I'd lived with twenty-two years before. His hair was still sandy brown, not a gray strand in sight, and his cheeks were still red and slightly puffy, like a child's. No middle age paunch. How is it, I thought, that in this trip of emotional reunions, everyone looks the same except for me? (I'd confirmed it moments before with a quick glance in the bathroom mirror.) Was Israel, despite a forever war, bombs exploding in pizza parlors and discos, battles on every border, ceaseless inner conflicts, vicious politics, somehow also a fountain of youth? If I'd stayed and married Michal, would I be as ageless and self-confident as Zehava, as handsome and authoritative as Charlie?

We hugged tightly, then spent several seconds searching each other's faces as if we weren't really sure who we were looking at. Charlie was the first to turn away. He looked around the shack, whistling his approval. "Not so bad, considering the neighborhood. Lots of memories for you on this block, I'm sure. You know it's all haredim now, right? Zehava's the last hold out. And even she spends most of her time in Tel Aviv, when she's not at the Knesset." He glanced into the bedrooms. "Did you lose someone already? Weren't you supposed to bring Hannah?"

I considered telling him about Kamal, the failed suicide bomber, but instead sighed. "Do you have teenagers?" I asked.

He shook his head. "No children. Never married." He studied me again, like he still hadn't made up his mind about me. I waited. "Well. Maybe since Hannah's away, we'll skip the tour. You and I can get straight to work."

Charlie sat at the dining room table and unloaded eight heavy files from his satchel. I felt a wave of jet lag, so I went into the kitchen to make more coffee. When Charlie saw me opening and slamming cabinet doors, looking for the coffee maker, he got up, gently pushed me aside, grabbed the *kumkum*, already lying on the burner, and boiled Turkish coffee. He brought the muddy mixture to a boil five times, then added five heaping tablespoons of sugar. We sipped quietly at the kitchen counter. After three mouthfuls, the caffeine shot through my veins, jolting me into wakefulness. Like cocaine, I remembered. He nodded at me, and we returned to the living room.

I'd contacted Charlie three years before, when I first considered writing about Chaim and the questions surrounding his death. The police connection made the story more attractive to my editors. Charlie surprised me by urging me to pursue the case. He told me the Jerusalem police, even after twenty years, kept the Lerner file open. He promised help from his department. Charlie was now, as he'd dreamed, a Jerusalem homicide detective.

Freshly caffeinated, I started telling Charlie my latest theory. "I'm almost sure it was an accident," I said. "I studied the balcony last night, and I can see . . ."

Four quick tongue clicks. I'd never heard four in a row. I stopped. "No," he said, as if the clicks hadn't gotten through. "It was murder."

I leaned back. "Sure, that's possible. But I don't think—"

He clicked again. This time, a machine-gut *rat ta tat* of tongue clicks. "Judah, it was murder."

"Charlie, with all due respect, I've been studying this story for years. And, you know, I lived it when I was here." I saw again how keenly he was observing my face. It was like he was waiting for me to say the right thing, interrupting me whenever I got it wrong. I took another sip of Turkish coffee. Caffeine ripped through me. A cobweb cleared. "You've got a new lead," I guessed. "Something you've kept out of the newspapers."

He nodded.

"Well, show it to me."

"In a minute. We'll talk it through. But we're going with homicide. And, what do you know, I'm a homicide detective. And you're an investigative reporter. Let's investigate this thing."

"This murder," I said. I remembered Chaim's broken body on the sidewalk below the balcony. The EMTs tried to revive him, but a four-year-old could tell he was dead. No one alive could have a body twisted into that pretzel shape.

"Murder," Charlie repeated. "Let's go with that, at least for now. If this is a murder, who are the obvious suspects?"

Of course, I'd thought about this. Homicide was always a possibility. It kept me up several nights, especially those early heartbroken days after Chaim's death, and even for several years after I fled Jerusalem. I had my own scattered theories that I embraced and then discarded. But there was an obvious, textbook answer to Charlie's question, even if I didn't like it. "The family," I said, softly, as if I was afraid someone was listening in.

"Nu?" Charlie said.

I wasn't sure what that meant, but at least it wasn't a tongue click. "Zehava," I offered.

He drew a wheel with his forefinger. "And?"

"Michal," I said. "But she wasn't—"

"She's family, Mr. Investigative Reporter. We don't exclude anyone at this stage. Correct? Except for . . ."

He waited. A quiz. Not a hard one. "Yoav," I said. "He was at the hospital in Haifa. Probably a dozen or so doctors, nurses, fellow soldiers, maybe more could testify where he was when Chaim fell. And he was under guard. He couldn't get out."

"Exactly. So. Two family suspects. Zehava. Michal."

I waited. A new lead, he'd said. I wondered.

"Seems unlikely," he said. "Don't you think?

I breathed a sigh of relief. "Yes. Very unlikely. I spent a lot of time with them that year. Zehava clearly adored Chaim. She protected him—from students, from journalists. And Michal?" I stopped to think. Mousy, quiet Michal. I remembered her buying packages of pitah to give to beggars in the old city. She cried at the end of *Casablanca*, when Rick sacrificed his relationship with Elsa. Sentimental Michal. She had some issues with Chaim, I remembered, yes, but she also admired him, called him amazing, introduced me to him. She was also my first love. "I just can't imagine it."

Charlie nodded, stuck his tongue in his cheek. He tilted his head, thinking things over. "Okay, *tov*," he said. "Anyway, they have alibis."

I exhaled. "Oh?"

"Five neighbors heard the body fall. A thump, like a load of flour hitting the pavement. Before that, someone saying, 'Whoops.' Chaim's voice. Like he dropped something. Nothing that alarmed them, but a sound, and they all heard it. Nineteen-hundred hours. Seven p.m., the way you Americans say it. Every witness confirmed the time. That's when they heard the loud bump. Michal and Zehava were nowhere near the apartment. Two witnesses confirmed. *Tov*. We eliminate the family. It wasn't Yoav, Zehava, or Michal. So, who?"

"Is this some kind of test? You're the one with the new lead."

"Just trying out some theories with an old friend. Humor me. We take his family out of contention, at least for now. What's left?"

I thought about my last month in Israel. "Political extremists," I said. "He came out against the Lebanon War. The Occupation. He gave that speech in Pisgat David."

Charlie nodded, then gave the forefinger in a wheel gesture. He was looking for more.

"Religious extremists," I said. "The talk to the Modern Orthodox rabbi convention. The book, where he claimed that God wasn't all-powerful. The heresy accusations."

Charlie shoved the two thick files at me. "Bingo," he said. "That's what I've got here. Religion." He pointed to the folder on my right—ten inches thick. "And politics." He patted the one on the left. It was at least two inches thicker.

We started with the thicker file. Charlie pulled out newspaper clippings (all in Hebrew, so gobbledygook to me) highlighting fringe political movements that at the time advocated violence. He'd already narrowed it down to groups that specifically mentioned Chaim and at least implicitly threatened him. He read me an entire article on a trio of former paratroopers who threw eggs and rolls of toilet paper at the houses of several musicians who'd protested against the Lebanon War. But that seemed far from murder, and they were never accused of any violent crime. We put them aside. Next, Charlie showed me a CIA intelligence report on a Tel Aviv University student club that heckled the lectures of leftist professors. Most significant: when the campus police raided the group's student offices, they found photographs of their victims with targets drawn across their faces. Still, a drawing isn't throwing someone from a rooftop, and anyway, Chaim taught at Hebrew University in Jerusalem, not at Tel Aviv University. He set aside the report. I wondered how Charlie had gotten his hands on it.

We went through half a dozen articles, intelligence reports, and police interviews all describing nationalist groups that either explicitly threatened bodily harm against leftists or used violent imagery or language. Charlie even read out loud, then translated, some of the key findings of the Mossad report on the Yitzhak Rabin assassination. A conspiracy theorist could concoct a frightening and compelling narrative about a nascent right-wing coup threatening Israel's democracy. But Charlie was no conspiracy obsessive, and he admitted he only shared these files to demonstrate that a political murder was not out of the question, not now or twenty-two years ago.

"But throwing someone off their own balcony and making it look like suicide—that doesn't fit any of these groups," Charlie said. He was stroking his bare chin, like a scholar lost in thought, or a *yeshiva bucher*. He clearly enjoyed thinking deeply about murder. "The crime is a little too clever, too subtle. There were reasons why Chaim might have killed himself, right? Trauma from the Holocaust, his sore hip. In fact, suicide is what most people figured, what most of his friends and family believe today. But a political murder isn't supposed to be a mystery. Sure, the perpetrators wouldn't want to get caught, but they'd want the world to know why they did it. It's like terrorism. The medium is the message. None of these groups would kill someone and then make it look like something other than murder. What would be the point?"

I nodded. I decided to reserve my comments until I heard his whole theory. Anyway, I had nothing to say.

"I'm figuring it was personal," Charlie continued. "To grab hold of someone. To see the fear in his eyes while he's tumbling backward. There's something intimate about murdering another human being with your bare hands. But we've eliminated his intimates, right? Zehava? Yoav? Michal?"

I paused. "I guess," I said.

"Right. So that's why I want to start your investigation with this guy." He reached into the folder, took out an eight-by-ten black-and-white photo, and pushed it under my face. "Meir Alon. Ring a bell?" he asked.

It was a scowling face, staring directly into the camera. Long, full, black beard, beady eyes, white shirt with dark tie, and a black yarmulke that covered his whole head. At first, it looked like one of the dozens of male Orthodox Jews one would see walking the streets of Jerusalem at any given moment. But Charlie waited, and I studied the photo while my memory slowly dredged up an incident from the Kotel tunnel. I nodded. "It's the guy from the Zohar class," I said. "Some assistant minister somewhere. He told me to stop Chaim. He kept repeating that sentence. 'Stop him.' Chaim laughed it off. But for me, it felt—" I looked at Charlie. I couldn't come up with the right word.

"Threatening," Charlie said.

I paused and then nodded. "Threatening," I agreed.

"I remember you telling me the story. The guy freaked you out—that's what you told me. Well, he's not an assistant minister anymore. He's no one's assistant. He's the head of Et Ratzon, a political party. He'd like to be prime minister. And he's also a writer. Or maybe we could just call him a polemicist. A propagandist. I've been going through his books and articles, now that I'm actually fluent in Hebrew. He started writing about Chaim weeks before the murder. Called him a traitor to other Holocaust survivors. Said he needs to be dealt with. But then, after the murder, he wrote about him even more! Called him the epitome of leftist self-hatred. No wonder he leaped off the roof, he wrote. He hated himself so deeply, hated his Jewishness, his country, his comrades. Hated God. It was harsh stuff, Judah. Even for Israel."

I picked up the photo with my finger and thumb. Strangely, it was a glossy print, as if it had been distributed by his fan club. "Did the police even question him?"

Two tongue clicks. Israeli for "no." "He's a VIP. At the time, he was already influential in the government. They would have needed more evidence than a bunch of mean articles. Anyway, the police conducted almost no interviews at the time. Remember? It was suicide. Case closed."

"So we go to see him?" I asked.

Two clicks. He smiled. He was enjoying the rudeness of the sound. It was now part of his birthright. "Not we," he said. "You. You go see him."

"Wait. Charlie. I thought—"

"You're a journalist. From America. You'll get him talking. A cop shows up, he'll just shut down. Call a lawyer. I'll help you come up with some questions. I'll go over some of his articles with you. But you've got to go on your own."

I had to admit that from his point of view, it made sense. I wondered briefly about journalistic ethics. Suddenly, I wasn't writing a book, I was helping the police department of a foreign government in its investigation. But if this was the best way to get information, it was, by definition, my way.

"I arranged some appointments," he said. He looked at his watch. "You'll see Alon in one hour. A car will pick you up in thirty minutes. Right after that, you're seeing Kaplowitz. The Kabbalist."

"Oh!" I said. I'd thought that Charlie would help with Hebrew, maybe allow me to bounce ideas off him, help me order in restaurants, catch taxis. But here he was, setting up my appointments, providing me with confidential intelligence, arranging transportation. "Okay," I said. "Where are we going?" I pictured the tunnel by the Kotel. At least it would be cool.

"The Knesset," Charlie said. "Alon's office."

"He's in your parliament? The guy who accuses a Holocaust survivor of killing himself because of self-hatred?"

"Not just in the Knesset. He's in the cabinet." Charlie shrugged. "That's Israel." He finished his coffee and got up. "But don't worry. We've got some good guys in the Knesset too."

◆◆◆

I set off two security alarms as my driver walked me through a maze of hallways and staircases to Alon's office. The first was my metal watchband, the second my belt buckle. Both times, the guard looked me up and down quickly and signaled me to keep going. *Profiling*, I figured. *Too old, too slow, with a paunch. Not a likely terrorist in the waning days of the Second Intifada.*

I was surprised to find Alon's office door wide open. I tapped on it a few times; he didn't respond, so I walked in. I felt the dust and pet dander right away in my sinuses. The walls were covered with dark-brown bookshelves, still not enough space for all of his volumes. Books spilled on to the dirty white carpet and extended from the shelves halfway into the room. Five of the stuffed armchairs overflowed with books and folders. Four high towers of books teetered on his desk. I remembered Chaim telling me that Alon was an intellectual lightweight, a nonreader. Either he'd changed, or Chaim got him wrong. A dun-colored cat danced among the paper, files, and volumes. Alon was signing documents, ignoring me. One glance at his wrinkled face, and I could see that the photo Charlie showed me was many years old. Alon's thick beard was now fully gray, and the yarmulke covering his head was so wide, it reached his white eyebrows. A *haredi*-style black hat and long dark coat hung on the coat rack. Meir looked much older and more religious.

I cleared my throat, and he looked up. "Loeb," he said. He squinted at me over the top of his bifocals. "You've gained weight. You look a lot older."

I was impressed that he remembered me. "You also," I said.

His mouth, covered by a thick layer of gray whiskers, turned down in a scowl. It seemed to be his default expression. He gripped the bottom of his long beard with both hands, as if he was wringing water out of it. "Who do you seek?" he asked.

Now I was even more impressed. He remembered the topic of the Zohar class on the day that he and I spoke. "You mean I seek God? God's other name is 'Who,' right? God is an interrogative," I surprised myself. I remembered the old rabbi's lesson like it was yesterday. "To seek God is to question."

He waved his hand, as if he were shooing away a fly. "Mystical double-talk," he said, with only the slightest of Eastern European accents. "Our sacred rabbis tell us that Kabbalah is for mature men. I say it's for children. Fairy tales and word games. Sit!" He pointed to the only chair in the room not overflowing with books and papers. He took a cell phone out of his pocket and set it on his desk. "I have ten minutes. I understand that you wish to speak about Lerner. You have questions. Ask."

He spit out the name *Lerner* like an epithet. I was surprised he made no effort to hide his distaste. "You didn't like him," I said.

"I despise him," he said. "With a great, satisfying passion. You know what Peretz used to say about Sholem Asch? These two Yiddish writers? Peretz would say, 'I wake myself up a half hour early every day so I'll have more time to hate Asch.' That's how I feel about Lerner. There are not enough hours in the day to contain my hatred."

I looked for some hint in his eyes that he was joking, or at least exaggerating. But his scowl never wavered. "Do you mind telling me why?" I asked.

"I'd love to. I relish articulating my hate for the man. We are on the record, I assume? I hope so."

Actually, it hadn't occurred to me to record the conversation. Jet lag had deadened my journalistic instincts. But I nodded, took out my iPhone, found the voice memo, and pressed record.

"He thinks . . . he *though*t, I should say. Thought. Past tense. I often forget that he's dead. My hatred, you see, is so alive in my heart. Anyway, he thought he owned the Shoah. That his stories were the only stories. Such enormous arrogance concerning our worst tragedy."

"Funny," I said. "I thought Chaim was one of the humblest men I'd ever met. Considering his accomplishments. He seemed really grounded. Down-to-earth. That was my impression."

"You were a boy. A foolish boy, lovestruck."

"I'll grant that. But what do you mean, he thought he owned the Shoah?"

"The lessons. The morals. The theology. The wisest men of our generation, our greatest Talmudists, scholars, theologians—the ones who survived the *hurban*—probed these mysteries and failed. But he's solved all the riddles. And what is his answer? Jews must have *less* power. We must *withdraw* from Lebanon, *withdraw* from Hebron and Bethlehem and Shechem. Wherever we assert our power over our enemies, enemies who pledge to destroy us, we must give up that power. Why? So we don't become Nazis, like the Germans. Can you imagine a philosophy more obscenely heretical? Never mind the insult to our soldiers, our commanders, the implication that these suffering and selfless and brave boys have become sadistic killers. For that alone—that blood libel—I could never forgive him. Never. But listen to what he prescribes, this policy genius. Less than forty years after the wicked Esau's army herds us into gas chambers and mass graves in the forest because we have no guns and planes and tanks, we cannot defend ourselves. Saint Lerner, using the moral authority of the mere random accident that he happened to survive where millions did not, commands us that we lay down our rifles, ground our fighter jets, and relinquish our weapons. Forty years later. After one generation. And why? You'll forgive me, but the demonic logic escapes me. Because we were weak? So now we must always be weak? Because we've witnessed the genocidal fury of the goy? Now we must not oppose it?"

I leaned back in my chair a few moments into Alon's diatribe. At first, I tensed up, prepared to flee, positive his own words would propel him across his desk, into my chest. But his dispassionate tone never changed. He spoke calmly, never modulating his voice, like a seasoned bureaucrat arguing against other bureaucrats for an electricity rate cut or a Talmud scholar offering a minor textual correction to his *chavrusa*. It occurred to me that he'd given this speech before, that it was his canned response to inquiries regarding Chaim, that, despite the fiery vocabulary, he was boring himself.

"And then," he continued, "the holy martyr—the martyr who miraculously didn't die—enlightens us as to the true nature of The Almighty. The Almighty, it turns out, is not almighty. He is The Less Than Almighty. Lerner invents for us the *shlepper* God. God as *schlemiel*, that is his contribution to twentieth-century thought. God, you see, so very much wants to help. He cries. He moans. But the Nazis are stronger than Him, poor thing. Cancer defeats Him, earthquakes leave Him puzzled and shaken. What do you want from Him, this pathetic loser? Stop nagging Him and celebrate His powerlessness! Weep with Him. His sadness is His most noble characteristic. Certainly not his power. Only Chaim Lerner would think that Jews would want to worship a God who is less than all-powerful. Because only Lerner, the Saint of Auschwitz, worships powerlessness. Look what he did. He created a God in his own image. Lerner is the one God of his own theology. Thank God he killed himself before he could convince even one more Jew of his catastrophic ideas." He reached across his right arm, unbuttoned the wrist buttons, and rolled up his sleeve. I assumed he'd heated himself up with his anti-Chaim polemic and would roll up the other sleeve. Instead, he gestured to me with his fingers to come close. He twisted his wrist and showed me his forearm. A tattooed number, his concentration camp ID. "You see?" he asked. For the first time, emotion entered his voice, but it was more disgust than anger. "Saint Chaim Lerner is not the only

Auschwitz survivor in the land of Israel. He's not the only one who can claim the right to speak on behalf of the victims. You see?" he said, thrusting his tattooed arm under my nose, as if he were demanding I smell it.

"I see the numbers," I said.

He took back his arm, rolled up his sleeve. "You see why I wanted to murder him."

What is going on here? Is he confessing? Did he and Charlie work this out ahead of time? Alon must have seen the horrified confusion on my face because he chuckled. "No, no, I didn't kill him. I'm not offering you a scoop. I'm confessing my feelings. And I want you to understand why many of us despised Lerner. We hated him when he was alive, and we hate him with an even darker, hotter passion now that he's been canonized by the church of the secular Jew in America."

He opened his desk drawer and took out a cigarette and lighter. I glanced at the sign just above his right ear. "No smoking," it said, in English, and, I assumed, Hebrew and Arabic. I wondered about smoke alarms. But he didn't light the cigarette. He just tapped the filtered side repeatedly on the desk, like he was beating out a quiet, obscure rhythm. "Other questions?" He looked at his phone. We'd surpassed the ten-minute mark at least twenty minutes ago. But he made no move to expel me.

I thought of the list of questions Charlie and I had worked on. I decided to throw in one that neither of us dared to suggest. "Where were you the night Chaim fell to his death?" I asked.

He waited a minute, as if he were expecting additional questions or considering how to phrase his answer. Then, he nodded twice and spoke calmly. "I was walking to Chaim's apartment. I live thirty minutes away. I had an appointment to speak with him at his home at seven-thirty p.m."

I had to contain myself from leaping off the chair. "Seven-thirty p.m!" I said. "May 5, 1983? Half an hour after the time of death? That's the time and date you were meeting with him? Is this some kind of joke?"

He kept his gaze on me and tapped his cigarette on the desk. "Do I seem like a joker to you, Loeb?"

"The night he died. Near the time of death. You were there?"

"I was running late. When I got there, I saw the ambulance. I inquired. They told me they were taking Chaim Lerner to the hospital. I assumed a stroke, a heart attack. God was finally punishing him for his sins. He was not a well man. Okay. I didn't see any point in continuing to the house. The family obviously had better things to do than explain to me what happened. I turned around and walked home. I didn't find out that he'd jumped to his death until the next morning when I listened to the news on the radio."

Charlie never told me any of this. Sneaky bastard. *Charlie never told me any of this.* It was a sentence that wouldn't stop journeying through my brain. One of the people Charlie considered a suspect, someone who admitted a murderous hatred for the victim was, by the suspect's own admission, present at the scene near the time of the murder. *And Charlie never told me!* "What did you tell the police?" I asked.

He shrugged. "The police never questioned me."

I stared at him. He stared back, daring me to voice my thoughts. Corruption? Alon was an important political figure even then. Could he have skewed the investigation? Incompetence? Seemed unlikely from the gang that won a war in six days, although they still couldn't defeat a ragtag group of Palestinian zealots. Coincidence? The guy who wished Chaim dead shows up at the time of death? Hard to believe. "You didn't think you should approach the police? You were practically a witness."

"I witnessed nothing. I assessed the situation. I realized I was not needed. I went home."

He studied a loose sheet of paper as I pondered what he told me. The cat leaped on his desk, miraculously avoiding the book piles, then hopped on Alon's lap. He petted the cat and cooed a slow melody in Yiddish. Could this old man have pushed Chaim off his balcony? Of course, he wasn't such an old man twenty-two years ago and was likely in better physical shape than Chaim. Still, murder because they disagreed on the lessons of the Shoah? Murder over who had the higher status as a Holocaust victim? Murderous hatred directed at an ideological opponent isn't exactly novel in human history even if I personally couldn't imagine that level of rage over politics. But there was something robotic in his delivery that undermined the angry words. And the coincidence was too shockingly obvious. I was missing something.

Alon gave me two minutes to stew in my thoughts. Then, he nudged the cat off his lap and touched his phone. "I'm afraid our time is up," he said. He remained seated but stuck out his hand. "It was a pleasure and an honor."

"Why were you going to Chaim's house?"

He slowly retracted his hand and reached into a desk drawer. He brought out a dusty unopened bottle of red wine and set it on one of his desk's few empty spots. Then, he grabbed a sealed, beige, card-sized envelope from the top of a pile of papers. "I was going to give him these things."

I looked at the bottle. Golan, a new product back then, Israel's first foray into fine wine. "A gift?"

"For his birthday. It was four days away, but I was flying to the United States the next evening. I always delivered his gift in person."

"A birthday present? For Chaim? And a card?"

"I never missed his birthday," he said, as if it were the most obvious statement in the world.

◆◆◆

I rendezvoused with Kaplowitz in the Kotel tunnel, where I'd met him years before as part of the kabbalah class. At the time, I thought he was a bodyguard or secretary. Now I discovered that he was indeed both of those things. But he was also the son of the teacher. He'd taken on all his late father's titles and duties. Unlike Alon, Rabbi Kaplowitz seemed overjoyed to see me. He grinned widely, kissed both my cheeks, then pulled me in for a tight embrace. I smelled dust and aftershave.

I honestly wouldn't have recognized him. In class, he was one of the duo of young haredim who waited on the rebbe, fetching coffee or mint tea, gathering his papers when the wind blew them away, glaring at students who interrupted or seemed not to be giving their fullest attention. The pair dressed alike, in dark coats and hats, and had identical long black beards. They were both thin and unusually tall for haredim—at least an inch taller than me, which would put them just past six, two. They could have been identical twins. Now Rabbi Kaplowitz carried the paunch of a man past his physical prime (like me), and his beard and hair had turned gray. But otherwise, he looked the same, which is to say he dressed and carried himself like a middle-aged haredi, frankly indistinguishable—to me at least—from the hundreds of male haredim now crowding the Kotel tunnel.

After hugging me, Kaplowitz retained contact by gripping me on my right upper arm and pulling me into a wide, brightly lit room about 100 feet into the tunnel on the right. I was surprised to see a fairly modern office, with a gleaming black desk, two computers—a desktop and a laptop—a laser printer just to the side, a copier, fax machine, two leather couches, an oak conference table surrounded by eight high-backed chairs, and five overstuffed armchairs in a semicircle around the desk. Kaplowitz dragged me to the couch, set me down, and then sat next to me, our hips nearly touching. Strangely, he was breathing heavily, as if dragging me to the office had been a particularly exhausting activity. He leaned forward and caught his breath, then looked around the room, gesturing at the desk, copier, table, and chair. "They gave me this office." He wheezed, his voice soft and mournful, as if he was bemoaning a particularly harsh punishment, as if the sleek, modern office were a prison cell. "An office here, another in Pisgat David. Offices, computers, copy machines. I belong in the beis midrash with my books." He shrugged, looked me in the eye, and smiled lovingly. Still nearly attached to me by his hip, he reached across his body and touched my shoulder. "You spoke to our friend Reb Meir Alon?"

I nodded. Charlie must have told him. I wondered again what exactly Charlie had choreographed for me. Was he simply placing me in front of possible murder suspects? Or representatives of larger groups, political forces, ideologies, that, consciously or not, had conspired to end Chaim's life, either by murder or suicide?

"Ach, a politician," Kaplowitz said. He sighed, but his voice retained its warmth. "We have enough of those." Kaplowitz's accent was a little thicker than Chaim's and Alon's, and he hesitated before enunciating certain words (like "politician"). But I marveled at how everyone I met with spoke perfect English while I, despite spending nearly a year in Israel with an Israeli girlfriend, could barely muster ten words of Hebrew. "And you spoke about Chaim, may his memory be a blessing?"

"Yes," I said. "Well, I didn't hear him categorizing Chaim's memory as a blessing. More like a curse."

He chuckled, a sound I could only compare to Santa laughing. He even jiggled his paunch as he laughed, slapping his lap, as if urging me to climb aboard. "Alon and his vendettas," he said. "Some of these so-called religious politicians, they are my brothers, my friends, but they leave out the religion. They forget that the Torah is a Torah of compassion and forgiveness."

"Compassion and forgiveness," I repeated.

"Of course."

This wasn't my purpose, but I decided to wade into politics. It really wasn't avoidable in this country. "For Arabs? For the Palestinians?"

"Especially for the Palestinians. They are the stranger here. The Torah commands us precisely to love the stranger. Thirty-six times."

I considered that. "You're the rabbi of Pisgat David?"

"That is my honor."

"It's a settlement, right? On Palestinian territory? It's exactly where your neighbors would like to build a state. And how much do your residents love those strangers? Haven't you just created more hostility? How is that compassion?"

He unleashed, once again, his Santa chuckle, as if I were an especially adorable child who'd just said the darndest thing. "We are arguing politics today, Judah? That's our agenda? Let me first point out that anywhere people live together is a settlement. New York is a settlement. Ramallah. We settle where God commands us to settle."

"Even if there's already someone living there."

"No one was living in Pisgat David when we arrived. It was an empty hillside."

"You know what I mean. It's where Palestinian shepherds brought their sheep to graze. It cuts off three Palestinian villages from each other. You steal from their fields. You take their water."

"Yes," he said, without hesitation. "And those are crimes. Those thieves should be punished. I agree, it's very hard for our neighbors. We must find a way to compensate them. And you're correct. Some of my people despise our Palestinian friends. Sometimes they steal. Harass. They don't show the compassion our Torah demands. I've failed as their rabbi, in many ways. But nevertheless, we must be there on that hill. God commands us. As for the Palestinians." He shook his head. "It's tragic. We must provide an alternative for them. We must open our hands with generosity."

"Alternative?"

He shrugged, sadly. He seemed genuinely pained. "They cannot stay. But, you know, Abraham and Sarah sinned grievously. They didn't provide Hagar and Ishmael with enough food or water when they expelled them from their home. God in his great mercy rescued Ishmael, and He thereby rescued the great Arab people. If it had been left to the mercies of our father Abraham, Hagar and the child would have died in the desert. We must do better."

"Better—in kicking them out? Expelling the Palestinians?"

Again, the sad shrug. "The Torah demands sacrifice."

But who is supposed to sacrifice? I wondered. I was about to ask when Kaplowitz patted my lap. "Theology, politics, Torah," he said, smiling. "Worthy topics. But not why you're here, Reb Judah. You came to discuss Chaim. Shall we?" He leaned back, creating space between our bodies for the first time since we'd embraced.

"What did you think of him?" I asked.

He closed his eyes and tilted his face toward the high domed ceiling. "I loved him. Like a brother. I adored him. How I loved him."

There was a window in the door that opened to the tunnel. I could see the outside space filling up with *haredi* men, crowding around the wall, pushing their way in so they could touch the sacred stones while they prayed. It must have been an official time for services. I heard mumbled cries, responses, and song. But Kaplowitz showed no inclination to join the flock. He kept his face pointed toward heaven, his eyes tightly shut. "You loved him?" I asked. "Everything about him?"

He opened his eyes, tilted his head, smiled, and regarded me with the delight of a loving parent. "Not everything. Even a mother finds some fault in her newborn. But almost everything. Almost.

He was a brilliant thinker and a lover of Israel. A wonderful family. A generous soul. No meanness, no jealousy. He survived the Shoah, guided us through our worst experiences, and then this? Such a tragedy."

"A tragedy?" I said. "You think it was an accident?"

"Reb Judah. By now, you must know what I believe. There are no accidents. Especially here in this holy land, in this holy city."

"What do you think happened?" I asked.

He sat up straight and frowned. Tears flooded his eyes, moistened his beard. "The Holy One," he said, wheezing again. "God gives and God takes. God took him."

"God took him? God killed him?"

"What choice did He have? Chaim dared Him to do it. He called the Holy One less than all-powerful. A dangerous heresy. Awful. God showed His great power. A true tragedy."

I was astonished. A new suspect—God? "You mean God pushed him over the balcony? A heavenly wind?"

"A wind. Murder. Suicide. A drunken stumble. Those are mere details. Interesting maybe to you and our dear friend Charlie, to earthly investigators. For me, there is only one answer. It was the will of God." He breathed in deeply, then exhaled slowly and twisted his lips upward, forcing his naturally joyful face to reassert itself. I watched him transform himself from mourning to gladness.

"What were you doing that night?" I asked. "Around seven p.m."

He turned to me. "That night? The night Chaim died? Reb Charlie certainly told you. It's why you're here, correct?"

"Charlie told me shockingly little," I said.

"Ah. Well, he's a complicated man, our Charlie. Multiple agendas, not always easy to sort through. That night. The night God took my friend. Well. I ate dinner with my wife and seven of my eight children. I'm blessed. We watched the news. We studied the parsheh. My youngest son—now he has five boys of his own and the sweetest bride—led us through birkat hamazon. I said goodnight, bid them farewell. I walked. A pleasant, clear night. I walked."

I felt a coolness on the back of my neck, as if a breeze from that night broke through the barrier of time and space. I hesitated to ask but forced myself. "Walked where?"

"Reb Judah, you must know. I walked. I walked. To Chaim's house."

I dropped my pen and paper. The pen clattered across the stone floor. Kaplowitz chose to follow it with his eyes rather than face me. Then, he looked up. Thick tears leaked from his dark-brown eyes, soaking his whiskers. "It was almost his birthday," he said.

♦♦♦

"Charlie, what the fuck!"

"Calm down," he said.

We were sitting in an outdoor café on the Ben Yehuda plaza. For a city that had recently endured a wave of suicide bombings, the pedestrian mall was packed. Large groups of teen tourists, with matching T-shirts, backpacks, and baseball caps, marched across the cobblestone, singing songs in Hebrew, Spanish, and English. Young Israeli couples crowded the outdoor restaurants; roughly half the men wore knitted yarmulkes, the rest bareheaded. Hundreds of others, including haredim dressed in black, priests with their collars and vestments, Arabs with white robes, and moderns in shorts and tank tops, hurried through the plaza, clutching shopping bags. It was Friday afternoon—a leisure time for many, and for many others, the time to shop, clean, and cook for Shabbat. We were waiting for Hannah and Michal, who were finishing up their interview with the wannabe suicide bomber at a nearby prison. Charlie nursed his Maccabi beer; I was still fighting off jet lag, so I sipped a steady stream of espressos.

"Two guys who wanted Chaim dead," I said. I held up two fingers. I noticed my hands trembling. So was my voice. "Two. And they both admit they were at the scene the night of the murder!"

Charlie laughed. "Murder? You're calling it murder? I see you're coming around."

"What else am I supposed to think? This is your so-called new evidence, right? This is why the police reopened the case?"

"Well, it's new. There's no previous record of it."

"How could that be? No one talked to them twenty-two years ago? You didn't interview known associates? The Kabbalah circle? Rabbis in Pisgat David? They hated Chaim back then. Openly."

"Yeah, well it was officially a suicide. From what I can tell, the decision to call it suicide was made right away, at the highest levels. And the family agreed. It's what Holocaust writers do. They write and write and write. Then, they kill themselves."

I nodded. Again, the writers. Paul Celan. Thadeus Borowski. Jerzy Kosinski. Jean Amery. Holocaust survivors who used fiction or poetry to reflect on their Shoah traumas. All suicides. I shook my head. "That's not evidence. Anyway, Applefeld is still alive. In Jerusalem. And Eli Wiesel."

"I'm just telling you the official story. Chaim killed himself like Paul Celan, like the others. He was Hitler's final victim. Number six million and one."

I shook my head. "Charlie, this is starting to feel like a conspiracy. Two men—a powerful politician, an influential rabbi—admit that Chaim had to die. They have motive and opportunity. They were both at the scene. No alibis. And they represent large populations. And no one thinks to interrogate them until today?"

"Why do you think I brought you here?" Charlie said. For the first time, I could sense a chord of impatience in his tone. He took a swig of his beer.

"You brought me here? I don't understand."

"You think your editors, your publisher, would have sent you here if I hadn't told you that we'd reopened the case? That there were real questions about Chaim's death?"

I thought about that. He was right that the true crime element—the ongoing criminal mystery—intrigued Stan, my brother-in-law agent, and the editors who approved the project. A suicide that's possibly a homicide. It intrigued me, convinced me there was a story here that many people would want to read. But something in the way Charlie phrased the last two sentences caught my attention. "You said you told me that the police here had reopened the case. Not that they'd reopened the case, just that you'd told me."

He signaled the waiter for another beer. "You're good with words," he said. "Good at writing, good at listening."

I watched Charlie's half smile. It took my still jetlagged brain another minute to work things out. "The police didn't actually reopen the case. You just told me that. So I'd tell my agent, my editors. You wanted me here to investigate a closed case."

He twisted off the top of the beer and swallowed a good quarter of it before putting the bottle down. "It's like you said. These are important guys. Important twenty-two years ago, much more important today. Alon's a freaking deputy prime minister. He winks at his faction, and the government falls. Kaplowitz is probably the most popular rabbi in Israel. Certainly the most powerful rabbi in the settlements. You think I could get my bosses to bring these guys in, park them in an interrogation booth, grill them? I needed some outside pressure. I needed you."

Charlie was wearing his light-blue police uniform. I supposed he was on duty, though he'd just polished off three beers. I studied his shirt. I couldn't decipher the writing or the various badges, but his chest was well decorated. I assumed he'd risen far up the ranks. He needed me? "How did you find out about Alon and Kaplowitz?"

"You think I didn't remember all the stories you told me about Chaim? The people he'd pissed off? The big shots in the Kabbalah circle, the folks he insulted at Pisgat David. When you first emailed me that you were thinking of a Chaim Lerner book, but you doubted your publisher would pay for it, I decided to ask around. I'm pretty high up in the force, so I've met Kaplowitz and Alon. Lucky for me, they were the first two I talked to from the Kabbalah circle. I was stunned at what they told me. I knew I had to bring you out here. So I lied. It was the only way."

"The only way for what?"

He polished off the last of his beer. "To find the killer."

I watched him dig into his pocket for his phone. I was nervous, irritated. But surprisingly free of fury. Why wasn't I angrier? No one likes being misled or manipulated. But his machinations had brought me here, back to Jerusalem after twenty-two years. And, for some reason, it's where I wanted to be. Or maybe I was just too tired for anger.

Charlie laughed. "Just got a text from Michal," he said and handed me his phone. "Read it."

We'll be there in ten minutes. Hannah says to tell Judah we've figured it out. We solved the case. We know why Chaim killed himself.

◆ ◆ ◆

I could tell Michal and Hannah were arguing as they walked up the cobblestone and toward our café. Hannah was punching her right fist into her left hand, a rhythmic slapping I could hear from thirty feet away. Michal was wagging her finger uncomfortably close to Hannah's ear, as if she could inject her argument through the ear canal and into the brain. I was intimately familiar with the gestures both used when quarreling.

By the time they reached the table, the argument had resolved into a sullen, stony silence. Our waiter showed up as they sat down, and to my astonishment, Hannah unleashed several sentences in Hebrew. I heard the word "toast" and understood the words "choco" (chocolate) and "cham" (hot), but the rest sounded like native talk. "You learned Hebrew?" I asked.

She shrugged. "It's not that hard to learn enough to order in a restaurant." She looked at me, irritated. "You lived here for a year. You can't order in Hebrew?"

I was about to snap back, but Michal rescued us from another argument. "Hannah prepared excellently for her trip. She knows more about us than many Israelis her age."

"Yeah," Hannah said. "I do. And I definitely know more than *you* about my own father."

"Hannah," Michal said. "Of course you do. I just don't think it's appropriate—"

"Who are you to decide?" Hannah said, popping her fist into her palm. "Just because you were his girlfriend a hundred years ago."

"Hey, Hannah," I said. "I'm right here." I looked at Michal. "You don't have to talk about me. Just ask."

"Michal videotaped my interview with Kamal," Hannah said. "The guy who wanted to blow himself up in a pizza place. He was cool. So cool. I want to show you the video. Dad, I think you can use it for your book. It explains everything. But Michal thinks it'll make you sad."

"It made you cry," Michal said.

"That's different," Hannah answered. She unzipped a side pocket of Michal's bulky black backpack and pulled out a hand-sized video cassette player. Michal stared and frowned while

Hannah rummaged through her property. But she didn't object. "We can watch it right now," Hannah said. Then, she barked a guttural word in Hebrew at Michal, who barked back. *Amazing*, I thought. *They've known each other for barely two days, and they're fighting like mother and daughter.*

The waiter brought two hot chocolates and a cheese toast for Hannah. Michal stared at the steam coming from her cup. I looked at Charlie, who just shrugged. Hannah waved the cassette at my face. "Okay," I said. "Let's watch Kamal."

Hannah set the palm-sized screen on the edge of the salt and pepper shakers and pressed play. A thin, olive-skinned, clean-shaven young man sat on a concrete bench with his hands cuffed in front of him. Hannah sat off to the side, with only her left cheek and hair visible. Hannah asked questions in English. Michal translated the questions and then the Hebrew answers from Kamal. Hannah first asked him to describe the incident.

"The target was Sbarros in Hod Hasharon," Michal recited, after Kamal spoke in Hebrew. Michal spoke in a steady, matter-of-fact tone, like a court translator. Kamal, on the other hand, injected every word with drama, modulating between high and low, as if he were chanting a sacred text, moving his bound hands in rhythm to his tale. "It's a city less than a twenty-minute drive from *Dahaisha*, the camp where I live. Three kilometers north of this Jewish city was an Arab village called *Sylia*. My grandparents lived there and were expelled by the Jews in the *Naqba*. My grandfather loses his place at Cairo University, the medical school. Because he is now a refugee, he cannot attend. He ends up a janitor at a Christian school in Ramallah, and he dies young. A heart attack, a broken heart. I go to Hod Hasharon to revenge my grandfather. My mission—to blow myself up and take as many Jews with me as Allah allows. Great sadness at my home before I leave. I don't tell my mother or father where I am really going, what I am doing. I lie to them. I tell them I'm going to see Milah, my fiancé in Jenin. But they know. They hear me recite the martyr verses before I go to sleep each night. They see me, every day, become inflamed with rage and Muslim furor. They offer hospitality to my new friend, brother of the *shaheed* of Tiberius. And they see my bulky coat. It's November, not so hot, and I'm wearing a heavy coat. They know."

"Did they try and talk you out of it?" Hannah interrupted, and Michal quickly translated.

"*La. La. La. La*," Kamal said. "He says no," Michal translated.

He went on to explain his journey. A car ride to Ramallah, then he's smuggled into South Tel Aviv in the trunk of a van, soaking himself in sweat from fear, anxiety, and the heat of an unseasonably warm day. From Tel Aviv, he took a public bus. A few people looked askance at his bulky coat, but this is before the great wave of terrorism. No one stops him. It's only when he reaches the front door of the restaurant that a uniformed soldier just passing by notices him. "My brother," he says to me. "Let's talk for a moment. He puts his hand on my shoulder and smiles. Can I buy you a beer, buy you a slice of pizza? His hand slides down the side of my arm, and I realize he's frisking me. But he's rubbing the left side. The trigger for the bomb is on my right. I don't even think for a moment. My reflexes push me. My right hand jerks up toward the trigger, just below my shoulder. The soldier understands what I'm doing. He bear-hugs me and pulls me away from the restaurant. I wiggle and squirm, but he is strong. Well, really, I am weak. As he wrestles me to the ground, he whispers in my ear, 'You and I will die right now, but you are not going into that restaurant.' He is stronger, but my fingers are skinny. I reach past his thick forearm. I find the trigger and pull. Nothing happens. I wiggle and pull again. Nothing. The bomb is a dud. God did not want this. God saved fifty people in the restaurant. God saved the soldier. God saved me." He whispered the last line, but Michal recited it firmly and loudly in English.

"Why did you do it?" Hannah asked. "You mentioned revenge. Was that your motive? Vengeance?"

"Yes, yes, of course. Revenge. But not just revenge."

"Was it the virgins?" Hannah asked. "All those virgins in heaven?" Michal hesitated but then translated.

For the first time, Kamal smiled. "Yes, the virgins! Sounds wonderful, does it not? Forty-nine virgins, or some say seventy-three. Who can resist? No, I tell you, that's not me. It wasn't me, even when I was an insane suicide killer. Of course, they bribe us with stories of virgins. And cake and honey and all good things in heaven. It meant nothing to me. To be honest, I was more motivated by the money my family would get from Hamas, enough, maybe to move from the camp, move to Ramallah, or maybe even London or Detroit."

"So, revenge and a reward," Hannah said. "Not in heaven, but here, for your family. That's why you did it. What else? Religion? Did you think Islam commanded you to fight the Jews and kill them?"

He shrugged. "Religion? Maybe. Maybe this was a bonus. I was following the Sharia. God would be pleased. Maybe? But really, it was not for religion. You will think I'm crazy. I was. I was stupid crazy. The number one reason? Send a message with my death, with my mass murder. *Significance.* This is the word I've learned in this jail. I wanted to live a significant life, a life of meaning for my people. But this was not possible. I was poor and stuck in a muddy, smelly refugee camp. My life had no significance. I could only find significance in death. My death and the death of innocents. Yes, I knew they were innocent. They were not the oppressor. But I was sending them to heaven as a message to all humanity. Look at us, I was saying to the whole world—to America, to Russia, to China, to Egypt, to Syria, and, yes, to Israel. Help us. We are so desperate. Save us. You know we record a video before we go. A statement. We explain our goals. We think every child in China watches this video. Every Muslim in Indonesia. They will watch the video and come to our defense. That is our narcissism. That is our madness. But it is also the reason why we blow ourselves up. Why we blow you up."

He spoke for several more minutes, but Michal stopped translating. He looked at the camera, at where Michal was standing, puzzled.

"Why did you stop translating?" Hannah asked.

"It wasn't important," Michal said. "He was just correcting something from before. But I'd already corrected it."

"*La*," Kammal said. "No!" He switched to English. "I was telling lady that I was coward! Suicide is coward. Is cruel to family and weak, coward and wrong. Everyone who do suicide is selfish coward. That is what I say. Is important."

The camera caught a single tear rolling down Hannah's cheek, the only cheek visible. We also heard a sniffle. I looked at her now, watching the screen. Her cheeks were dry, but her eyes seemed full. "It's not the same, Hannah," I said. "You can't compare the two."

"I know!" she snapped. "I'm not a total moron. Mom didn't try to take fifty innocent men, women, and children with her when she hung herself. I know that." She sipped her hot chocolate. "This is cold," she said.

Michal clicked off the video. "That was it. Our time was up, but anyhow, he was done telling his story. He's an important source for us. He helps us understand their methods, as well as their motivations. People think it's all virgins and Sharia. Or revenge, the cycle of violence. You heard what he said. Significance."

I nodded. "Hannah, you said you solved the case. You understand why Chaim killed himself. What did you mean?"

"Well, you heard it," she said. "Significance. He was sending a message."

"What message?" Charlie asked.

"I don't know!" Hannah said. "About Lebanon, right? Or the Occupation. I was thinking, maybe the message was for Holocaust deniers. Dad, you told me how much their books tortured him. He was sending a message to the world. The Holocaust is real. I'm real."

I stared at my fifteen-year-old child. How did she become such a perceptive soul? How did she learn to think so deeply, with such empathy? She certainly didn't get it from me. There was, however, a slight flaw in her reasoning, which I felt compelled to point out. "But Hannah," I said. "If the point was to send a message, why didn't he leave a note? The suicide bombers record messages. But for Chaim, without a note, how would the world get the message?"

Hannah looked at Michal. "Oh, yeah," Michal said. "We forgot to tell you. We found the note."

CHAPTER 11

April-May 1983

Zehava described a "splendid" shop in the Christian Quarter of the Old City where she assumed Michal would buy her wedding dress. She couldn't wait to accompany her daughter-in-law-to-be to the store. Maybe she'd buy herself a new dress there and a few more Persian rugs. Perhaps I'd like to tag along, she offered, buy some souvenirs for my family.

Chaim wondered about the ceremony. He hoped they would consider asking Rabbi Kaplowitz from his Zohar circle to perform the rituals. Of course, Chaim himself would prefer a non-Orthodox rabbi, but this, unfortunately, was impossible in Israel. But Rabbi Kaplowitz was blessed with an open mind, and perhaps he'd even permit Chaim to rewrite one of the marriage blessings, even if he just recited it in English, or even Arabic.

They spoke over each other, responded to each other with their own particular passions, or spoke to me, each in their own turn. In my memory, I hear them talking simultaneously, and, through a cruel miracle, I understand them both perfectly. I felt like I'd been transported to a parallel universe, one where I hadn't enjoyed a passionate eight-month love affair—my first—with Michal, where I was merely a friend of the family or maybe just a distant cousin. The vehicle that brought me to this strange new world was a bullet to the chest, one that spilled no blood but stayed lodged in my lungs, robbing me of speech or even breath. Michal would marry Yoav. Would marry someone who was not me. It could only be true in a bizarro, fallen world where nightmares become reality.

But, of course, reality intruded, harsher than any bullet. Even in the nightmare, I recognized that it wasn't my imagination, a hallucination, or a tasteless practical joke. I admitted to myself that I'd suspected a romantic connection between Michal and Yoav from the first time I'd heard about his existence and Michal's connection to the Lerner family. I'd also harbored nagging insecurities about our relationship. Why would a bright, lively, beautiful Israeli woman like Michal flirt with an ordinary, decidedly unworldly American like me on the first day we met? Why would she allow herself to fall in love with me, when she knew I would inevitably leave and she would stay? I knew now that she flirted with me as an experiment, to test the relationship with the troubled, missing Yoav. And the relationship passed the test, which is to say I failed it. She chose Yoav over me, which was undoubtedly her preference all along.

I got up from the table in the middle of a muddle of happy wedding talk. A mild headache, I told them. Not enough sleep. I'd go back to the dorm, get a few hours of rest before finishing up my theology paper. Zehava nodded, grinned, and squeezed my hand, then turned back to Chaim to ask him if the Arab store sold wedding rings. Chaim tilted his head at me and squinted, as if he was just now seeing something he'd missed. But Zehava touched his arm, and he turned his head back to her. I left without saying goodbye.

I knew I couldn't return to the lonely desolation of the Mt. Scopus dorm. I thought of marching across the street and down two houses to Michal's place. I'd force my way in, convince her to change her mind, fight for her. But this wasn't an American romantic comedy where one lover rushes after the other and she changes her mind at the movie's final scene. Boy meets girl, boy loses girl, boy regains her. Or if it was, it was Yoav's story, Yoav's journey—Yoav the hero. I was the bit player, the impediment, the comic distraction that the golden couple overcomes.

I walked straight through the *haredi* neighborhood. After taking just two steps, the street seemed to suddenly explode with life. Young mothers, many of them pregnant, pushed double or triple strollers through the hard cobblestone. It was Shabbat; cars were forbidden, but strollers were allowed through a legal fiction called an *eruv*—a string around the city, making it a single house. Alongside the mothers and strollers were children, three or four or five or more, some crying, some laughing, all holding on to each other's hand, like it was some kind of solidarity march. *Haredi* women and children. I wondered where the men had gone. Studying? Napping? Wherever they were, I knew I didn't belong with them, and I certainly didn't belong with the women and children. Or with the secular men, who served in the army, nor, come to think of it, with any Israelis. They spoke a language I'd never learn, conducting themselves with an aggressive energy I would never be able to emulate. I was a stranger in this strange land. A ten-month tourist whose time was almost up.

I found myself walking through Wadi Joz, the Arab neighborhood filled with car repair shops and skeletons of broken-down vehicles. Teenage boys kicked soccer balls on the twisty sidewalks, dodging the dented fenders, broken glass, and loose tires. A tall, skinny kid, thirteen or fourteen—Bar Mitzvah age—shouted at me in Arabic. He could have been asking me how I was doing, cursing me out, mocking my American clothing, or threatening to murder me for all I knew. I stopped and shrugged, figuring if he wanted to stab me, I'd let it happen. But he pointed at the ground next to my sandal, and I saw another soccer ball. I kicked it to him with all the grace of a great-grandfather in a walker. He waved at me, and I turned left, toward the Old City.

Damascus Gate teemed with pedestrians. Mostly it was Palestinian men in dark jeans and T-shirts pushing their way through the walled entrance, leaning on each other's shoulders. But there were also black-robed women, with scarves covering their hair, older men with kaffiyehs and canes hobbling through, and a smattering of foreign tourists lugging cameras and backpacks. I wedged my way into the line, twisting through the gate. The crowd carried me into the city, and I quickly took the right fork into the Arab market.

My program discouraged trips to the Arab quarter. If we must go, they told us, never walk alone. In the past month, there had been three violent attacks against Jews in the Old City—two with knives and one with a bullet that just missed the head of a visiting American rabbi on his way to pray at the *Kotel* on a Friday afternoon. My only visits up to that day had been with Michal, who strode fearlessly through every maze and alleyway. Now, surrounded and pushed by eager shoppers, bellowing shopkeepers, and tourists, I felt no fear whatsoever. But I did wish someone would stab or shoot me. It seemed like an appropriate way to end my suddenly shattered life.

I moved forward and then turned at random whenever a fork in the road appeared. Somehow, I must have wandered into the Christian Quarter because the shops now included a variety of crosses—tiny silver ones for necklaces, fist-sized white ones to hang on your rearview mirror, multicolored mosaic ones—artwork to decorate any room in the house. At the end of the road was a church, with a giant crucifix hanging over the entrance. I felt suddenly faint and thirsty. I thought of entering the church, finding a priest, begging for water. But I noticed a large, colorful, well-lit shop just to the left of the church. *That's it*, I realized. Michal's favorite store, the one she dragged me to the day after our first quarrel. I realized this must be the same shop where Zehava longed to go—to accompany Michal, her future daughter-in-law, as she tried on and purchased a wedding dress for her marriage, to someone other than me.

I walked into the store. Near the entrance where I stood were cheap tourist knickknacks like postcards, card-sized mosaic tiles with Hebrew last names, T-shirts with writing in Hebrew, Arabic, and/or English, olive-wood necklaces with dangling crosses, cheap blue and white *mezuzahs*, knit yarmulkes, and ceramic upside-down hands—*hamsas*—mystically significant for Arabs and Jews. But off to the right, in its own department, I could see the fancier jewelry. And in the left corner, women's clothing, including colorful Bedouin wedding dresses, complete with veils and head coverings. Was that Michal's dream? To marry Yoav as a Bedouin?

I walked slowly to the dresses, passing the leather goods department and an alarming variety of gleaming stainless-steel knives. I reached for a Bedouin dress and caressed it, slowly running the unpleasantly coarse material through my thumb and forefinger. *Not a good choice for a summer wedding*, I thought, as if I had any role in planning Michal's marriage to Yoav. I heard a man clear his throat behind me—an alarming, guttural sound. I quickly withdrew my hand from the dress and turned.

"It's all right. It's all right," the man said. He was tall and thin, with jet-black hair, a skinny black mustache, and a tawny complexion. Rafik, the store owner. "You are marrying a Bedouin?"

"No, no, I was just . . ."

"Of course not," he said, laughing loudly. He touched my shoulder. "But weddings on the brain, no?" He looked around the store. "Where is she?" he asked.

"Who?" I asked. But I knew.

"You woman. This is my store. I own it all. I see you with her. We smoke, you remember. You shop. And her alone, many times, ten times maybe this year alone. Great customer. Pretty girl. You are lucky man. But you know what, my advice, you let her buy the dress. For you, what you do, mister groom, I will show you the rings. Many, many beautiful rings, wedding rings, engagement rings. Only the finest. Give you best price."

"No, no," I said. "I'm not . . ." What would I say to him? Would this stranger be the first person I tell about the most consequential moment in my life—that I'd lost the woman I'd hoped and expected to spend the rest of my life with? I couldn't imagine describing this pain to my parents or Charlie or my friends back home, much less to this odd storekeeper.

"You're not ready," he said. "I understand. But let me show you something. So you'll know. When you're ready, you come see me. Only best price." He attached himself to my arm and dragged me to the front of the store. Behind the cashier, hung on the wall, were signed black-and-white photos of his most famous customers, all in golden frames. I recognized Moshe Dayan, Yitzhak Navon, and Arik Sharon. Below them, Israelis pop stars Yehudit Ravitz, Shalom Hanoch, and Arik Einstein. I did a double take when I saw the photo at the very top, the one with the most writing, all in English. It was Zehava, ten years younger, maybe more. With dark hair, no wrinkles, and a bright, warm smile. She was beautiful. Rafik released my arm, then reached up, removed the photo from the wall, and showed it to me. She'd written, "To my friend, Rafik. My favorite store in all of Israel. Always the best prices for my dresses."

"You know her, I think," Rafik said.

I nodded slowly. "I do. But how did you know?"

He pointed to his ear. "I listen. You'll forgive me. I eavesdrop on the conversations of all my favorite customers. So I know their hearts. I know what merchandise to order for them. To make special price for the best rings and bracelets and drums and dresses. It is what brings me joy. I listen to you and your love. Michal, is it not? I listen to her sweet voice. You are lucky man."

The smell of the *shuk* suddenly intruded. Spices, coffee, cardamom, sesame, leather, cinnamon, donkey sweat, church wax, shit, fruit, rotting vegetables, onions, human perspiration. Mixed together, it was not a bad odor. Good, in fact, when you're in a good mood, when you're exploring, when you're young and in love. It had, of course, been there all along. It followed me, in fact, all through Jerusalem. It was the smell of that awful and awesome year. I noted its power for the first time at that moment, facing the grinning shopkeeper telling me that I'm a lucky man. The *shuk* smell overcame me. It nauseated me, sent me to my knees in a fit of coughing. Rafik lifted me from the rear, pointed, and then shoved me toward his bathroom. I vomited all of the Lerner's breakfast into Rafik's toilet. When I came out, he was holding a small silver flask. He extended his long arm all the way to hand it to me, avoiding my breath. "I have made you sad," he said gently. "I spoke too much. I misjudged. This is gift for you. This will help your heart." I grabbed the flask and hurried out.

After exiting the Old City through the Jaffa Gate, before beginning my ascent to Mt. Scopus, I twisted off the flask's cap and sniffed. Alcohol. Vodka, tequila, or gin—the truth is, I had no idea. When it came to booze, I only knew beer and wine. I took a slug from the flask, then took three more steps and drank some more. By the time I reached my room, I was drunk. I threw up again in the bathroom—the rest of the food and a stream of noxious liquid—and passed out on my bed.

By the time Charlie woke me up, stomping down the hallway, dropping his bag on the floor, flicking on the light, it was evening. He took one look at my face and asked how long I'd been sick. Then, he spotted the flask on my desk, sniffed the air, and smiled. "Oh, that kind of sick, huh?"

I told him the "wonderful" news I'd heard from Chaim and Zehava. The saintly troubled Yoav getting married—to Michal! It seemed a simple story to me, even timeless; girlfriend chooses another, breaks the other boy's heart. But Charlie probed for details. What, exactly, had Yoav told Chaim over the phone? Could I repeat some of the Hebrew? How, precisely, had Zehava reacted? If I can't recall the words, could I describe her facial expression, the tone of her voice? Describe Michal's body language when she talked about Yoav. What Hebrew words did she use? I realized that Charlie was practicing his undergraduate criminology skills, investigating my heartbreak as if it were a crime. But there was nothing mysterious about Michal marrying Yoav. In fact, it solved a number of mysteries. Why Michal was so close to the Lerners in the first place. Why she didn't want to tell them we were together. Why she would never look me in the eye when she spoke about Yoav. Why she had no social life and no friends when I met her; she was spending all her free time with Yoav—her almost fiancé. I explained all this to Charlie.

"But you're missing the big mystery," he said.

I waited.

"Why introduce you to the Lerners at all? Why risk them finding out that you were together?"

Yes, that was a mystery, or at least a legitimate question. The problem was, I didn't want to know the answer. Any solution only hurt more. Maybe she wanted them to know she had other options. Maybe she figured they'd tell Yoav, and that would make him jealous. Maybe she thought of our relationship as a meaningless fling. Every answer blew up the love-story narrative I'd been carrying until just the day before: adventure, meaning, and true love in the Holy Land.

"Listen, Judah, you at least have got to go see her. You've only heard the news through Zehava and Chaim. Maybe they got something wrong. Maybe they misunderstood. Or maybe Yoav is lying to them. Or maybe he's hallucinating. He's got mental problems, right? Or, I don't know, maybe you can change her mind. Fight for her."

For the first time in hours, I perked up. Every one of Charlie's possibilities was ridiculous—wishful thinking—especially the last one. But what did I have to lose? Anyway, the idea of never seeing her again felt like a bottomless pit. I sat up and reached for my sneakers.

"Uh, Judah," Charlie said.

I looked up.

"Clean up a little bit first."

♦♦♦

I jogged most of the way to Michal's apartment, down Mt. Scopus, through Wadi Joz. It was just past midnight when I climbed the three stairways and rang her buzzer. She didn't answer, so I sat on the floor and leaned my head against her door. She'd either arrive early the next morning, or she was there and would eventually wake up and leave the apartment. Either way, I'd catch her, confront her. I had just closed my eyes, feeling my mind drift off, when the door swung open. I fell backward into Michal's legs.

♦♦♦

"I did love you," she said. "I mean, I do . . . I do love you." We faced each other at her kitchen table. Michal wore red running shorts and a gray tank top—her usual bed clothes. She sipped her coffee, which had to have gone cold by now. I hadn't touched my glass of water. She'd just finished weeping her way through a forty-five-minute story—one she could have told in two minutes. She and Yoav were middle school pals, high school sweethearts, then serious young adult lovers. They rarely quarreled, but ten months ago, Yoav enraged her when he applied for an officer training program. It meant more time away from her, more potential danger for him, but most importantly, it meant involving him intimately in the Lebanon conflict, a war Michal despised. They fought by phone, she hung up on him, and the next day, she met me in Chaim's class. Yoav never called back, so she figured it was over, and she'd found somebody new.

But then Zehava called and told her about Khalel, in Northern Lebanon, how Yoav had shot two ten-year-old boys and was admitted to a military psych ward in Haifa. Zehava begged Michal to go and see him. She refused. It was over. But every week, sometimes every day, Zehava asked again. Michal put her off. She was with me, happy, though the happiness was always mixed with guilt. But Zehava persevered, insisted. Zehava, who'd always been like a mother to her. Zehava, who never stopped calling her "my daughter." Finally, last week, Michal relented. She visited Yoav in the military hospital. And then . . .

She stopped the story. I could figure out the rest myself. I asked her if she ever loved me, and she answered yes, of course.

"But, Judah, seeing Yoav so helpless in the hospital. You can't imagine."

"You're marrying him because you feel sorry for him?"

"That's not it," she said. She took another sip of cold coffee, then massaged her forehead. It was 2 a.m. "You have to understand. I love you. But I also love him. You can love two people. But then you have to choose. That's what I realized. I fought it at first. But it wasn't something I could defeat. It was love. I love him."

"More than you love me," I said. It wasn't a question. The answer was obvious, so she didn't answer. But she did nod, slightly.

"Why?" I asked. I don't know why I asked that, possibly the stupidest question someone could ask about love. I don't think Michal intended to destroy me with her answer, but I'm not absolutely sure she didn't. Anyway, she said it, dry-eyed and clear-voiced.

"Listen, Judah," she said. "Sometimes there is no why."

◆ ◆ ◆

At first, I intended to stay in Israel, to finish out the year. I forced myself out of bed every morning after at most two hours of sleep, showered, shaved, and tried to eat. I attended all my classes and actually stayed more engaged than I had before the breakup. Charlie showed me all the dingiest Jerusalem bars, most of them in the eastern, Arab parts of the city. We went out drinking every night, listened to local bands, ogled the belly dancers. After the mystery booze from the shopkeeper, I stuck to beer. I joined the other American students playing ultimate frisbee in Sacher Park every Friday afternoon. For the first time, I spoke up during the lunchtime political arguments at the Frank Sinatra cafeteria. I defended Israel's government, blasted the cowardly leftists. It was a Jerusalem spring—green returning to the trees, the weather warmer every day, and sunny.

But I was mimicking renewal. Really, I was devastated. How did anyone live with this pain? It wasn't like the movies or songs—I didn't see her face everywhere. The problem was, I didn't see her face at all, and the absence felt like a wallop to the chest, every minute of every day and most of the night. The only thing that temporarily eased the ache was talking about her. But I quickly bored Charlie with my tale of woe, and there was no one else who knew our story.

Except there was—the Lerners. But, I quickly concluded, not Zehava. I didn't really know her, and anyway, she always seemed maternal in her interactions with Michal—a feminine force that I didn't understand and didn't want to confront. But I was still interning for Chaim, sorting his papers, managing his fan mail, and helping him edit an English language collection of his short stories. It was one of those stories that convinced me to talk to him about Michal. The story was called "Blue Jews." It was part of his "Planet of the Jews" series, a set of sci-fi stories that follows a band of Jews who flee Earth to escape a renewed outbreak of fascist anti-Semitism. The Jews land on a habitable planet in a distant star system where they navigate various natural and social threats. In the story that inspired me, a group of rotund, blue-skinned aliens land on the planet claiming to be fellow Jews. They show off their fluent Hebrew, share their stories of enslavement and then liberation, and chant their law code, which includes striking similarities to the biblical book Deuteronomy. Most impressively, they pray with an inspiring melodic fervor. Their prayer services become the planet's single most attended pastime. Secular Jews, who'd scoffed at ritual and rejected God, now strap on *tefillin* every morning and *shuckle*, dance, and sway with the visiting blue Jews. A religious renaissance blooms. Until, one day, the community wakes up to find the alien Jews have flown away. And taken with them several complex, crucial pieces of equipment. And the community's only handwritten Torah scroll. The blue Jews were, in reality, con men and thieves. A nasty communal disillusion replaces the renaissance. Rabbis become atheists and resign. Synagogues empty. New, nihilistic cults emerge, dedicated to cynicism. Their most sacred ritual: suicide.

I had only the vaguest notion of what Chaim was getting at in the story. Something about the disenchantment of the modern age, perhaps alluding to how the Holocaust robbed modern Jews of their faith. But I was curious about the disillusionment, of waking up to find that your apparent blessed reality was not at all what it seemed, that someone or something had deceived you, or that you had deceived yourself. And this disenchantment provoked thoughts of suicide. Thoughts, not actions. I was not suicidal during this period, but the notion of suicide as a response to disenchantment intrigued me. I thought of all the Holocaust writers, Chaim's spiritual colleagues, who'd killed themselves. I decided to seek him out, to talk with him about my own episode of heartbreak and disillusion.

Apart from teaching, Chaim rarely worked at the university, but he offered to spare me the bittersweet memory of hiking through Wadi Joz to his apartment, three doors down from Michal's. We met instead at his university office three weeks after I'd last seen her. I wasn't surprised that papers and books covered every surface—the floor, the chairs, the shelves. I waited while Chaim cleared a path for me through journals, books, and manuscripts and then slowly transferred the heaps on the chairs to the larger heaps on the desk. We sat facing each other. He took a moment to catch his breath. I wondered about his health. I knew about the hip, the knee, but was there more? Something internal, more ominous? Despite his ready smile, Chaim always seemed haunted, or, better, invaded, and not only by memories.

"Ah, Judah," he said, rubbing his goatee. "My dear Judah. I didn't know. I hope you believe that, yes? I thought you and Michal were just good friends. University colleagues. I understand now. I misjudged. You are suffering. I see, even from the way you sit. She's made you suffer, yes?"

His tone and affect were so parental that I found it difficult to speak. I nodded and fought back tears.

"Matters of the heart," he said. "So deep and so painful. Time, my friend. Time will heal."

Time will heal. A cliché from one of the great thinkers of the twentieth century. And nonsense—it's not time that does the healing. But the words didn't matter. He saw me. He heard me. I was grateful. "I'm ashamed," I said.

"Ashamed?"

"You've suffered so much. My puny heartbreak—"

"Nonsense. Nonsense. Never compare sufferings. It's not a competition. Your hurt is genuine. There was a cause, yes? Heartbreak can torment you like a kapo. I don't judge your pain. You shouldn't either."

I swallowed. "Thank you."

"Some advice?" he said.

I nodded. I couldn't speak.

"Suffer," he said. "Don't try to talk yourself out of suffering. Allow the suffering its place, yes? But don't only suffer. The world has suffering, but that's not all it has. Even in the camps, yes? There were moments of reprieve. Suffer. But enjoy. Or marvel, or rest. There is suffering in life, but also so much more. Yes?"

I was utterly captivated and convinced by this advice. To this day, I wonder why. Maybe his conversational tic—adding the word yes to many declarative sentences—drew me in, forced me to assent. Maybe it was the raw fact of his love, unearned, and therefore even more precious. Clearly, the stunning effect of his words doesn't transfer to the written page, or even, now that I think of it, to memory. Years later, when my wife killed herself and I spiraled into depression and addiction, I recalled Chaim's advice verbatim. It was utterly worthless.

"Have you thought of travel?" he asked.

That confused me. Another tour around Israel—alone—was the last think I wanted. I'd already traveled with Michal to the Sinai, the upper Galilee, Golan, Eilat, Tel Aviv, Masada, Ein

Geddi, Haifa, Nahariya, Akko, and Bethlehem. Not to mention Cairo, Alexandria, and Aswan. Where else would I go? But I misunderstood.

"Maybe go home," he said. He shrugged, losing some confidence in this particular piece of advice. Still, he continued. "Maybe your adventure here . . . perhaps it has run its course, yes? Is this country the best place for you now?" He shrugged again, as if any answer to that question was beyond him.

In fact, I had considered leaving. But I wondered, *Does he want me to leave? Is he—gently—kicking me out?* Would it have been impossible or horribly awkward to continue my work for him when his son was marrying the love of my life? Was the simplest solution—for me and for everyone involved: Michal, Zehava, Yoav, Chaim, even Charlie who now suffered my tales of woe—to leave this place where, unlike them, I so obviously didn't belong? Was he offering me sage counsel, or was he getting rid of me? Was I his student or a nuisance? I still don't know.

◆ ◆ ◆

Anyway, I took his advice. I decided to wait a week until May. In a manic, caffeine-fueled rush, I avoided sleep, meals, and normal hygiene, and I managed to finish all my final papers and exams. Three days before my scheduled flight, I knocked on Michal's door. My goal was to say goodbye, to tell her I was leaving. And also, maybe, to induce guilt. To bequeath to her some of the pain she'd inflicted on me. And possibly, deep down, in a psychic place I hid even from myself, I harbored the hope that I might change her mind.

But no part of me expected or hoped for what actually happened. We barely spoke. Right after opening the door, she drew me in to the apartment, both of her hands tugging on my shoulders. When I told her I was leaving, she raised her finger to her lips, shushing me. She knew. Chaim had told her. Let's not talk, she said. She pulled me to the bedroom. It's impossible to exaggerate the wonder and astonishment I felt. She guided us through sex. Genuine intercourse, lovemaking, the one intimate act she'd withheld from me.

It might not have been her first time. In a full and complex love life, I don't know how memorable it was for her. And even for me. Michal, after all, was not the love of my life. She was a nine-month chapter in a much longer book. But she was my first. My first intercourse, my first love. So it was impossible to forget. In addition to every caress, every novel sensation, every touch, every scent, I remembered the exact date and time. Many, many years later, those memories would prove fateful.

In the morning, I held her from behind and wept. It was the first time I cried over Michal, the first time I cried adult tears. As I moved into adulthood, I avoided crying. I choked back tears whenever a sad movie or song touched a chord. Honestly, for a good part of my life, I didn't have reasons to cry. It was only when Mary got sick—really, only when she died—that the tears broke through, and weeping became a daily activity. Now I can cry anytime. But back then, pulling Michal into me, the tears surprised me, revealed hidden vulnerabilities that shocked and frightened me. Michal waited patiently for the fit to pass. Then, she turned and told me Yoav would be there in half an hour. I had to leave. She wordlessly watched me get dressed and pushed me away when I tried for a farewell hug. "I love you," I said, but she didn't say anything. I left.

Three days later, a Mercedes taxi picked me up at the dorm at 8 p.m. for an 11:30 p.m. flight. Charlie helped me heave my suitcases into the trunk. I hugged him goodbye and hopped in. As the Mercedes turned left down the hill, I felt an urge to say goodbye to Chaim. I remembered that his birthday was in four days. I knew he ate dinner at 8 p.m. every weeknight. It would be a good time to catch him at home. I'd wish him a happy birthday. I gave the driver the address and told him we'd be making a quick stop.

Darkness overtook Jerusalem in the ten minutes it took us to reach the house on Jeremiah Street. Constellations shone brightly in the cloudless night. At first, I mistook the ambulance's flashing red lights for the stars of heaven. My heartbeat accelerated as the car moved slowly up the narrow street. Shielding my eyes from the headlight's glare, I looked straight ahead and confirmed what I'd suspected. The ambulance was parked right in front of Chaim's building. I yelled to the driver to stop and jumped out. Four muscular men carefully lifted a prone, twisted body onto a stretcher and rushed it into the ambulance. As I ran closer, I saw two figures huddled on the lawn, hugging themselves to keep away the cool Jerusalem night. Zehava and Michal. Across the street, a dozen or so neighbors congregated, wondering who needed the ambulance. My driver called out, warning me that I'd miss my flight. I ignored him. Michal was the first to recognize me. She wore her achingly familiar purple tank top and black sweatpants. She ran to me and threw one arm around my neck. "It's Chaim," she screamed. "Chaim! He's dead!"

"My God," I said. "What on earth?" I looked at the house, as if it held an answer. I studied the spot where the ENTs lifted the body. Right below the side balcony.

"He must have fallen," Michal said. "Oh, my God, Chaim. What was he doing up there, by himself? He fell."

"He didn't fall!" a voice cried out, bereaved, clear and certain. Zehava. She wore blue jeans, a black blouse, and sneakers. I didn't spot any tears, but her eyes were bloodshot red, as if she'd been weeping for hours. Her curly gray hairs stuck out in every direction. She glared at me, horrified, furious, as if I had brought this madness to her family. She wrapped her arms around Michal. "He jumped!" she said.

My driver caught up to me and grabbed my arm. "You will miss flight!" he said. He pointed to his watch.

"Go, Judah," Zehava said. "Now! You don't have to stay. Go!"

I looked at Michal. "Yes. Go," she said breathlessly. "I'll write to you. I promise. But go."

I let the driver guide me back to the Mercedes. Just before I got in the car, I heard Zehava's voice, talking to Michal, to the neighbors, to Jerusalem, to history. "He didn't fall," she announced. "He jumped!"

Part 3

CHAPTER 12

July 2005

It turned out the suicide note Hannah claimed to have discovered was a short story. A piece of fiction by Chaim Lerner. Hannah found it in an out-of-print collection she'd bought at a used bookstore in Greenwich Village—research for her suicide project. She read the story the week before our trip, but she only realized its "true meaning" after listening to the failed suicide bomber.

We were still nursing iced coffees and hot chocolate at the café. The crowd around us was thinning; Friday afternoon would soon become Friday evening, Shabbat, when Jerusalem shut down. The heat wasn't breaking, but we sat in the shade, and the caffeine and ice cream relieved my weary jet lag. "Hannah," I said, when she admitted the suicide note was a fantasy tale Chaim had published at least ten years before his death, "I don't think you can count a story as a note."

"Don't be so quick to judge, Judah," Michal said. She looked at Hannah. "Your daughter has a brilliant interpretation of the story. And how it connects to Chaim's suicide." Hannah blushed. Again, I was amazed by the intimacy between these two—the fondness and the quarrels, something I never would have predicted. Maybe Hannah was so desperate for a mother, she latched on to anyone who was about the right age. "Go ahead, Hannah," Michal said. "Tell us about the story. Tell us your theory."

Hannah reached into her backpack and pulled out a thin paperback. She flipped to the story, cleared her throat, and seemed poised to read it out loud. But then she touched her lips and looked at me. "I'll just tell you the story," she said. "And then I'll tell you what it means. If I don't convince you, you can read it yourself."

I looked at Charlie. I was afraid we were wasting his time. But he didn't seem at all impatient. He gazed at Hannah like a fan waiting for his favorite band to start playing. I told her to go ahead.

The story was called "The Magic Eyeglasses." It was about a company that invented glasses that enabled the customer to see the very best in whatever they examined with their eyes. If you looked at a person, the glasses brought into sharp focus whatever features could objectively be considered beautiful. If it was a homely boy with disheveled hair and torn clothing but excellent teeth, you saw the teeth, and your brain extrapolated the rest. The boy you beheld became beautiful. If you saw a dented, rusted old clunker of a car, you saw the perfect engine, the clear window, or the functioning door handle. And therefore, you saw a beautiful automobile. The glasses even worked at a molecular level. If you saw dogshit, you saw the enzymes and molecules that aided digestion, so the object became admirable.

Not surprisingly, there was a market for these glasses. Who wouldn't want to see the very best in our world? But, also not surprising, the product stirred some controversy. After all, the glasses abetted what can only be called fraud. The old clunker isn't really beautiful. Neither is dogshit. The glasses are deceiving you. Not everyone wants to be deceived.

Nevertheless, they sold at a brisk pace, making the company that manufactured them and the quirky genius who invented them comfortable and successful, if not obnoxiously wealthy.

As it happened, a man in a nearby town—Jayme Cohen—had a similar power, but it worked in an opposite fashion. This guy only saw the bad in things, the flawed, the imperfect, the unpleasant, the ugly. When he looked at a beautiful woman—a world-renowned model—he only saw the one hair out of place, the microscopic pimple under the blush, or the slight asymmetry between her right and left earlobes. Beauty became ugly. Ultimately, Jayme entered the perfect profession. He became a critic for the local newspaper. And his reviews were flawless. No one could deny the truth of his observations. He never lied, was impervious to bribes, and highlighted facts that were undeniable. And he had a meticulous sense of detail, which gave him extraordinary, persuasive powers. The problem, of course, was that every review was negative. Every restaurant was an overpriced failure, every film a lazy fraud, every book a bore, every bottle of wine—well, you get the idea. As a result, every new restaurant in town went bankrupt within weeks of opening—a victim of poor reviews. Every play closed after one night—even high school performances, which should have been granted a measure of grace, but Jayme's ruthlessness matched his integrity. He could only tell the truth. He could only report what he saw with his own peculiar eyes.

It was those peculiar eyes that drew the attention of the eyeglass manufacturers. To be honest, they thought of it as a publicity stunt. Still a little disappointed at the brisk but not overwhelming traffic in their remarkable product, they figured they could goose up sails with one perfect commercial. They would film Jayme Cohen—famous critic, famous fault-finder—trying on the glasses and then commenting on whatever he chose to see. The fact is, the advertisement's producers didn't put much thought into what Mr. Cohen would look at. Because it didn't matter. The glasses made excrement look lovely and wholesome. After considering a few objects at hand in the empty lot where they were filming—a stop sign, a field of weeds, a burly male director, a charmless Volvo—they chose, almost at random, an ill two-year-old toddler that the camera woman had brought with her to work that morning. No one could later explain why they decided on a human object for filming, and, in fact, there was no explanation because they hadn't thought about it at all. The sick kid was there, wheezing, crying in his stroller, calling attention to himself, so they used him. They readied the camera, gave the glasses to Jayme. He put them on, took one look at the now screaming child, and dropped dead. The startled toddler opened his eyes wider than anyone could imagine, then screeched mournfully as if he'd just lost both parents. He was beyond comfort. His cry penetrated every house in the city and continued for days. Finally, his parents packed him into their Volvo, along with all their worldly possessions, and drove themselves and the weeping child away. For all we know, he's still crying.

I stared at Hannah. She hadn't once looked at the text. Her rhythm, drama, syntax—the music of her voice—sounded almost exactly like Chaim, particularly when he told stories. The only thing missing was the odd "yes?" every once in a while. She'd *performed* the story, but it was a Chaim performance: witty, old world, and wise. *She never knew him*, I thought. *And she's fifteen. How is this possible?*

Michal applauded, and then Charlie clapped loudly. "Now tell them," Michal said. "How is the story a suicide note?"

"Yes. Well. I think it's obvious." She leaned forward, made eye contact with each of us. "Jayme is clearly Chaim, right? I mean, it's his name, the same name in Spanish. He only sees the bad—he only sees the Holocaust. He can't see the success of Israel or the democracies in Europe or the next generation in Germany. All he sees is Auschwitz. And he annoys everyone by writing about nothing except the Holocaust. He's like Jayme the critic. He makes sure no one enjoys themselves because there's always the Holocaust. It's everywhere. And he has to point it out all the time. For Chaim, it's one book after another: theology, fiction, history, whatever—it's all just Holocaust. And people love his books because they're *so* true. But they hate them too, because they're so depressing. He makes Israeli Jews think they're victims, he makes Europeans feel guilty, and he reminds the rest of the world how shitty human beings are. Everyone buys his books, but they wish he would stop writing them."

Not bad, I thought. It occurred to me how much Hannah would have liked Chaim. And he would have liked her. "Go on," I said. "The glasses?"

"Yes!" she said. "The glasses. The magic eyeglasses are what the world really wants when it comes to the Holocaust. We want to stop seeing it everywhere. We're sick of Holocaust comparisons. What's that called? Godwin's law. We're tired of every political argument bringing in the Holocaust. And it's like I said before. Jews are sick of feeling like victims. Europeans are sick of the guilt. That's what Chaim is saying in the story. The world wants new lenses. So we don't see the Holocaust everywhere."

"Jews are sick of talking about the Holocaust?" I said. "It seems more like we want to talk about it all the time."

"But not so much in the 1970s and 1980s in Israel," Michal said. "It was different. We were ready for the Holocaust victims to retire, to stop reminding us of all that suffering. Shoah fatigue. Chaim knew about it; he complained about it. It was only in the nineties, after *Schindler's List*, that Israelis really opened their hearts to the victims. But Chaim missed it."

"Plus, there were the Holocaust deniers, right?" Hannah said. "I read about them for my project. In America and Germany. Michal told me Chaim was really pissed off about them."

Michal clicked her tongue twice. "Not pissed off," she said. "Depressed. Despairing."

"Exactly," Hannah said. "Maybe the magical eyeglasses are the Holocaust deniers, who give us permission not to see the Holocaust because it's not there. That's why the glasses in the story don't sell so spectacularly at first. Because you can't totally hide the Holocaust. The glasses give you a quick illusion to ease your guilt, or your feelings of victimhood. But it doesn't last. So the manufacturers—let's not call them the Holocaust hiders because they're not all deniers—need Jayme to put on the glasses. If they can get the greatest Holocaust writer to see the world without the Holocaust, everyone will win. Even Jayme will be happier. That's why the character agrees to put on the glasses. Because even he is sick of himself, sick of the gloom, the pile of bodies, the trauma. He's ready to see something else."

"But he can't," Michal said.

"He can't," Hannah agreed. "He can't live in a world where he can't see the Holocaust. But he realizes that he also can't live in a world where all he sees is the Holocaust. So. What do you do when you can't live in any possible world?"

She looked at me. *Is she thinking of her mother? How can she not be?* "You kill yourself," I said.

She handed me the book with the story. "Read it yourself."

Charlie shook his head in amazement. "That's your daughter!" he said.

"Her mother was a great reader," I said. I looked at Hannah. She held my gaze and smiled. "A truly deep thinker. But maybe not as deep as her daughter."

"So, that's it," Michal said. She clapped her hands. "The verdict is suicide? Case closed? You've got your proof now? Enough to write your book?"

I looked around. We were the last ones in the café. The waitress sat at the neighboring table, reading the newspaper, waiting for us. The city was ready to close for Shabbat. "I wouldn't say case closed," I said. "But that's a chapter, for sure. Thank you, Hannah." She blushed.

Michal took out a credit card. "*Hevre*," she said. "Shabbat dinner is at Zehava's place. Two hours. *Yallah!*" Before I could protest, she'd paid for the coffee, ice cream, hot chocolate, and cheese toast. She winked at me after signing the bill. I wasn't sure why, but I liked it.

♦♦♦

Yoav sat at the head of Zehava's Shabbat table. A colorful Yemenite yarmulke covered his balding scalp. He lifted the silver Kiddush cup and cleared his throat. Chaim and Zehava were secular Jews, but like most nonreligious Israelis, that didn't mean they ignored Friday night or embraced creative or progressive practices. Chaim had been the man of the house, so he'd led the traditional Sabbath Eve rituals. But with Chaim no longer with us, the task fell to Yoav.

I watched Michal while she watched Yoav chant the blessing. Studying them at our first meal together, shortly after we'd landed, I'd suspected something was amiss in their relationship.

They clearly avoided touching each other, and Michal couldn't stop herself from rolling her eyes whenever Yoav gave a political opinion, or really any opinion at all. I'd known for years about specific troubles in their marriage, but that first night, they looked like a couple who truly couldn't stand each other. But now I wasn't so sure. Yoav smiled at Michal as he sang with a confident, surprisingly pleasing tenor. I wouldn't use the word "adoring" to describe Michal's expression—Michal didn't do adoring—but she looked pleased, warmed, relaxed. I was surprised to see Charlie looking at Michal. Apparently, he'd become close to the family after I left. *Is there something between him and Michal? None of my business*, I thought.

During dinner, at Michal's urging, Hannah retold the magic eyeglasses story and then took Zehava and Yoav through her interpretation. Zehava beamed and blew Hannah a kiss, but Yoav clicked his tongue several times and shook his head. "It's a simple story. Optimism, pessimism, that's all. You are certainly a very smart young lady, but you don't need all these complications, all these hints and symbols. My father was a very simple man."

"Really?" I said. Simple was the last word I would have used to describe Chaim.

"Simple," Yoav insisted. He touched the top of his yarmulke of many colors, making sure it was still in place. "There was right, and there was wrong. That was it for him. The difficulty was assigning degrees of responsibility for different levels of wrong. Or give rewards for various levels of right. But there was always just right or wrong. You know the Schiller story?" He looked at Hannah.

"Uh, no," she said. "Did you say Schiller?" She scrunched her forehead, thinking. She'd read a lot of Chaim's writings preparing for the trip, but apparently nothing about a Schiller.

"Yoav," Zehava said.

He waved her off. "Doesn't matter," he said. "It's perhaps not in any of his books. I will tell it to you. It's a story so you understand my father. And why he . . . why he died the way he did."

A German named Otto Schiller had been Chaim's civilian boss in Buna, the Auschwitz rubber factory. Before the war, Chaim trained as an industrial chemist in Cracow. He was able to parlay his specialized knowledge into a lifesaving role as a slave laborer in the factory. Chaim was tortured, beaten, worked to exhaustion, and humiliated. But, unlike his father and sisters, not to mention the million or so other Auschwitz victims, he was kept alive as an asset of the German war effort. After liberation, Yoav explained, Chaim abandoned chemistry and became one of Hebrew University's first PhDs in modern English literature. "One day," Yoav went on, "in early 1970, I was ten. Before Abba's great fame but after he'd published his two memoirs. He receives a postcard inviting him to speak at an English literature conference in London. The mailing was signed by the organization's vice president, Otto Schiller."

Yoav's voice shook slightly as he told the story. The occasional word slipped into upper registers, as if he were frightened, speaking under the gun. The obvious nervousness transformed my read on Yoav. For years, I'd thought of him as the winner, the macho soldier who won Michal's heart. But he sounded anxious and insecure, as if nothing in his life, none of his relationships, stood on a firm foundation. But, honestly, what did I know?

"Otto Schiller," Yoav repeated. He rubbed his scrawny beard, a gesture that reminded me of Chaim. "A coincidence, surely. The Schiller from Buna was a chemist, and how many chemists turn themselves into literature professors? Anyway, it's a common name. Can't be the same person. He ignores the card. One week later, a five-page, single-space letter arrives from Otto Schiller, in German. It's the same man. The slave boss, now, like Chaim, a scholar of English literature and a university professor. He explains in the letter that after the war, he wanted nothing more to do with chemistry, the field that turned him into a necessarily harsh boss. 'Necessarily harsh manager.' Those were the words Schiller chose. Not 'slave master,' or even 'unnecessarily cruel boss.' Necessarily harsh manager. Okay. Still. Germans were masters of euphemisms, and Chaim had no interest in policing the language of all his correspondents. But Schiller puts my father in a bind. He tells him he's inviting him to the conference not for Chaim's academic brilliance but so Schiller can sit with him at his favorite London pub and ask for forgiveness. That takes up less than half a page. For the remaining four and a half pages, Schiller explains himself. He claims the civilians also had no choice. In effect, they were also enslaved, though he admits they got paid, and the civilian living conditions were far superior to the dirty, crowded slave bunks. He reminds my father of the three, possibly four times he smuggled him food. My father has no memory of this at all. He further reminds my father that he scrupulously avoided beatings or any physical pressure. My father concedes that this is true, that numerous others whipped him and his fellow slaves, but never Schiller. Perhaps Schiller ordered the beatings, but perhaps not. He's willing to grant Schiller the benefit of the doubt when it comes to physical torture. Schiller denies knowing about the genocide, the gas chambers, the crematoria, the whole demonic infrastructure. My father is genuinely baffled by this claim. He's heard it from so many Germans and Poles that he can't dismiss it out of hand. But, he would always say, the smell? The smell?

"My father," Yoav continued, "does not want to travel to London to meet this German, not at his favorite pub, nor any pub, nor anyplace. But you know my father. He is a serious man. And he has no choice but to understand Schiller also as a serious man, though whether he's serious in a good way or bad way—that remains to be seen. He's serious because he's asking a serious question. Is forgiveness possible for Nazis? Well, probably not. But the civilians, the Schillers? They were bystanders, so that's unquestionably a sin. But sins can be repented and forgiven—that equation is central to any form of ethics, certainly to Judaism. My father needs to think this through. For him, that can only mean one thing: writing. He writes Schiller a long letter—six pages. I think, *Ima*, do you have it?"

Zehava shook her head. She watched Yoav carefully, as if he were a dangerous animal liable to pounce.

"Okay," Yoav says. "It doesn't matter. I remember it. He read it to us, three or four separate drafts, you remember *Ima*. I was only ten, so, not really understanding, I merely memorized it. He wrote it in English. An interesting and I would say appropriate choice. First, he tells Schiller he has no memory of receiving stolen food from him. If he were dealing with any other topic or event, he would be willing to concede that, in the rush and panic of stress-filled days, perhaps he forgot. But he tells Schiller that when it comes to the *lager*, the camp, God has cursed him with perfect memory. He remembers everything. So, Schiller is mistaken. He doesn't write 'lying' but 'mistaken.' There was no smuggling of food to him. As to his refraining from physical torture, my father writes yes, that is also his memory. Which means that Schiller, indeed, preserved some modicum of decency in that most indecent of places, and such an effort should be acknowledged, even praised. However, and I remember this line verbatim, he wrote, 'In a world with no Auschwitz, it is sufficient to preserve a modicum of decency. But in a world with Auschwitz, which is to say our world, the world that you and I endured, it is necessary to restore decency, not merely to preserve it.' Then, he wrote that he accepts the invitation to speak at the English literature conference, and even to accompany Schiller to a pub where they could discuss Milton, Shakespeare, Chaucer, or anything Schiller proposes. But not forgiveness. That will not be forthcoming. At least not from my father."

Yoav stopped to sip from his wineglass. It was only the second sip he'd taken all night. We waited for him to finish the story. But he was quiet—waiting for us, for the right question. Like his father, Yoav was a skilled storyteller. He knew when to tell, but he also knew when to withhold. Finally, it was Hannah who asked, "What happened at the meeting?"

"Nothing," Yoav said. "There was no meeting, no pub in London. It took over a week for my father to compose the letter. The day he finished, he was about to walk to the post office and send it off. But the phone rang. It was Schiller's wife. You remember, *Ima*."

Zehava nodded. She hadn't stopped staring at her son the whole time he told the story.

"God knows how he got our phone number," Yoav continued. "She called to give my father the news. Schiller was dead. He died of a heart attack two days before. The wife felt my father should know."

Again, Hannah interrupted the silence, "Your father killed him?"

Yoav laughed. A chilling sound after such a sober story. "Only if you believe thoughts could kill, which I guarantee my father did not believe. No, it was his weak heart. Perhaps he knew his days were numbered, so he reached out to my father before the time came to face God. He never got to read my father's beautiful letter."

"I don't understand," I said. "It's a fascinating story. But you said it explained how your father died. I didn't get that. Am I missing something?"

"You are," Yoav said quickly, the first time I heard real confidence in his high, shaky voice. "Think about it. My father labors over a masterpiece of ethical reasoning. He dedicates his fine, creative, empathetic mind to a crucial area of moral logic—how to judge the bystander. And no one reads it. Really, no one cares. Maybe one person would care, but that person died. My father lived in a world that, in theory, demanded fine moral reasoning. But, in reality, no one was demanding this genre of thought. Not even here. Especially not here, with our morally complex invasions, anti-terrorist violence, enhanced interrogations. He couldn't live in this world. He chose not to."

◆◆◆

Hannah and I made our excuses not long after Yoav's lesson in moral reasoning. Charlie also pleaded exhaustion and accompanied us down the alley to our cottage. Outside the front door, Charlie asked Hannah if she could go up to her room by herself and let him talk to me in private. "No," she said without hesitation.

"Hannah," I said.

"No! I want to hear everything. That was our deal."

Hannah had a habit of making up "our deals" on the spot. But, as was often the case, I was too tired to argue. Plus, deal or no deal, why keep secrets from her? The fact is, so far, she'd been extraordinarily helpful. The suicide bomber interview was fascinating. And her analysis of Chaim's odd story was far from foolproof, but it was intriguing and worth exploring. Besides, no one on the planet knew me better than she did. There was no one else I trusted more. Which was a scary thought.

"Doesn't matter," Charlie said. He took a breath. "Listen, Judah. I have some advice. Go home. Write your book."

"Are you kidding?" I said. "I just started. I've got nothing to write."

"You've got everything! Short stories that explain the suicide. Yoav's story about Chaim's moral reasoning. Hannah's interview with the suicide bomber. And c'mon! A possible government conspiracy."

"But that's exactly it. I have those two interviews, but nothing else. I have to run down that lead."

"Judah, they're not going to tell you anything more. Trust me. They only said what they said because they figure we know about them visiting Chaim that night. But you're still a foreign journalist. No one will talk to you anymore. But so what? You don't have to solve this. Just raise some questions. That's enough for a successful book. You know what, write an article first. I'm sure you can find a newspaper or journal that would publish it. Whet the public's appetite. Then, write the book. Suicide? Murder? Accident? You have enough to ask the questions, suggest some possible answers. You're not going to get more."

I looked at him. Charlie and I were roughly the same age, but during our year together, he was the big brother, offering helpful theories on Israeli women, reminding me to eat breakfast, to go easy on the Maccabi beer. I don't know if it was the gun under the bed or just his personality, but I'd pegged him for an adult the first time I met him, someone from whom I felt comfortable taking instruction. I marveled at how our roles hadn't changed. But I'd become a little more sophisticated. I noticed Hannah was staring at me, waiting for a reply. Charlie surprised me by taking out a Time cigarette, but not lighting it. He'd told me he quit ten years before. "You want me to write an article so you'll be able to open an official police investigation. That's what you've wanted all along. That's why you sent me to Kaplowitz and Alon in the first place. You already knew their stories. But right now, like me, you've really got nothing solid. Just some weird coincidences, not enough to investigate cabinet ministers. But an article in a respected American newspaper—that will force your bosses to act. That's what you really want."

He smiled. He lit the cigarette, looked at it, then tossed it on the ground, grinding it out with his sandal. "Not bad, Judah.

Not bad. Yeah, I left that part out. I need something published, fast. Listen, you already knew I was using you. I apologize. But I wasn't lying just now. No one will talk to you anymore. So what's the point in waiting? Write an article. Then, I can swoop in with all my resources. Then, you can write the book. I'll give you exclusive access."

I looked at Hannah. She shook her head quickly. "How about this?" I said. "We work together. You'll open all the Israeli files on Chaim's death, get the important ones translated for me and Hannah. I'll follow up with Alon and Kaplowitz. One more interview with each. But this time, you'll be in the room. In uniform. It will look like the start of an official investigation. Let's see if they open up a little."

Charlie nodded. "Hmm," he said. His hands shook slightly, and he tapped his foot. His body language screamed desperately for a cigarette. Ten years after quitting, he still hadn't beaten the urge. "Me in the room." Earlier, he'd told me he *shouldn't* be in the room, that his presence would only shut them up. But that was when he was using me, lying to me.

"You've got enough evidence to justify bringing them to your office," I said.

He brought a finger to his lips, as if he could smoke it. "Worth a try." He shrugged.

"One more thing," I said. "If we're investigating, we have to investigate all possibilities. You and I. We have to interview the family."

"Even Yoav? We talked about this. He was in a hospital. They wouldn't have let him out."

"Yoav too," I said. "He might still know something. He was pretty pushy about suicide. Like he's trying to talk me into it."

Yoav nodded. Hannah yawned, but then also nodded.

"And Michal," I said.

He stared at me. "Michal? Judah, I'm not sure—"

"She's in the family. I'm an investigative reporter. I have to do my job. For a murder investigation, you have to interview the family. The entire family."

"They do have alibis. Zehava and Michal. I told you. They've been checked out. It's not like the original cops were total incompetents."

"Great," I said. "Still."

"I want to be in the room for those interviews!" It was Hannah. I was wondering when she'd pipe in. I couldn't help but notice she was smart enough not to insist on helping with the Kaplowitz and Alon interviews. She knew they wouldn't put up with a fifteen-year-old in the room. But Yoav, Michal, Zehava? Hannah was practically family.

A creepy, ghostly moaning, like a police siren in a cartoon horror movie, radiated from Charlie's breast pocket. His emergency cell phone. He fished it out and barked a few Hebrew words. Two seconds later, he shoved the phone back in his pocket. "Terrorist bombing," he said. "A nightclub in Talpiot." He gave a quick wave and ran to his car. I had to stop Hannah from following him. Police sirens wailed in the distance.

Hannah woke me up the next morning, knocking on my door, then pushing it open. She held her open laptop on her left forearm, as if it were attached to her person. "Five dead," she said. "Including the bomber. All teenagers. The bomber too."

I looked at my watch. 7 a.m., Israel time.

"I guess the Intifada's not over," Hannah said.

◆ ◆ ◆

Three days later, Charlie and I sat at a metal card table across from Interior Minister Meir Alon. This time, we used an empty office at police headquarters, a confusing warren of nineteenth-century-style buildings in the Russian Compound. Charlie insisted on holding the interview at 6 a.m. Fewer witnesses, he told me. Plus, the optimum time to catch someone in a lie. He took the lead.

"Let's hear your story again," Charlie said.

Alon looked around the room. A single uncovered light bulb overhead. No books, no plants, no portraits of bearded rabbis, no photos of Israeli jet planes over Auschwitz. No windows. No laptops. When Alon arrived, no offer from Charlie of tea or even water. No handshake. Just a gesture with his head that he should sit. Alon squeezed his beard, glared at Charlie, then barked out several sentences in Hebrew.

"English please," Charlie said. He pointed to me.

Alon nodded slowly. "English?" Alon said. "English? Okay. Fuck you. Fuck you, motherfucker."

I couldn't help but laugh. Surprisingly, Alon laughed too. Then Charlie.

"Okay," Alon said. "Okay. I get it now. This has nothing to do with the police. Two old friends playing some kind of game. But there's no law that I have to cooperate with journalists. I assume I'm free to go."

Charlie smiled. "Minister. Did I ever imply otherwise?"

"Just wait," I said. "You know it looks bad. You bragged about hating Chaim. You admit you were at the scene right after it happened. I could write that up tomorrow, add a little bit that only I know, and suddenly, the whole country will see you as a murder suspect."

"Oh, so now you extort me?"

I leaned back in my chair and waited. He looked around the room again. "It's not bugged?" he said. "I'm not being recorded?"

"I guarantee I'm not recording you," Charlie said. That surprised me. In fact, I was recording the conversation. The recorder was in my pocket.

"There is more to the story," Alon said. "But I suspect you won't want to publish it. Chaim is suddenly, after all these years, your liberal icon. And you would like to make him a martyr, a murder victim. But there is so much you don't know about him."

"I don't understand," Charlie said. But I suspect he did. I got it right away.

"You were going to blackmail him," I said. "Get him to back off his political statements."

"He was a defeatist leftist. And ignorant. Maybe he was a smart theologian, what do I know? But what did he know about Hezbollah, about the Shiites on the northern border, about the unholy alliance between Fatah and the ayatollahs? We needed to finish the job in Lebanon. And annex Golan, annex Judea, and Samaria. He and all the other leftist intellectuals, they were enemies. This was war."

Charlie shook his head. "You crazy maniacs. And now you're in power again. God help us."

"We are protecting the homeland, Lieutenant. And what is your solution? Withdraw, and make peace? Another salami slice off the homeland? That worked so well in Lebanon? In Samaria, with your cursed Oslo accords? Area A, Area B—you are feeding terror. How many more pizza parlors do you have to rush to and clear out the bodies after they blow up our children? Now is the time for strength. Build new settlements. Make them pay!"

"More settlements? You fascist jerk, why do you think they're so eager to blow themselves up?"

"Leftist coward!"

"Wait," I said. "None of this is the point. I don't need the left versus right play right now. I already know all your lines. This is about Chaim. The Holocaust survivor. The mystery of his death." I looked at Alon. "What did you have on him?"

He smiled. "Oh, I think you know. You were his secretary. What do you think we had on him?"

Of course, I knew. "Women," I said.

"Not just women," Alon said.

"Students," I said. The fact is, I'd heard the rumors. I never saw anything, but, looking back, I realized that Michal probably had. By the time I'd left, she stopped singing his praises. Like too many prominent men, Chaim took advantage of his charisma and budding fame. I was disappointed but not astonished.

"We had testimony," Alon said. "Photos. That was my plan, that night. Show him the documents. Get him to withdraw from politics. So you see, I didn't have to kill him. All I had to do was threaten to kill his reputation."

"There's nothing in the files about this," Charlie said. "You never told the police investigating Chaim's death?"

"Why ruin a man's reputation after he's dead?" Alon answered. "Anyway, as I'm sure you know, there wasn't much of an investigation. It was suicide. Everyone agreed."

"Yeah," I said. "And by not coming forward, you saved your own reputation. You'd be outed as a blackmailer."

He tilted his head. "I suppose," he said. "Though I don't think that revelation would have hurt me among my supporters."

Charlie laughed bitterly. "You're right about that."

"I can leave?" Alon said. "You have your scoop?"

"Just one more question," I said. "Were you so sure Chaim would give in to blackmail? My sense of him was he didn't care that much about his reputation. And it's not like he would have lost his job. Not in those days. And Zehava? Yoav? They probably knew."

"Oh, they definitely knew. We had recordings, of both of them, yelling at Chaim about the girls. The issue with the family wasn't so much Chaim's reputation. I think you know what it was about."

It took me a moment. It was a long time ago. But the answer was obvious. "Zehava," I said. "A scandal would have hurt her career."

"Probably ruin it," Alon said. "Women in politics were not so common back then. She was a rising star. Today, she *is* a star. But a scandal back then? A predator husband, not a sainted icon? That would have been the end. Chaim would have followed all of my instructions. He would have completely withdrawn from political activity. For Zehava's sake, not his own. That was his weakness. He whored with the students, but he loved his wife."

"Enough," Charlie said.

"What?" Alon said. "You expected a murder confession? But I've given you the truth. Clearly, it was suicide. He must have figured out why I wanted to see him. And anyway, he felt guilty. He betrayed his wife. Betrayed all his deluded fans who saw him as the holy saint of Auschwitz. Took advantage of vulnerable young women. He came face-to-face with the real Chaim Lerner. So he jumped off the roof."

"Enough!" Charlie said. "Just get the hell out!"

Alon looked at me. "I have no power over you, Mr. Loeb. Write what you want. But if I see my name in any article or book from you, I will make it my business to end the career of your good old friend Charlie. Yes, I'm blackmailing you. I've practiced that art many times. I'm good at it."

Alon was a big man with a belly that, in sitting position, extended past his lap. And he was in his late seventies, so lifting himself from his seat was a project. Neither Charlie nor I offered to help as he pressed down on the metal table, maneuvered his legs under his bulk, and made it to a standing position. Once up, he quickly regained his dignity. He marched from the room like an advancing soldier. We watched him disappear down the twisty corridor.

"God, I hate that guy," Charlie said.

I wasn't sure he did. There didn't seem to be any heat in Charlie's statement. No red face, no frown. He was even smiling a little. I wondered if Charlie's hatred for Alon was of the same species of hatred that Alon had described to me, his hatred of Chaim, how he woke up early in the morning so he'd have extra time to enjoy it. Had I stumbled into some dark swamp of a feud, when all I wanted was to get to the bottom of Chaim's death? "Should I back off?" I asked Charlie. "Was his threat for real? Can he ruin your career?"

He laughed. "When it comes to my career, he's the least of my problems." He checked his watch. "Let's go," he said. "We don't want to be late."

I looked at my phone. It was 6:45 a.m. "Late?"

"To the Zohar class. In the *Kotel* tunnel. Your friend Rabbi Kaplowitz Junior teaches it now. He added a seven a.m. session for the late risers. We'll make it," he said. "I'll use the car siren."

◆ ◆ ◆

The class was gobbledygook to me. All Hebrew or Aramaic, spoken so rapidly that even if I understood every tenth word—an optimistic aspiration—each thought would blow by so quickly, I'd miss everything. That part of the lesson was just like twenty-two years ago. But otherwise, things had markedly improved. Instead of a dozen or so folding chairs in a circle, we sat in an auditorium on plush movie-theater type seats. At least 100 males participated, about a third with black hats and beards, another third in suits with knit yarmulkes, and a third, including me, in jeans and T-shirts. Among the black hats were a dozen or so schoolboys, black hats in training, with the right uniform—a black coat, white shirt, no tie, black hat, black pants—but no beard. Most of those paid strict attention, though two of them looked like me—bored, irritated, and lost. Kaplowitz spoke at a lectern. A video camera filmed him from the back of the room. He smiled frequently, and the crowd laughed every few minutes. He was clearly an excellent teacher—for those who understood. I noticed Charlie laughing heartily at every Hebrew joke. He was either enjoying himself or doing a good job of faking it.

After the hour-long class, he approached us immediately, even though we were sitting in the back. He embraced Charlie with the warmth of a long-lost relative and kissed both his cheeks. Then, he did the same to me. I thought of Santa Claus, Mr. Rogers, Barney the Dinosaur, imaginary creatures whose friendliness could move you to tears even if they barely knew you. He ignored his many disciples all vying for his attention and guided us to his tunnel office. Three chairs waited for us in a triangle. He pointed, smiled widely, and sat. We did too.

"Nu, Charlie," he said. "You are ready to join our little class? Our Zohar study group?"

"I just might do that," Charlie said. "It's a little early, though. You don't happen to offer an eight a.m. session?"

He laughed and turned to me. "And you, Yehudah. I felt your strong attention. It's time for you, no? With your daughter. You will move here to be with us. Join our class?"

The absurdity of the suggestion almost made me laugh, but it occurred to me that he wasn't joking, and the laugh would be on me. Charlie had instructed me to take the lead this time, so I started right in. "Were you planning on blackmailing Chaim?" I asked. "Is that why you went to see him that night?"

"Of course, I was," he said. "Reb Meir and I, we don't agree on much. I'm sure we never will. But on this matter, we were united. Chaim had to be stopped."

His quick answer surprised me. I'd suspected, but I was far from sure, that he was in on the blackmail. But here he was confessing immediately. With no remorse. "I thought you loved him," I said.

"I did. I do. With all my heart."

"I don't understand."

"I've explained it to you. It wasn't personal. It wasn't political or even theological. Chaim's thoughts on the Master of the Universe were dangerous. He was a clever man and could have gained some influence, even among the *haredim*. We needed to stop him."

"Rabbi Kaplowitz," Charlie said. "You've just confessed to blackmail. And you've given us a motive. You understand this could make you a suspect for murder?"

"For murdering a man who killed himself? A man I loved? I still mourn for him."

"Well, let me ask you this," I said. "His theology offended you. You considered it not just heretical but dangerous. I assume you weren't the only one in your circle who felt that way."

"Of course not," he said. "We all felt that way. Our teacher, Rabbi Shach. My father of blessed memory, certainly. The other students at my Yeshiva. The participants in the Zohar circle."

"Maybe," I suggested, "one of them didn't love him quite as much as you did?"

He rested his hairy chin on his hand and looked up, searching for answers. "Violence?" he said, quietly, tentatively, as if he'd just learned the word and was practicing his pronunciation. "From my circle? I can't deny that it's possible. Religion is a serious business here. Many American reporters miss that about us. And this Holy Land of ours—it seems to trigger heated emotions, wouldn't you say?"

"And," Charlie said, "if someone from your circle acted on those heated emotions with violence toward Professor Lerner, you would be sympathetic?"

"Never," he said. He tsked his tongue three times and shook his head. "Never bloodshed. Never."

We sat still. The quiet in the room allowed the outside noise to penetrate. Male voices. Chanting. Cantillating. Melodic mumbling. *Davening*. Twenty-two years ago, this *Kotel* tunnel was largely empty, especially mid-morning on a weekday. But now, it was evidently prayers twenty-four seven. Strangely, as if to amplify my thoughts about Jerusalem's growing spirituality, the chanting seemed to rise in volume, as if someone was slowly turning a nob. Just when I felt it might reach a dangerous volume, all the prayerful noises were, in a flash, replaced by three quick, extraordinarily loud blasts. Explosions. Then screams, anguished and beseeching. Then sirens, blaring from just a few feet away and also from a distance, dopplering toward us. Then smoke. First the smell, then the stuff itself, thin, like a wispy cloud, seeping through the door crack, but darkening, growing, ominous, as if it were leaking from hell.

Charlie grabbed his phone, glanced at me quickly, and rushed out.

I looked at Rabbi Kaplowitz. He sat up straight, frowned, and shook his head, but he seemed remarkably calm, considering the screaming that, by now, was louder than the previous prayers, and the dark gray, thickening smoke slowly filled his private office. "This Holy Land," he said, a lament. "Master of the Universe. This Holy Land."

CHAPTER 13

Excerpt from *Here There Is No Why* by Judah Loeb, 2005

Zehava Lerner was born in Kansas City, Kansas, in 1935. Her parents owned a Western-wear clothing shop in The Plaza district. Zehava worked there, sweeping the floor, stacking jeans, folding shirts, and eventually waiting on customers every weekend and summer starting in 1949, the year she entered eighth grade. To this day, it's not unusual to see her in Western blue jeans, plaid shirts, and cowboy boots. She "made aliyah" (moved to Israel) in 1953, on her own. She's an attractive woman at age seventy, slim, with smooth skin and dark-brown curly hair. She has a vivacious, almost flirtatious manner. She laughs often and occasionally punctuates a point by touching my hand or arm. When speaking English with me, I detect a slight heartland twang, and I'm told that even after living in Israel for more than fifty years, she still speaks Hebrew with an American accent. Nevertheless, no one doubts that Zehava Lerner is a true Israeli patriot. She's an important political leader, an accomplished negotiator, and an essential advocate for Israel in Washington and on the world's stage. She's written several books in English, making Israel's case—all bestsellers. Our conversation was interrupted several times by phone calls from Israeli, Palestinian, and American political leaders (she wouldn't tell me who). She's also the widow of Chaim Lerner.

We spoke in her spacious Knesset office. As leader of the opposition, she merits one of the few views the Knesset offers—a window facing the rolling Judean Hills, dry in the summer, but dotted with white, Arab-style houses. The journey from Kansas and selling jeans to Israel and the Knesset—that is from the periphery of the Jewish world to its very center—seemed almost unfathomably long. I started by asking about that journey.

"Yes, quite a trip. But sometimes, a journey toward something is actually running away from someplace else. For me, Kansas was middling: the middle of the country, middle class, middle of the road politics, at least back then. And nothing but America as far as the eye could see. I felt I was escaping mediocrity. I wanted to go to a place that I could only imagine."

"Like Dorothy Gale?"

"Ha. Yes. Exactly. Don't underestimate the power of Dorothy Gale's hold on a teenage girl from Kansas City. By the way, when I got to Israel, *The Wizard of Oz* was the only thing people knew about Kansas. Now, Israel's not exactly the Land of Oz. But for an American Jewish kid back then, it was kind of the place 'over the rainbow.' In a world clearly hostile to Jews—remember this was less than ten years after the Holocaust—Israel was an enchanted forest, the place of our dreams, and a very real shelter from the world's hatred."

"You thought the world hated you?"

"In 1953? Eight years after the Holocaust, and the Arabs still trying to destroy us? Yes. We all thought that."

I'd return to Zehava's views of the world and Israel. But I wanted to get to the point of the interview: Chaim. "How did you meet Chaim Lerner?"

"Oh, this would be a terrible scandal nowadays. He was my professor at the Hebrew University. I became his teaching assistant. He flirted with me shamelessly, especially late at night in the library when there was no one else around. Of course, I flirted back. I had a crush on him from the first lecture, the first sentence. Not that I could understand him. He was always too deep for me. But still. Something about his singsong voice. Like a bird."

"Can you describe your marriage?"

"Well, I can't say it was all enchanted forests and journeys over the rainbow. Chaim resented the time my political career took me away from our small family. He felt I neglected Yoav. That I wasn't fully committed to the marriage. We didn't argue. He kept it inside, but I could tell. Those disapproving blue eyes. And then there was Chaim's tendency to daydream, really to warp off to some distant dimension. It could happen during meals, kicking around a football with Yoav, or kissing me goodnight. That wasn't easy to take. But I was happy. I fell in love, and I never fell out of it. I do believe he tried to be happy, tried to live normally, tried to live. Obviously, something was missing."

"Why do you think he killed himself?"

"It shouldn't surprise you that I've given this subject a lot of thought. Not voluntarily, by the way. Really, it's the last thing I *want* to think about. I won't bore you with the crazy theories that float through my brain in the middle of the night. How he haunted me, how he *still* haunts me. What I've come up with is this: you're asking the wrong question. The right questions are, why didn't he kill himself sooner? How did he stay alive for so many years after the Shoah?"

"I'm not sure what you mean. Can you explain?"

"No! Of course not. I can't explain. But I can offer some thoughts. Think of Chaim's true colleagues. Not his friends at the University and not his fellow survivors. His true colleagues."

"Other Holocaust writers."

"Of course. The folks who not only experienced the horror of horrors but who also took it upon themselves to transmit the experience. To give meaning to the thing that actively defies meaning. They all killed themselves. This obsessive writing. It was as deadly as the gas. Borowski. Celan. Kosinski, Amery, Levi. Poets, memoirists, novelists. It killed them."

"Eli Wiesel?"

"Yes, there are exceptions. I have my opinions about Eli. I'd prefer not to share. I'll just say Chaim went deeper. I think you'd agree. You also could have mentioned Aharon Appelfeld. But he never wrote about the Shoah, did he? Always just before, the season before, the day before. Never the horror itself. Appelfeld knew what he was doing. He knew what to avoid, the places you shouldn't go."

"After Chaim's death, some Jewish intellectuals in America called him Hitler's final victim. Do you agree with that?"

"I'm not sure I would phrase it that way. I'm not a historian or a philosopher. I'm just a politician. But, yes, it was the Shoah. He survived it just a bit longer than other victims. If you want to be a poet, call him Hitler's final victim. I just say trauma. Trauma kills."

"Post-trauma, right? What you're describing is a kind of PTSD?"

"I suppose."

"Do you think Israel itself suffers from PTSD? Does that explain some of Israel's political choices?"

"To be perfectly honest, I resent the question. In my opinion, the great majority of Israel's decisive policy moves have been rational and humane. We're not some haunted people exorcising our demons. Chaim's actions are not symbolic of post-war Judaism. You're like those critics who invented something called the Masada Complex, merely because we choose to defend ourselves. It's nonsense. We're not suicidal maniacs. We're not the ones blowing ourselves up in pizza restaurants. Anyway, you're asking me to be a psychologist. And to the whole country, no less. But we're getting far afield from discussing Chaim. You have to understand: politics wasn't his thing. He would have been the first to admit that. I think he hated politics, but he was too polite to tell me. But I can assure you, he was no politician."

"What was he, then?"

"What was he? Chaim? Chaim? A storyteller, certainly. A thinker. A teacher. But if you asked him that question, I'm pretty sure I know how he would answer. A theologian. Chaim was a theologian. He wanted to teach us about God. More than that. He wanted to rescue God."

"I don't understand."

"His book. His last book. The bestseller. The only one people still read. Chaim wasn't religious. But that's a complicated sentence, isn't it? Here, we would say Chaim wasn't *dati*. He was *hiloni*—secular. But he recognized that God was at the center of Jewish consciousness. The Jewish people invented God. Jewish national consciousness depends on a covenant with God. There could be no Judaism without God. These were Chaim's core beliefs. So, in his opinion, the most urgent Jewish task for the twentieth century was theological. It wasn't building the Jewish homeland. It was creating a theological framework that explained God in light of the Holocaust. And he did. Better than anyone else. One simple declarative sentence."

"God is not omnipotent."

"Exactly. God wanted to help. God couldn't. He tried to save the million children. He tries to cure every innocent child with a cruel disease. He failed. He fails still. Every day."

"'Our Imperfect God.' The God who failed."

"Well, the God who failed but nevertheless keeps trying. Now, if you think about it, maybe this is why Chaim took his own life."

"I don't understand."

"He worked so hard to redefine the central Jewish definition of God. Maybe he ended up believing it himself. He was the first victim of his own project of disillusionment. He believed in God, believed that God wasn't all-powerful, and couldn't live with a God who, time and time again, fails. Psychologically, it was worse than atheism. At least an atheist can say it's all bullshit. But Chaim had to live with a God who disappoints over and over again. Sooner or later, the disappointment kills you."

"Fascinating."

"Thank you."

"But—couldn't it just have been an accident?"

"Chaim never used that balcony alone. He wasn't there by accident."

"Did he love you?" [JL: *This question was asked by the author's daughter, Hannah Loeb.*]

"Of course he did, sweetie. He was the love of my life. We were deeply in love. Until his dying day."

"One more question."

"Of course."

"Could it have been murder? Do you think someone might have killed Chaim? Pushed him over the edge? Made it look like suicide?"

"What a perfectly insane question. Everyone loved Chaim. He was Israel's soul. Who would murder him?"

CHAPTER 14

July 2005

"'Did he love you?' What kind of question is that? To a *widow*?"

Hannah and I were eating ice cream at a shop on the Ben Yehuda mall. I remembered Israeli ice cream as doughy and sickly sweet, but like so much else in the country, the ice cream had leaped forward in quality. It was the best gelato I'd ever tasted, and I'd been to Rome several times. Also, the shop was gloriously air-conditioned, and the heat outside was brutal and punishing—the air dry enough to burn away sweat. It was as if Jerusalem had traveled a few million miles closer to the sun.

"But you didn't even ask about the girls," Hannah said. "The blackmail." She quickly licked away her remaining salted caramel and then gobbled down the waffle cone. She asked if she could get another, maybe try the Israel version of rocky road.

"Why not," I said. I looked at my butter pecan cone. Almost gone. "Get one for me too."

"It was a tricky interview," I said when Hannah returned with two overflowing cones. I spoke in between licks. "She's not a suspect, right? Charlie told us she's got an airtight alibi. So what were we trying to get out of her?" I sounded to myself like a journalism professor—and not a particularly bright one. And I suddenly realized that I should have given this particular lecture before we interviewed Zehava. But I'd thought Charlie would take the lead. He'd texted me only an hour before that there was no point in him being there; Zehava wasn't a suspect in any crime. Anyway, I didn't expect Hannah to ask any questions. That, of course, was a misjudgment. In retrospect, it was surprising that she didn't butt in more with her inquiries.

"Some insight into Chaim's state of mind?" Hannah suggested. "Why he would have killed himself?"

"Exactly."

"But Dad. Didn't it occur to you that he might have jumped because of the blackmail? Because of how much he hurt Zehava? That all of this had nothing to do with the Holocaust? He just couldn't live with the guilt of hurting her. That's why I asked her if he loved her."

Nothing to do with the Holocaust? But, in my mind, everything about Chaim—every choice, every relationship, every involuntary action—had to do with the Holocaust. Still, Hannah was unquestionably correct. The smart thing—the journalistic move—would have been to ask about the blackmail.

"I didn't want to hurt her feelings," I admitted. "She was always so kind to me."

"Dad," she said firmly. I was surprised by how adult her voice sounded. The effect was undercut a bit by watching her teenage tongue dance around her cone, like a dog ensuring that every bit of the delicious treat was lapped up. "We have a book to write. No compromises from now on, okay? Hard-hitting investigative journalism."

I nodded. I couldn't speak. I was too busy lapping up my own cone.

◆ ◆ ◆

Our next interview was with Michal. We met at her office at the David Institute on Keren Hayesod Street in Talbieh, one of Jerusalem's toniest neighborhoods. I was surprised that Michal enjoyed a spacious corner office. I didn't realize she'd become the executive vice president. I'd discovered years ago that Michal had journeyed far from her left-wing positions as a college student. Shortly after 9/11, she sent me a stream of op-ed columns excoriating the peace negotiators she called the "Oslo Criminals," including the assassinated Yitzhak Rabin. I googled the David Institute the moment after I heard she'd taken a job there. Its main interest appeared to be the inherent Jewish right to settle and annex every inch of biblical Israel. So I knew Michal's politics, and I knew she was a well-known and successful attorney. But, until I saw her office, on the top floor of this sleek building, in this fancy neighborhood, I didn't realize she was one of Israel's leading figures on the intellectual right, the ideological faction that most hated and feared Zehava's party. I imagined years of interesting dinner conversations at the Lerner table.

Michal seated us at a long oak conference table and offered coffee. Hannah accepted; I didn't. Michal brewed two cappuccinos on her machine, then added sugar and vanilla to Hannah's. *Ice cream and sweetened cappuccino*, I thought. *That's all Hannah's eaten today. Some father she's got.*

"You found the body," I said.

"I did," Michal answered. "You were there."

Strange, I thought, *that we'd never discussed that night*. Now, here, it was twenty-two years later. Maybe that's how long these things take. "What did you think when you found him?"

She paused a few seconds, letting her coffee cool, then took a sip. "At first, I figured he slipped. He had a hard time walking those days. You remember. But Zehava figured it out right away. He never hung out on that balcony. Overall, he preferred to be indoors."

"Why do you think he did it?" I asked.

She shrugged. "God, who knows? He had a million reasons, right? PTSD. A bum leg. Don't underestimate what chronic pain can do to you. Especially an active guy like Chaim. Also, not everyone knows this, but he suffered from depression. Even before the war, so maybe this had nothing to do with the Holocaust. Or, I don't know, some people say it was that last book he wrote about God. Took too much out of him. You know, I spent a few months thinking about it. But Yoav and I had our lives to live. At some point, what does it matter why he did it? Dead is dead."

"Disappointment with Israel?" I suggested. "Could that have been part of it? He gave that statement about the Lebanon War."

She shrugged, smiled. She was done thinking about suicide. I was momentarily jealous. "Hannah," Michal said. "Another cappuccino?"

"Yes, please."

"Hannah," I protested. "Your hands are shaking. You won't get any sleep tonight."

"Oh, Hannah's got the constitution of an Israeli," Michal said, scooping coffee into the slot, steaming the milk. "She can drink coffee all day. Hannah, you'll have to come back to visit us, maybe stay for a summer. I can put you to work at the Institute." She placed the cappuccino in front of Hannah.

"Yeah, for sure," Hannah said, pouring sugar into her steaming cup. She took a sip, added more sugar. "What about all the women Chaim fooled around with?" she asked.

Michal looked at me. *Why*, I wondered, *does everyone look at me when Hannah says something inappropriate?* "Excuse me?" Michal said.

"The two old religious guys told us that Chaim had seduced a lot of his students. Is that true?"

Michal exhaled sharply and nodded. She answered Hannah but kept looking at me. "You know, Hannah," she said. "I think it might be true. I certainly heard the rumors." She sipped her coffee. "I think I mentioned it to your father. Maybe? I mean, back then."

I was almost sure she didn't. But, on the other hand, how was it that I knew?

"Did you know he was being blackmailed?" Hannah asked. "Or these guys were planning on blackmailing him, except he died?"

"No," Michal said slowly. She leaned back in her chair. "I didn't. Huh. I guess it doesn't surprise me. But I'm not sure any blackmail would have worked. It's not like today. I'm not excusing him. It was gross. Awful. But times have changed. I doubt he would have suffered any consequence at all back then. He wouldn't have gotten fired. Maybe Zehava would have left him? But probably not."

"Do you think that may be why he killed himself?" I asked. "He realized he was about to be blackmailed. Or he felt guilty."

"I don't know," Michal said. "I'm just hearing about this now. Sure. Why not? Like I said, what difference does it make? Judah, I'm really not sure what you're doing here."

"What was your alibi?" Hannah asked.

"Hannah!" I said.

"No, Judah." Michal said. "It's okay. Hannah, you're amazing! What would you like to know?"

"Charlie keeps telling us you have a solid alibi. I'm just wondering what it is. Where were you when Chaim died?"

She paused, stole a look at me. "Hannah, I'm afraid my answer might hurt your father's feelings. But I'm happy to tell you. I was shopping for wedding dresses. With my future mother-in-law. In fact, I took the dress home with me that night. You know, it's not like the police ignored the case completely back then. They asked all of us about our alibis. Zehava and I told them, and we gave them the receipt, with the date and time. I think they even interviewed the shopkeeper. Oh, Judah, I think you know the place. Remember? Rafik's Boutique. In the Arab Market. The Old City. He sold me my wedding dress."

◆◆◆

That night, Charlie dropped off several boxes of evidence at our cottage. He'd gotten the important interviews transcribed and translated into English, along with all the relevant police reports. One box contained documentary evidence, like Chaim's calendar, his handwritten Lebanon statement, and receipts. I asked him if he could find the wedding dress receipt. After a few seconds of fishing around, he found it and showed it to me. The writing was Hebrew and Arabic, but I could read the date and time. I showed it to Hannah. "The police talked to the guy?" Hannah asked. "To what's his name? The owner? Rafik?"

"I guess," Charlie said. He leafed through the interview file. "Here it is," he said. "Interview with Rafik Salahmi. Translated into English." Hannah grabbed it.

"Hannah," I said. "Maybe tomorrow, after we interview Yoav, we take the afternoon off. Do some shopping in the Old City. Buy some souvenirs. I know just the place."

CHAPTER 15

Excerpt from *Here There Is No Why: The Death and Life of Chaim Lerner* by Judah Loeb, 2005
Interview with Yoav Lerner

Yoav Lerner is the only son of Chaim and Zehava Lerner. The Lerners spoke English at home while he was growing up, which explains his fluency in the language. He's the chief software engineer at IsraTech, Israel's leading high-tech firm, headquartered in Rishon Letziyon, with offices in Boston, Houston, and Johannesburg. Before assuming his position at IsraTech, Yoav served in the Intelligence Branch of the Israel Defense Forces for sixteen years. He was, understandably, reluctant to share details of that service; though, as you'll read, some facts leaked through.

I hate you ridiculous journalists who would rather concoct convoluted philosophical existential theories than stick to the facts. There are two problems with this approach. One, you get the facts wrong. Not some of the time. Not most of the time. All of the time. I have never read a single article or magazine feature or journalist's volume about Israel without serious errors of fact. Two, journalists, particularly American journalists, are morons, with extremely low intelligence. So—this is what you do. You take the wrong facts and mold those inaccuracies into bizarre theories. You write fiction, literally.

I'm not talking about bias. Bias is different. Of course there's bias. From the beginning, or at least since our victory in 1967, the media favored first the Arab side, and now the Palestinians. But, honestly, I don't condemn this blatant bias. I share the political views of these journalists. I agree that Israel is now the aggressor, often the cruel aggressor. My problem is not your politics. My problem is your idiocy. Your laziness. Your arrogance, so richly undeserved.

Take my story, for example. I know you're growing impatient. You ask about my father, and I give you a sermon about reporters. But before I give you the obvious answer about how my father died, I have to show you how American journalists misread a story, how their bumbling incompetence infected my father. The story starts with the massacres in Sabra and Chatila, two Palestinian refugee camps in Beirut. My unit was stationed a few kilometers south of the camps, which were really more like decrepit suburbs than camps. The word "camp" is gloriously misleading, yes? Auschwitz was a camp, a hell on Earth. Gas chambers, firing squads, starvation. Ramah or Interlocken—those are also camps. Volleyball, swimming, horseback riding. Sabra and Chatila? Something in between, yes? But you see what I mean. Journalists never tackle the subtle questions, not with the intellectual delicacy they demand. What is a camp? That's the essential question.

We heard the shots. We heard the guttural Arabic commands from the loudspeaker. We heard the screams. Yes, the screams sounded like the cries of children. We assumed—it was a logical assumption—that they were executing children. The next day, we found out that hundreds of civilians were murdered. Four hundred, five hundred, maybe more. Dozens of children. Mothers and babies.

We did nothing. We didn't intervene. I stayed at my post monitoring radio transmissions inside my tent. I heard the most vicious, devilish rhythms one could imagine. Screams, then shots, then screams. Over and over again. Rhythmic, like a drum machine. You could dance to it. With each scream, I touched my rifle, ready for orders. None came. Ten thousand Jewish soldiers stood idly by while our allies murdered children.

Then, suddenly, quiet. No shots, no lunatic Arabic commands from the loudspeakers. The killing stopped. Maybe they killed them all, yes? Or they were afflicted by sudden pangs of conscience? Or they got tired, but they'd resume in a few minutes. Five minutes into the eerie silence, we got our orders. We rode into Chatila, on jeeps and halftracks. Two hundred and fifty of us, maybe fewer. I rode in the rear, as always, monitoring radio communication.

I saw the bodies. I won't describe them for you. Our people have produced enough atrocity porn. Usually, it's us. Now it was them. I will only ask you, Mr. Investigative Journalist, to imagine a mother lying down holding two babies close to her bosom and spotting three neat bullet holes. One in her skull, and two in the heads of each of her infant twins. See if you can hold that picture in your mind for two minutes straight, and then forget about it.

We marched through the camp. We disarmed every Phalangist soldier we saw. They cooperated with us fully. They handed us their rifles—weapons that we had given them. They had made their point to the Palestinians: if you don't leave, we will kill all of you. They had murdered enough babies to get this message across. So they disarmed and slunk off.

Technically, we halted the massacre. They killed four hundred. They stopped. We marched. How easy it is to play a quick game with that chronology. Switch around the second and third occurrence. We marched, they stopped. A few of our own Israeli journalists—also moral midgets and imbeciles—wrote it that way. Two or three Israeli reporters got it mostly right. When the Phalangists heard we were ordered to intervene, they stopped. So we didn't physically halt the massacre, but word of our coming forced them to stop. Would they have kept killing if they hadn't heard we were on our way? What a ridiculous, moronic question. Maybe yes, maybe no. Maybe six hundred instead of four hundred. Maybe two hundred children instead of fifty. How can anyone know? How can it matter? It's atrocity porn, yes?

But here's what I read in the American press. We did it. Yes, that is what many of your cowardly, lazy reporters first wrote. They wrote this libel, this smear, because they weren't there. They heard from this source, who heard from this source, who had a brother-in-law in the PLO's headquarters in Beirut. The Israelis perpetrated the Sabra and Chatila massacres. This was the first article my father read. Later, he read something closer to the truth, but still not the truth. He read that Israel "allowed it to happen." "Allowed" it. What does this strange English word mean? It sounds very much like they first asked our permission. Or that our forces surrounded the camps and that we stepped aside and gracefully waved our hands, inviting them in, so they can murder children.

Listen, the truth was bad enough. We didn't intervene. We condemn the entire non-Nazi world for not intervening in the death camps. My father viciously and righteously condemned the bystander. But when the time came for us to intervene, we did nothing. We stood by. We were the bystanders.

My father didn't read the article that condemned us as bystanders. Because there was no such article in the American and British media. He read that we did it. Jewish hands drip with blood. That's what he read first, yes? Then, he read that Jews didn't carry out the atrocity, but we allowed it to happen, which, in some moral calculus, could be accurate, could be not quite accurate. It doesn't really matter; it is just as bad.

But wait, listen. Stop writing and listen. You can't do both at the same time. I can see what you are concluding. You're ready to submit your brilliant thesis. Chaim Lerner killed himself because of Sabra and Chatila. Victim had become perpetrator. My father's worst nightmare. This would be typical of a journalist's moronic intelligence. My father didn't kill himself because of Sabra and Chatila. Frankly, like most of us, he didn't care enough about the Palestinians to kill himself because of their misery or our collective guilt.

He killed himself because of me.

I'll explain. Please stop writing everything down. I see your recorder. You won't miss a word. But I insist you listen closely, with no distractions. Yes? Good.

Approximately one month after Sabra and Chatila, around the time you started sleeping with my fiancé, my unit was sent into a small Lebanese village. Most of the residents of this village are Palestinian refugees. But it's not a camp. It's a village. What's the difference? I could tell you, but let's just agree that it doesn't matter. I can't tell you the name of the village or the mission. If I tell you, I'll get arrested. And why would you need to know those facts? Little facts like those have no interest to most journalists, most certainly including you. So, we rode into town, mostly on roofless halftracks, like marauders in a dystopian science-fiction movie. We create havoc by the mere fact of entering the village in our souped-up vehicles. I rode in the back. You know why. It's not cowardice; it's my assignment. But I am afraid. We are all afraid. Every Israeli soldier is afraid. But not of dying. Dying is irrelevant. Not because we've become suicidal, that somehow we don't care about our own bodies.

It's irrelevant because . . . I'm not sure. I think because it's impossible to imagine our own deaths. Anyway, for me, it was impossible. My fear, our fear, was of two possibilities. One, that we would screw up and embarrass ourselves. It's true. We're like high school students—we were just a few years out of high school!—so our greatest fear is humiliation. And—we're afraid of killing innocent civilians. Those were our two fears. And when it came to those two possibilities, I was a coward.

We ride into town. I'm in the back seat of the rearmost halftrack. One hand is on my rifle, and the other is on the radio. I'm listening with my ears and watching with my eyes. Impossible, but that's what I do. Suddenly, a hail of rocks flies at us. Not unusual. Normal in the West Bank or Gaza, like rain in the winter. Slightly less normal in Lebanon because weapons of war are so plentiful and available. In Lebanon, stones usually meant children. Little children couldn't lift or fire weapons, so they gathered rocks and threw them at us. We had shields, armored vests. Plus, these were children. How hard could they throw? It was a nuisance, not a threat, never deadly. Nevertheless, our orders are clear. Both hands on the rifle. Don't shoot, but stand your ground, protect your face, and intimidate. But the Palestinians in these villages are decidedly not morons. They come up with a brilliant strategy. They've learned that we don't fire back on stone throwers because we know these are merely young children. Boys and girls. So they greet us with stones but then suddenly switch to live fire. They convince us first that there is no deadly threat; then, they provide the deadly threat.

But that's not the full extent of their genius. Here's how it goes. First stones, from behind buildings and homes, so seeming from nowhere. We don't see the children. Then, the children pop out from their hiding places and continue throwing stones as hard as their nine-year-old arms can throw. We don't fire back. It's not a deadly threat, and we don't shoot at children.

But then—live fire. Also, at first, from behind a building or a home or a statue or a fountain. Our orders are to fire back at live rounds, but the only available targets are children. So we stand our ground. Some of our soldiers get shot. Some die. Very few, but some. And now, the brilliant part. The live shooters reveal themselves. Good for us, yes? Because now we have targets. Now we can defend ourselves. We don't have to aim at stone-throwing children. Except—the shooters are children! They enlist children! We can't fire, but we must. In the confusion of this strange wartime morality tale, they shoot many of us. What can we do? We fire back. This is what happened to me. This is why my father killed himself.

Remember, I'm at the rear. Attacks come from the front. They assume our best fighters are at the front, so that's where they aim. Not an inaccurate assumption, by the way. Often, the battle is over before any fire even gets to me. But this one time. In this one village. You know I can't say when or where. We are attacked from the rear. First, like always, stones. From children. I put up my shield and crouch. I'm safe from stones. But I know what happens next. Bullets from behind a fountain. My driver pushes me into the back of the halftrack. We crouch and wait. My commander orders us to return fire. That's what I hear. That's what I hear. The order to fire back. My driver doesn't hear the order. I understand. He's not lying. It's noisy when people are shooting at you. But I hear the fucking order. I pop up from under my seat and fire two continuous rounds, at two targets—two Lebanese Hezbollah fighters with Kalashnikovs. By pure luck, I hit both targets. I am an exceptionally poor shooter. Everyone in my battalion mocks me. I fail every firing exam. This is the first time in my life I hit the target, and I do it twice! Straight and sure, the center of the chest, the heart. I kill both fighters.

Except they are not Hezbollah fighters. It's two ten-year-old boys. No uniforms. No Kalashnikovs. I swear to God, I saw weapons. But I don't see them now. I just see two dead boys.

Before I went into the army, my parents had a conversation with me. It's a conversation that many Israeli parents have with their children. They told me that if I find myself in a situation where it seems very much like my life is threatened, but I'm not one-hundred-percent certain, shoot anyway. If I'm wrong, they said, we'll deal with the consequences together afterward. But at least I'll be alive. I know they meant it at the time.

But this war—the Lebanon War—haunted my father. To this day, people don't realize how much. He couldn't look at it objectively or strategically. For him, it wasn't an operation to weaken a terrorist organization on our border. It was David and Goliath, and we were Goliath. Worse. He never told me this directly, but I know he believed it. If he'd lived long enough, I'm sure he would have said it to me. Sabra and Chatila. Shooting at children. He smelled Nazis. And the smell was coming from his people. His own son. He didn't really think we were Nazis. But I knew his nightmares. He told them to us when we were children. Many survivors dream they're back in a camp, back in the forests, back in Auschwitz. My father's recurring dream was that he became a Nazi colonel in the Israeli army. And instead of hunting down Jews, he chased and murdered Arab children. His dream escaped the land of nightmares and burst into reality. Except it skipped a generation. I was the child-killing Nazi, not him. His son joined Pharoah's army and murdered innocent children. He couldn't live with that. He killed himself because of me.

Eventually, the army cleared me of all responsibility. But that was after he jumped off the balcony. And you know that I tried to make him happy by asking Michal to marry me. It didn't matter. He was doomed. It was my fault.

A voice from the back of the room. Young, female. My daughter. "Where were you the night your Dad died?"

"Excuse me?"

"What's your alibi for the murder?"

"Murder? Have you lost your mind?"

"Where were you?"

"Where was I? The army was still investigating the shooting in Lebanon. I was in jail, you fucking nitwit.

CHAPTER 16

July 2005

"My old and beautiful friend!"
Rafik's store hadn't changed much. Somehow, I remembered the route—through the Damascus Gate, taking the first right fork past fruit and vegetable stalls, then leather goods, then bloody, butchered calves, then a series of smoky, dark cafés, and then olive-wood crafts. Along the way, we dodged women in multicolored robes and scarves carrying trays of pita on their heads, boys whacking donkeys, men in suits or jeans or white robes and kaffiyehs hurrying to work, and a smattering of European and American tourists, far fewer than what I'd seen twenty years before. The Intifada had evidently hurt his business. It was the smell, more than anything, that triggered a flood of memories, and that guided me toward the store. The air was redolent of donkey dung, mint tea, leather, and tobacco from water pipes. The odors led the way—an olfactory GPS. As we crossed the invisible boundary into the Christian Quarter, the souvenirs turned decidedly

Christological: crosses, with and without the loin-clothed Jesus, fish necklaces, and New Testaments in many languages. At the next T intersection, straight ahead, was Rafki's Boutique—still the biggest store in the shuk.

As if he'd been expecting us, Rafik greeted me at the entrance. He looked like an exact replica of the Rafik I remembered—tall, thin, glasses with thick lenses, black wool slacks, and a white dress shirt. The only difference was his hair, now gray, and his five o'clock shadow, which had turned from black to salt-and-pepper. He pumped my hand, then looked me in the eye for several seconds before kissing both my cheeks. Was it possible he remembered me after twenty-two years?

"Of course I remember," he said, though I hadn't asked out loud. He stepped back and took in Hannah, looking up and down. "My wonderful and fascinating customer from Cleveland, Ohio. Friend of my greatest customer." He winked at me and turned to Hannah. "And this must be your beautiful, wonderful wife!"

Hannah blushed. "No," she said. "I'm not—"

"Joking, my dear. Joking! You, of course, are much too young for this man. For, uh, Judah! I remembered. You are too young for Judah. And much too beautiful. Your mother must have been magnificent."

"She was," Hannah said quietly.

He touched my shoulder. "Why have you stayed away so long? And what are you buying for your beautiful daughter today?"

I told him I was a reporter investigating Chaim Lerner's death. I asked him if the name sounded familiar.

"Of course," he said, frowning. "A famous man. The Israeli police talk with me for hours. Like I am suspect."

"Do you remember what the police wanted from you?" I asked.

"Of course. One doesn't forget when Israeli police scream at you. They ask if I sell Bedouin-style wedding gown to, uh, your former beloved, loved one, girlfriend."

"Michal," I said. "You mean Michal."

He nodded. "Michal."

"And you told them yes?"

He looked left and right, as if we'd been followed, then ushered us through the store, past the leather jackets, the CDs and cassettes blaring Arabic music, the Bedouin knives and dresses, and into his back office. He shouted a few words in Arabic, and a teenage boy brought in a samovar of tea, three espresso-sized cups, and a tray of round sesame cookies. Rafik pointed to the red-cushioned chairs and poured the tea. We sat, and Hannah grabbed a cookie. "Of course, my wonderful friends. I tell the police what is true. Yes. I tell them yes. Your, well, so sorry, not yours, I mean Michal. Michal was with the wonderful Zehava. My favorite customer. Zehava a very important woman. And she pay for dress."

"And you remember the exact day they were here?" I asked.

"It was nighttime. My wonderful wife, she sews and fits and helps the ladies with, uh, their dressing things. But only at night. She works at the health clinic during the day. Down there." He pointed toward the Damascus Gate. "There was receipt. With date. Time."

Hannah reached into her backpack and took out a sheet of paper. "You mean this?" she said. I had no idea she'd brought evidence with her to the *shuk*. She handed the page to Rafik. He glanced at it.

"Yes, yes," he said. "No computers back then. My wonderful wife, she write this with hand." He pointed to the bottom. "Her beautiful signature." He showed me the entirely illegible scrawl. It looked like a lizard crawling across the page. He seemed to be waiting for a reaction.

"Nice," I finally said.

"And this is date," he said, pointing to another line, this one much clearer: 5/5/83, 19:00. It took me a moment to remember that Israelis didn't use a.m. and p.m. for time. The receipt confirmed both Zehava and Michal's alibi. Four of Chaim's neighbors heard the bump at 18:30, on May 5. At that time, Michal and Zehava were purchasing a wedding dress so Michal could marry her beloved fiancé in a glorious virgin Bedouin gown.

After we finished the excellent tea and cookies, we shopped. I picked out a silver chai necklace that I'd either keep or give to my sister. After thirty minutes of indecision, Hannah chose a Grateful Dead T-shirt with the names of the bandmembers in Hebrew ("They've even got Pigpen," she enthused. *How does she know about the Grateful Dead?* I wondered). When I took out my wallet to pay, Rafik clicked his tongue several times and gently touched my chest, pushing me away. "You are my very special friends," he said. "No money."

I wasn't sure if this was some new form of *shuk* haggling. Maybe the customs had changed since my last visit. Was I supposed to offer something substantial, and then he'd counter with a lower price? But Hannah grabbed the gifts, rushed out, and yelled, "Thank you" over her shoulder.

I ran after her, back toward the Damascus Gate, and managed to grab her shoulder. She shook me off, but then saw it was me. She grabbed my hand and pulled me into a café. "I had to get away from that creep. You saw how he looked at me." Actually, I hadn't, or I hadn't thought it was so different from how he looked at Michal twenty years ago, or at me, for that matter. Weirdly attentive, but greedy for money, not lustful. But maybe I was wrong. A young, male waiter at the café looked at Hannah the same way when he led us to a table. Before he even offered us menus, Hannah ordered mint tea and sesame almond cookies—the same refreshments Rafik had served. I looked at her. "What?" she said. "They were good!"

We caught our breath for a few minutes. Hannah wolfed down three cookies. I nibbled at one. "The real reason I ran out is because I need to read my email. I didn't want Rafik to see it. Actually, I didn't really want you to see it, but I'll need to talk with someone about it, and it's probably going to have to be you." She showed me an email on her iPhone and pointed to the "From" line. It was a word in Arabic.

"Hannah."

"Oh, sorry. I forgot you didn't bother to learn Arabic. It says, 'Penitent.' Can you figure out who it's from?"

It didn't take long. "Your suicide bomber."

"My bomber," she confirmed.

"But how?" I asked. "They get email? And why is he writing to you?"

She shrugged. "How am I supposed to know? Sometimes there is no why. Do you want to hear it?"

I didn't. I wanted her to delete it, right away. But I didn't say anything. I knew she would read the whole thing, out loud, no matter what I said. I nodded and leaned in. Hannah read.

Dear Hannah,
A good friend translates this for me. English is better for him.
I Google you last night. I discover sad, sad story about your mother. I start to see why you interest in suicide so much. But Hannah. You see, of course, I am not acting like your mother. I was murderer. I am murderer. I try to murder. This is much more important than I am suicide.
Your mother not murderer. What I see in Google, she was beautiful woman. But she became sick. And scared. So she want not to live. I understand some of her feel. She is lost and afraid. I too. I understand. But she not try to kill. Very different.
Also different. It very sad, but she die anyway. I see it on Google. She kill herself, but soon, disease kill her. She not want you to see her sick. So she does this thing for you. I waste all

my life ahead of me. She die anyway, and soon. So, Hannah, don't judge your mother. Very important to love your mother. She love you.

Hannah, you ask so many question about note. Did I write note, when, how I write it, who it for—so many question. I guess now that your mother doesn't write note. And this make you sad. Hannah, she was lost and sick and afraid, and you were little girl. Nothing to say. Nothing to write. So hard to think. I feel these thing too. The only note for you is she love you. Her love for you make you a sweet, friendly, loving girl, who talk to me like a human being, even though, really, I am murderer criminal animal. I mean to say the note is in your heart.

Your Friend,
Kamal

By the final paragraph, tears streamed down Hannah's cheek, though, oddly, her voice stayed clear and even. It was as if part of her was crying, and the other part was analyzing. But when she shoved the phone back in her pocket, one of the few times I'd seen her relinquish her phone without my nagging, she was sobbing. I fought hard to restrain my own tears. I'd learned years ago that weeping with Hannah was never a good strategy. My role was to comfort—and then, if necessary, cry later, alone. I moved next to her and put my arm around her. She wept into the crook of my neck. I wondered how many more times she would cry in my arms. Maybe this was the last time. She pulled me in close and trembled with tears. Ilana was right, I thought. I never should have taken this assignment. I certainly shouldn't have brought Hannah. Every investigative path here led to suicide. I rubbed her face in it. She sat weeping for another five minutes, then slowly disentangled herself. I took a napkin and wiped her face. She grabbed it from me and dabbed it on my shoulder, trying to dry my shirt. "It will dry in the sun," I told her. "So will your face."

"Can we get the fuck out of here, please?" she said.

"Of course," I said. "Let me just get the check."

"No. I don't mean this café. I mean this country. Can we please leave this stupid country?"

I signaled the waiter, who brought me the check. "Let's leave the Old City first. Then, we'll figure it out." I put some shekels on the table. Hannah reached for all the leftover cookies and swept them into her backpack. We walked quickly toward the Damascus Gate. New flight arrangements danced through my head. Could we leave tomorrow? Did I have enough information to at least bat out an article and then maybe a draft of a short book?

But by the time we reached the apartment, Hannah seemed to have calmed down. She was eager to try on her new T-shirts. She ducked into the bathroom, and thirty seconds later, she appeared with a photo of the Grateful Dead splayed tightly across her chest. Too tightly.

"What do you think?" she asked.

I hesitated. Her breasts pushed through the shirt. This was a fraught moment. "It's, uh, okay."

"Too tight? I think maybe it's too tight."

I breathed a sigh of relief. "I think so."

"I should have tried it on at the store. I hate the thought of going back there."

I looked at the smiling members of the Grateful Dead. Who was Pigpen? Why does Hannah know, and I don't? Then, a thought hit me. Walloped me. "Wait," I said. "What did you say?"

"I said I hate the idea of going back to the store. But it's okay. I will. Now that I think about it, he wasn't that bad. And we really should have paid him."

"No, what did you say before that?"

"That I should have tried it on? That it doesn't fit?"

"It doesn't fit," I said. "Your shirt didn't fit. You should have tried it on at the store. Hannah, where's the evidence file?"

She walked into her room and came back carrying eight thick files piled one on top of the other. The top one reached her forehead. She dropped them on the kitchen table. "What do you need?" she asked. I marveled that, somehow, she'd become custodian of the English language evidence, my private fifteen-year-old archivist.

I sat at the table and tried sifting through the papers. "Rafik sold them the dress on May 5, right?" I said. "But nobody buys a wedding dress off-the-rack. Michal would have had to try it on, get it fitted. Remember, that's why Rafik needed his wife. At night. For the fitting. So they must have come in at some earlier date, done the measurements, and left a deposit. Does the receipt we have mention a deposit?"

Hannah found the page in her backpack and squinted at it. "I don't think so," she said. She showed it to me. I couldn't decipher the Arabic, but, beside the signatures, the document only had room for two variables. "It's just the date and the price," Hannah said.

"Then there must be another receipt in here. The police would have asked for all the receipts. Unless—"

"Unless the whole alibi is bullshit," Hannah said. "And this receipt is a forgery."

I stared at Hannah. "Let's not jump to conclusions," I said. "Let's see if we can find the other receipt."

It took almost two hours: sifting, translating, Googling. But Hannah found it in the second-to-last binder A receipt from Rafik's Boutique. Same salamander-like signature—presumably the wife—a smaller amount of money, and another Arabic word that Hannah, searching the net, was able to define as "deposit."

"What's the date?" I asked.

She pointed with her thumb: 2/5/1983. "May 2," she said. "Three days before they picked up the dress."

May 2. I looked at the ceiling. Then took a deep breath and closed my eyes. When I opened them, I saw Hannah sucking her lower lip, her forehead wrinkled with worry. It was a familiar expression. She was often worried about me. Too often. *She looks so much like her mother*, I thought. May 2. "I think we're ready to leave this stupid country," I said.

"No, Dad, it's okay. I just—all that stuff from my bomber. You know, about Mom and the note. I just lost it. But I want to stay. I want to finish the job. I feel like we're close to figuring everything out."

"I'm ready to go," I said, with more firmness than I intended. "I just have to talk with Charlie one more time. We'll leave the day after tomorrow."

"Day after tomorrow? I don't understand," Hannah said. "We've barely started. You're giving up? You don't want to know what happened to Chaim?"

"I really don't want to know," I agreed. "But. Unfortunately. I do." I picked up the first receipt, turned it over, glanced at it, then put it down. "I know exactly what happened to Chaim."

CHAPTER 17

April 1983

It had been an unusually cold winter for Jerusalem. The wind and the rain defeated my layered sweaters, sweatshirts, and Israeli-style *dubon* winter coat. It even snowed several times, with a blizzard in late March, just in time for Purim. The cold evenings gave me ample excuse to sleep over at Michal's, our bodies warming each other most nights. The weather warmed up a bit in April as the calendar approached Passover. But that morning, a week before the spring holiday, I still shivered in my winter coat as I fruitlessly tried to follow the Zohar discussion in the *Kotel* tunnel. Chaim was oddly energetic that day. His arms jerked left and right. He abandoned his clear singsong voice, growing gruff, hoarse. I might have said angry if I had any idea what he was saying. *Maybe he's just trying to stay warm*, I thought. After class, he sensed my cold, so he held my elbow tightly as he led me through the tunnel. At the *Kotel* plaza, I tried to head uphill, but he yanked me back.

"The discussion was prayer," he said, though I hadn't asked. "You followed, maybe, a little bit? Yes?"

"No. Not at all."

He laughed. "It will come, Judah. It will come."

I suspected that Chaim harbored a fantasy that I would stay in Israel, finish my degree at the Hebrew University, and then come to work for him. And maybe marry Michal. I attributed that fantasy to him, but some of it, maybe all of it, was mine.

"They challenged my notion of God, when it came to prayer. Why pray, they ask me, to a God who fails? We are talking here about petitionary prayer, yes? To pray *for* something. The crudest form of prayer. But, yes, something not even the most sophisticated theologian, or even, frankly, the most committed atheist, will give up."

I shrugged. I was neither a sophisticated theologian nor a committed atheist. I just didn't pray. Sometimes Michal would drag me to a Friday night service in her neighborhood led by a charismatic rabbi who reached out to young adults. She liked the singing. We'd part at the entrance and go to our separate gender-restricted areas. The worshippers in the men's section crowded together like stoned fans in a mosh pit. The smell was not dissimilar to a locker room. I would spend the whole time swaying a bit to the hip Shabbat melodies and watching Michal through the bars of the *mehitza*—the male/female divider. She'd stand ramrod straight and close her eyes tightly for forty-five minutes, the length of the service. I fell in love with Michal at first sight, but I fell deeper—the hole pulled me further in—when I watched her pray.

Chaim continued, "I told them it's much easier to pray to my less-than-all-powerful deity. Because now we understand why we often, actually, really, most of the time, don't get what we pray for. I can tell myself that God really wanted to honor my prayers. Really, yes, he tried. He does not reject me. He is on my side. Prayer, after all, is relationship, yes? To get exactly what we want is not really the point, no?"

"Sounds right," I said. For me, prayer was either a crowded room in Israel, waiting for Michal to finish, or, in America, an itchy sweater, a too-tight tie. It was listening to a failed opera tenor, swapping whispered insults with my sister, and my mother, also bored out of her mind, shushing us. For me, prayer was like catching a cold. You knew it had to happen sometime, but you couldn't wait for it to be over.

"Let's try an experiment," Chaim continued. When he was in lecture mode, my responses didn't matter. I could have shouted, "Shut the fuck up," and it wouldn't have fazed him. "We will pray. You and me. An aggregate of two, yes? That is our research number. Here's what you must do. Pray that God grant you five things that you very much desire. Important things—that you really want, that you need. And, please, we'll be realistic. No praying to live forever, no asking for a billion dollars, no marriage to, I don't know the actresses anymore, for instance, Elizabeth Taylor. Yes? A bad example? Five things, Judah. Doesn't have to be in order. This is petitionary prayer. Ask for these things. Then, understand you will only get one of them. The rest you will have to relinquish. Remember, the God I imagine has limited energy, limited abilities, limited time. So choose wisely. You want five things. You want them badly, yes, Judah? Badly. But you only get God's help with one. What will it be? And how will you feel about losing the others? Come. Join me at the *Kotel*."

"Wait," I said. "Are these things I don't have already? Can I ask to keep something I already have?"

"Judah, I am making up this experiment as we talk. There really are no rules beyond what I've already explained. Petitionary prayer—you are asking for something. To our imperfect God."

He looked at his watch. "We'll give it half an hour. Meet me right over there," he said, pointing to the dark-bearded man handing out black cardboard yarmulkes. "By that lovely gentleman."

He limped quickly to the far corner of the *Kotel*. I walked slowly, straight ahead. At first, I thought of keeping my distance, five or six feet away from the stacked stones. But some inner momentum carried me forward. I found myself shouldering past a giggling group of black-hatted *haredi* teenagers and wound up with my palms and face flush to the wall. Without thinking, I kissed the Herodian stone. *Like a mother kissing an infant*, I thought. I offered affection to something that could not possibly reciprocate. Stones have no odor to speak of, but I could smell the weed grasses poking out from between the stones and the decaying, smashed up notes in the cracks.

I took a breath. *What do I want?* I thought of reaching for one of the torn prayer books in a box a few feet away, but I knew I wouldn't understand the Hebrew, and even if there was a translation, I wouldn't identify with the words, wouldn't know where to begin. The only faintly liturgical line to pop into my mind was a song lyric from the Rolling Stones: "You can't always get what you want, but if you try sometimes, well, you just might find, you get what you need." With that limiting sentiment in mind, I focused. I had some vague hope for a career in writing. I prayed for that. The prayer was granted; I became a journalist. Since I was three or four years old, I carried a morbid fear that my parents, and sometimes my sister, would die in a tragic accident, a fire, a flood, a car crash, or a freak fall. I prayed they would all live long lives. Got that one too. I was fairly healthy in those days, but I did suffer from occasional bouts of asthma. I carried an inhaler with me at all times. I prayed for health, that I'd always be able to control my asthma. My asthma eased considerably less than one year after my prayer. I had a difficult time making friends. Other than Michal and Charlie—and maybe Chaim—I'd made no friends that year. Back at Northwestern, I was shy, anxious, and insecure, with men and women, professors and students. I could joke around with the best of them, but I rarely pushed hard enough into genuine intimacy. I prayed that, in the future, God would bless me with a lifetime of many good friends. He did.

That brought me to Michal. At first, I thought I didn't have to pray about her. I felt so secure in the relationship, there didn't seem to be anything I needed or wanted to add. My cup overflowed. I was literally delirious with love for her—intoxicated, enraptured, and, like all deliriums, deceived. I thought of the wonder of waking up with a woman: the sight, the scent, the physical contact, the serenity. It wasn't just that I'd never experienced any of that before; it was that I got to experience it with Michal. All the firsts she provided—wild sexual pleasure (though not yet intercourse), naked, entangled intimacy, long kisses, two separate hands easily finding each other—were amplified because they happened with the person I knew was my one true love. I considered leaving Michal off the list, not because I didn't want her but because my love for her made Chaim's prayer challenge ridiculously easy. If she was on the list, the other four items paled into nothingness. She overwhelmed everything. Still, I put her on the list, and remembering Chaim's instructions, I instantly chose her over career, family, health, and friendship. If I could only get one-fifth of everything I wanted, I instructed God, give me Michal. He didn't. It was the only thing on the list I didn't get.

By the time I met Chaim back at the man giving away cardboard yarmulkes, I was astonished to feel my eyes fill with tears, though none leaked through to my cheeks. It was as if there was an invisible barrier halting any descent into weeping. I was also surprised to see Chaim with red eyes, blowing his nose. He took one look at me and smiled. "So, Judah," he said. "I would say our experiment succeeded. We approached the limited God, yes, prayed, and emerged with red eyes. What more can anyone realistically expect from this activity?"

I searched my pockets for Kleenex, but I hadn't brought any. Chaim handed me a clean tissue. "Is it like blowing out candles at a birthday party?" I asked. "You can't tell what you prayed for because if you do, you won't get your wish?"

Chaim tilted back his head and laughed hard—his charming laugh, the flattering one that convinces you you're not only worth listening to but are authentically funny, bringing joy to the world through excellent humor. Which is to say, he thought I was joking. But I wasn't.

"It's exactly like that, Judah," he said. "Exactly."

CHAPTER 18

September 1995

A week before Mary took her own life, we took a walk around the pond at Central Park. It was hot and sticky, normal for Manhattan in September, though we all grumbled as if ninety-degree weather in the fall were some kind of strange and rare curse. Mary hummed her favorite tunes from the show *Camelot*, laughed easily when I made fun of her squeaky singing voice, took my arm, urging me to walk faster, even though she was limping, and, in between songs, marveled at how beautiful the city was in late September. She behaved, in other words, like someone who loved life and was eager for more. I've since been reminded by far too many people that her jaunty attitude—dissonant, you would think, for someone who would kill herself the next week—was normal for suicides. Once they make up their minds, burdens lift, and moods improve. True, but Mary, despite the ominous, really hopeless diagnosis she'd received just six months before, never openly fell into gloom or frustration. She cracked jokes through her daylong chemo sessions, took up tennis and the ukelele, swung Hannah around the room every night before bed to the delight of both of them, and seemed to enjoy sex more than ever. Many of her friends found her friendlier, more outgoing even to strangers and quick with warm compliments. Was it all an act, performed largely for me and Hannah, so we'd stay cheerful? Evidently, yes. She did, after all, kill herself. But she fooled me. I thought her sunny disposition indicated bravery, so she'd fight for every minute of life. But it meant something else. I'm not sure what.

Part of her new volubility was a fascination with the past, both hers and mine. Specifically, our romantic past. She told me stories she'd never shared about old boyfriends. Mark, her high school sweetheart, the quietest, most polite of all her former lovers. Also, by far, the best athlete, a varsity basketball, football, and tennis star. If they hadn't been so young, she might have married him and stayed in Cleveland Heights, Ohio, wife of a lawyer. Then, there was Barry, who costarred with her in a summer stock performance of *Pippin*, who was too obsessed with an acting career and who, she suspected, cheated whenever he saw the opportunity. And there was Steve (Mark, Barry, Steve: what quintessential American *goyishe* names!), the University of Chicago physicist who had to be hospitalized with depression because she broke up with him—for reasons that she can't really remember.

Naturally, she asked for my old love stories. But for me, there wasn't much to tell. There was only Michal. Or, to be more drearily accurate, there were tragic teenage crushes, awkward make-out sessions, guilt, frustrated longing, and then Michal. Then sad crushes, bumbling sex a few times, guilt, frustrated longing, and then Mary. A happy ending. Except it *would* really end, far too soon, and we both knew it. I'd told her about Michal before, just as she had reported on her past boyfriends, but that September morning, strolling and holding hands like a young couple with time and the world ahead of them, we elaborated in ways that pushed the boundaries of polite revelations. She pushed me for more information. Not necessarily details, but the narrative structure. How she might fit the episode into the arc of my story. What it all meant.

I tried to explain the difference between a first love and the love of my life. I tried a few metaphors, but they fell flat even to me. Michal opened the door, and Mary was waiting on the other side. Michal showed me the way; Mary was the destination. Michal was adolescent youth; Mary was adulthood. Michal was desperation and longing; Mary was serenity. I couldn't help but sound like a failed pop song, maybe because I was a journalist who never aspired to deeper thinking or poetic prose.

So I tried a different tack. "It wasn't just a first love," I said. "It was an adventure."

"Okay then," she said, slowing down a bit, from fatigue, or just so she could concentrate better. "How was it an adventure? How were you adventurous?"

"Well, there was the obvious, right? My first time out of the country. Meeting people from all over America, and then from all over the world. And, remember, Israel was at war. The invasion was over, but it seemed like every day, there was a flare-up in South Lebanon. You'd see soldiers with guns all the time, on the buses, strolling downtown. In my own dorm room. I never got used to it. One time, on a bus, a soldier—younger than me—fell asleep on my shoulder. His gun ended up leaning on my knee, so it pointed up, at my crotch. I was afraid to touch it; I thought it might go off. And there was terrorism. Like there is now. Still."

"So you fell in love with the drama of Israel as much as with Michal?" she asked. She rubbed my hand with her index finger. Weirdly, it was something Michal used to do when we held hands.

"Sort of," I said. "I don't think I would put it quite that way. But, yeah, it was more than just Michal, for sure. It was . . ." I stopped to think as the reality hit me. "It was the Lerners. All four of them, and I'm including Michal. Even Yoav, though I never met him." Mary knew a little about my master-disciple friendship with Chaim. She'd seen all his books on my shelf and listened politely as I outlined his radical theology. And I'd probably mentioned Yoav and Zehava. But I'd never put the family at the narrative center of my junior year. "Think about it," I told Mary. "Chaim symbolized the Holocaust. The great trauma of Jewish history. Zehava—she was a charismatic Israeli political leader, still is. To me, she represented the heroic rebirth of the Jewish people through the Zionist project. And Yoav. Carrying the burden of the next generation. Suffering for his parents' trauma and paying for their mistakes. You had the whole twentieth-century Jewish story right there, in one apartment. And Michal. I don't doubt that she felt something for me, maybe even love. But her tribal loyalty—something I didn't understand, *couldn't* understand—was so much stronger than romantic love."

"I can see that," Mary said, still massaging the palm of my hand with her finger. She cleared her throat a few times, a symptom that by now had become so commonplace, it almost lost its ominous tinge. Almost. "Are you sorry you didn't stay? You could have been a part of that grand narrative. Building a country, rebuilding a devastated people. Guaranteed yourself a life of meaning. Any regrets?"

"Oh, hell no," I said. It was almost true. "I mean, there's the obvious. If I'd stayed, I wouldn't have met you. There would be no Hannah. There's no possible alternative life I would ever pick over this one. But also, the Lerners were all about the existential burdens of Jewish history. And those burdens weren't for me. I didn't see it as my history, so I wasn't interested in carrying the weight. It wore me down. That's why I got out." I hesitated before adding the next sentence. "Besides, Michal and I never would have lasted. She's become a right-wing kook."

"Excuse me," Mary said. "How do you know this?"

This was before the wide use of the internet. We didn't have Google or social media. No cyberstalking. If you wanted to know about old girlfriends, you had to actually stay in touch with them, maybe even see them in person. I laughed. "Don't worry," I said. "It's not like I write her every day or sneak away to call her. If I did, you'd have seen the long-distance bill. But I read Jewish newspapers. Zehava's still pretty famous. But now Michal's also gone into politics. On the other side. She writes these screeds attacking the Oslo process. She hints that the only solution is to expel all the Palestinians from Israel. She didn't actually support Rabin's assassination, but she blames the left. Turns my stomach," I said.

There were only a few lies in those sentences. Nothing to keep me up at night with guilt. Anyway, I think I know now why Mary was pushing me to talk about Michal, and it had nothing to do with jealousy, Michal's right-wing politics, or the burdens of Jewish history. Discussing Michal would bring me to the Lerners, which would bring me to Chaim, which would bring me to his suicide. Despite my own nagging suspicions, I never told Chaim's story to Mary in any way that would cast doubt on a verdict of suicide. At this time, twelve years after his death, the tragic tale of Hitler's final victim, the slow-acting murder forty years after the Shoah, was the universally accepted narrative regarding Chaim's death. Mary wanted me to talk about his suicide. She steered the conversation onto this morbid road because she had suicide on the brain.

Later that night, in bed with Mary for what I didn't know would be one of the last times, unable to sleep with my fears for Mary toxically mingling with my reawakened memories of Michal and the Lerners, I suddenly remembered Chaim's prayer experiment. I decided to try it again. It had failed the last time, but the whole point was that God sometimes—often—failed. So why not give the old guy—who I didn't believe in, but what did that matter, I still couldn't sleep—another shot? I quickly ran through four desires: health and happiness for Hannah, the same for Ilana and my parents, a more fulfilling career for me, the strength and courage to become a better husband to Mary in any time we had left together. And then, the big one. I went for it all. A cure. More time. A longer life for the love of my life. Like the last time, this fifth petition overwhelmed the others. Before it even formed in my brain, it rendered my previous desires puny and irrelevant. I'd give them all up, even my hopes for my daughter, for more time with Mary.

The result was even more catastrophic than the first attempt. Rather than more time, I got dramatically less, as if God were mocking me, punishing me for abetting Chaim's heresies. Or maybe that was the point of the exercise. The theological equivalent of *don't put all your eggs in one basket*. Or maybe it was all bullshit.

Nevertheless, I tried the exercise again five years later. I was four years out of rehab, four years sober. I was on a date with a young widow I'd met through JDate, one of the first online dating outfits, the only one, at the time, that catered to Jews. At my companion's suggestion, we started our date at a musical Friday night service for singles on the Upper West Side. For most of the service, we chanted along with the rock band, clapped our hands, danced in the aisle. It was fun if you like those activities, which I did, sort of. But then, there was the silent prayer. I hadn't glanced at a siddur since that day at the *Kotel* with Chaim. The rabbi told us we could use the words in the prayer book or pray whatever was in our hearts. I took the latter suggestion and once again followed Chaim's instruction, directing my petitions to my higher power. Health for Hannah, one. Sobriety for me, two. Career, three. Health for me, four. Five took a little longer. The other two times, wish number five had been everything, the request that crowded out all the others. But this time, there was no all-consuming need, and that very lack revealed a hole in my heart. *Would I ever fill it?* But the exercise called for five, so I needed something. I settled on love and left it to my higher power to figure out how that might fit into my current life. Now, which wishes would I relinquish? I meditated a few seconds, but I quickly realized there was no hierarchy to these needs. I couldn't pick one to give up or one to hold on to with the proper desperation. Again, I left it up to God.

This go-round, I got all five. Maybe the third time was the charm. Or the Old Guy finally found it in Himself to go to bat for me—and He succeeded. Or, more likely than not, it was still all bullshit.

CHAPTER 19

July 2005

"Back to New York, huh? Had enough of us, I guess." It was Charlie. Time to say goodbye. We met at the same café he'd taken us to when we first arrived. I would miss the perfect lemony Israeli hummus, the tangy olives, the fresh pita—somehow not at all the same in New York, even in Israeli restaurants. I invited Hannah, but she said she had "errands in the city." My mind conjured up all sorts of trouble—a trip to prison to visit her suicide bomber, back to the *Kotel* to confront Kaplowitz, and badgering Yoav about his alibi. But Michal called me and said she'd tag along with Hannah, keep her safe.

Charlie only ordered espresso, but he was on his fourth. I wondered why he needed all that caffeine. "Yeah," I said. "I've got enough to cast some suspicions, but I doubt I'll get any more solid evidence about something that happened twenty years ago, unless I move here for several months. I can't do that to Hannah. Anyway, the book isn't really a 'Who Killed Chaim Lerner?' sort of project. It's really . . ." I stopped. I didn't know what kind of book it was. "What do you think?" I asked.

"Leave it open," Charlie said. He called for a fifth espresso. "Let the reader decide. Throw in all the stuff about Chaim's theology. His politics, everything he stirred up. What kind of guy he was—you knew as well as anyone. The messy personal life. The young women. Yoav's story. Was it murder? Was it suicide? If so, why? Great questions, even without answers. Put in the evidence . . . and then give it to the reader. It's not your job to solve every puzzle."

I scooped up the final bit of hummus on my plate. I decided I'd order some more. After all, when would I be back? "Not my job to solve every puzzle. But it's your job, right?" Without asking, the waiter brought another order of hummus. After a week of eating at his café, he knew what I needed.

Charlie grinned. "Maybe not every puzzle. But, yeah, I'd like to take a crack at this one. And you know what I mean. Off the record. Alon and Kaplowitz are hiding something. But I need official permission to go after them. That's where you come in. Write fast. Sell a lot of books. Better yet, get an excerpt out soon, online. That's all I'll need."

I nodded. Write fast. It was my best quality as a writer, my one advantage over average journalists. But somehow, I didn't think this story lent itself to fast writing. "I've got to see Zehava one more time," I said. "To say goodbye. Thank her. Maybe tie up a few loose ends. Can you arrange it?" After my first night in the country, Charlie became my liaison with the ultra-busy Zehava. Michal refused to help.

Charlie smiled. He took a Hebrew newspaper out of his briefcase. "I can try. Crazy day for her though." He pointed at the headline, which, of course, meant nothing to me. But I couldn't miss Zehava's smiling face. Her gray hair fell down to her shoulders, and her teeth gleamed. She looked twenty years younger, the way she looked when I first met her. That is, she looked beautiful. "Looks like she's joining the government coalition. They made a deal. Just last night."

"Wow," I said. I grabbed the paper and brought it closer to my face, as if somehow the problem was with my eyes; if I only had better vision, I'd be able to read Hebrew. "What does it mean?" I asked Charlie.

"Just two possibilities," he said. "War. Sharon is broadening the coalition to get support for an invasion of the West Bank. End the Intifada once and for all. Or—peace. The rumor is, she has a great personal relationship with several leaders of the Palestinian Authority, including Arafat. So maybe Sharon's bringing her in to negotiate a peace deal with the Palestinians. I'm hoping for peace. Most nights, I'm up past midnight dealing with the latest bombing. Why do you think I'm mainlining this amazing espresso? Apparently, Zehava's got a proposal to end the fighting—and credibility with Sharon and Arafat. You really should study more about Israeli politics, Mr. Pulitzer Prize Journalist."

"I'll bone up on the airplane. You think you can get me in? Our flight leaves late tomorrow."

He took out his cell phone and punched in some characters. After less than a minute, he looked up. "Can you go now?"

"Now? To the Knesset?"

"Not the Knesset. Her place. Scene of the crime."

♦ ♦ ♦

On the taxi ride to Zehava's flat, I pondered the lies Charlie told me while he inhaled five espressos. Then, I thought back and counted the lies he'd told me since I arrived in Israel. *Three?*

I thought. *Maybe four?* Not really that many, when you consider how often people lie and, frankly, how often friends lie to each other. For all sorts of reasons. From genuine malice to some crooked scheme to a simple effort to spare a friend painful truths. In the past two days, lies were flying my way like incoming rockets from an enemy. Would I ever figure out why? Did I want to?

I told the taxi to stop at my apartment. I needed to grab my thick Lerner file, with all my notes, transcripts, and the key evidence Charlie provided. I climbed the three flights, unlocked the door, and took a quick look on the kitchen table—the file was missing. Paranoia, never really dormant with me, stirred and rushed through my bloodstream like the caffeine from five espressos. I'd left it on the table, the lefthand corner of the table; it wasn't there. The Shin Bet took it. The Israeli police. Or military intelligence. They'd detain me, here in the apartment, or if I rushed out quickly, they'd get me at the airport. Hannah would have to live with Ilana's family. Or they'd arrest her too. It took less than thirty seconds for these thoughts to tumble through my head. Then, I saw the file. It was on the coffee table, next to the sofa. Where, now that I thought about it, I'd left it.

◆ ◆ ◆

Zehava's assistant brought out mint tea and almond cookies. I'd never seen Zehava actually eat the almond cookies she proudly baked and so generously provided every time I visited. But she scarfed down two, with two big bites a piece, as if she'd never learned how to eat cookies. She apologized as she took her phone out of her pocket and laid it on the tray next to the tea set. She would almost certainly be interrupted while we were talking, she told me. And she needed to take every call. "I'm so sorry, Judah. But, uh, well, a lot depends on what happens in the next few weeks. Or, really, what happens today. There's more?" she said. "You have more questions for me about Chaim? Or you're just saying goodbye? Have another cookie."

I looked at the tray. There were only two left. Somehow, she'd eaten four. I was about to answer when her phone rang. She jabbered into it with her guttural, all-business Hebrew—so different in texture than her flawlessly polite English—then clicked off, punched in some numbers, and barked out what could only be orders. Then, she put down the phone and smiled, like a loving mother. "So sorry."

"Congratulations," I said.

"Oh, well, yes. I'm not sure that's the correct term to use, but thank you. I suppose it's a promotion, but it's also like I'm being sentenced to twenty-four seven work with narcissists and fanatics and fanatical narcissists."

"It's what you've wanted for the past ten years. A senior role in the government so you could conduct direct negotiations with the Palestinian Authority." I knew that because, despite Charlie's snide implication, I'd done extensive research on Zehava before coming to Israel. I'd also read all the English language newspapers that morning, so I was well aware that Zehava had joined Sharon's government. I was, after all, a Pulitzer Prize winner. I resented Charlie lying to me, but I hadn't been altogether honest with him, Michal, or Zehava. Or Yoav. Though they lied to me more than I lied to them. I think.

She shrugged. She reached for another cookie but then withdrew her hand. "Anyway. Come to say goodbye?" she repeated. It seemed to be her preference. "You'll have to come again when there's a few less suicide bombings. That's what I'll be working on." She sat back, tilted her head, and looked at me. She seemed to relax for the first time this trip. "You know Chaim adored you. He'd be proud of the career you've carved out for yourself. And of the way you've raised your beautiful daughter, on your own."

"I wonder," I said. "I sometimes think maybe Chaim would have been disappointed in my choices. I married a non-Jew. Raised a non-Jewish daughter. The Jewish line in my family ends with me. Also, I've done nothing Israel-related in my career. Chaim was by far the most influential teacher in my life, but I let him down."

She shook her head. She was about to offer something, no doubt something warm and comforting, but I had a little more to say.

"He was extraordinarily kind to me," I continued. "And generous with his thoughts and time. Even though, I have to say, he really didn't know me all that well. Lately, I've been wondering what I owe him. Justice? Is that my role here? Is it any of my business? I know now how he died, but I'm not sure why. But does why even matter anymore?"

"I'm not following," she said. Her voice dropped a register. I realized that was the biggest difference between when she spoke English and when she spoke Hebrew. In English, she went high, like a bird. In Hebrew, she went low, slightly threatening but also sultry, seductive.

"I have to ask you why you lied about your alibi."

"Lied?" she said. She smiled.

I nodded. "Lied."

"Really? Me? You're accusing me of lying?"

I waited, watched.

She seemed to reach for her tea cup but then thought better of it. "Judah," she said. "It's so simple. We went to buy a wedding dress in my favorite store in the *shuk*. Michal was with me. It was a crowded store. Dozens of people must have seen me. For sure, what's his name—Rafik? And his wife, she did the measurements. Judah, I hate to say this, but I think you're losing the plot. You know, it's a good thing you're leaving. I don't think you ever got over Michal, even after all these years. And I understand.

Especially now, after losing your wife. But Michal is happily married. And you have your daughter with you. It's unseemly."

"First of all, the store wasn't crowded. Rafik does his bridal fittings after hours, when his wife is available. So that's another lie. After a while, I have to ask myself. Why do you keep lying?"

"A lie? Really, Judah. Okay, I forgot. Yes, the store wasn't crowded. It was a long time ago, and I've had other things to think about in the meantime. Anyway, I do remember we gave the police the receipts. With the time of day, if I'm remembering correctly. And I know they interviewed the store owner. Probably his wife also." Her voice remained low and sultry—speaking English but with her Israeli persona. She reached again for a cookie and again changed her mind before her hand reached the destination.

"Okay, if you picked up the dress that night with Michal, you must have come earlier for measurements. When was that?"

She shook her head. "Probably a week before. Two weeks. I don't remember every detail. Maybe earlier. I think he said three days. They were so proud of how quickly they work. But listen, Judah, this is complete nonsense, totally irrational. We have receipts. And witnesses. I understand, the wife is always a suspect, but we dispensed with this years ago."

"We both know the witnesses don't prove anything. Michal would protect you. Rafik? An Arab shopkeeper versus one of the most powerful politicians in Israel? You could bribe him and his wife or threaten them pretty easily. They'd have all sorts of reasons to be on your good side."

"Judah, I happen to know he kept copies of the receipts. It's not just his word."

"You called him and told him about me. That's how he knew my wife had died. You figured I'd go snooping around, so you needed to make sure he was solid."

"Of course I did. If you're reopening the investigation, I need to make sure you're not led astray. Like the police, maybe you'd suspect me. I needed to make sure my alibi was still intact."

"I'm afraid it's not," I said. "At least not for the fitting. And if you lied about that, well, I have to wonder why."

"But I didn't lie! Michal will remember. I came with her."

"Michal wasn't there either. Not that night."

"How could you possibly know that?"

"She was with me."

"Judah, dear, she'd broken up with you by then. At least two weeks before. You're not thinking clearly."

"Yes," I said. "She'd broken up with me. Yoav asked her to marry him two weeks before, and she said yes. But she was with me that night."

She grew slightly pale. I wondered how long she would keep up the lies. "It was twenty-two years ago, Judah. You know exactly where you were that night? I only remember because you reminded me of the receipts. How could you remember?"

I looked out the window. I could see the corner of Michal's building and the window of her third-story flat. I imagined I was looking past the Jerusalem stone façade, gazing into the past. A heartbroken young lover, having clumsy sex for the first time with the girl who broke his heart. "It was an important night for me," I said.

Zehava stood up and ducked into the kitchen. For a moment, I had the ludicrous thought that she was fleeing. Or she'd come back with a gun. I'm not sure why, but I stood up. Maybe I'd have to flee. But she reappeared after four or five seconds with a lit cigarette. She held out the pack to me. I hadn't smoked since my junior year. I shook my head. She hesitated, composing her words carefully. I waited. "Judah," she said. "Can you even faintly imagine what it was like to be married to Chaim Lerner?"

"I honestly can't, Zehava," I said. "He was only kind and generous and witty and wise with me."

She smiled. She pointed to the love seat. She took the seat next to me, where Chaim would often sit during our talks—hip to hip. "Yes, you were his student. He wanted his students to worship him. Even the male students. He exhausted all his charm on them, on you." She pushed herself off the love seat, then hurried to the balcony, cracked the door open, and exhaled. She kept the cigarette dangling out the door. But the wind blew in the smoke, and I could easily smell the burned tobacco—the odor of a filter-free Israeli cigarette. Time cigarettes. Used to be my favorite. "The nightmares didn't start until ten years into our marriage. Ten years. When Yoav was eight—the perfect age to absorb all of Chaim's trauma. Every night for almost three years, Chaim would kick and groan and curse in Polish from one to three in the morning. I couldn't soothe him, couldn't wake him up, because he'd slap me if I touched him. At breakfast, while Yoav was eating his cereal, Chaim would recount every detail of the dream. Five nazis, always different boyhood friends in SS uniforms, with machine guns, chasing after him. They'd shoot him, and he'd feel the impact, cry out in physical pain, and not wake up. When Yoav himself started having the same dreams, I forced Chaim—believe me, it wasn't easy—to see my friend, a psychiatrist, who was also a survivor. She prescribed some pills that drugged Chaim to sleep every night, but the side effects were worse than the dreams."

She crushed out her cigarette on her teacup, then walked quickly to the love seat and sat next to me. Our hips reunited. I could still smell the unfiltered cigarette, and also her lemony shampoo. She described how Chaim's perpetual groggy state—the side effect of the anti-nightmare pills—made him cranky, especially in the mornings. The slightest irritant—a squeaky cereal bowl, a coffee spill, the wrong window open or shut, a grammatical error from Yoav—led to an angry tantrum, often in Polish, which scared and mystified both Zehava and Yoav. But, she told me, she could learn to live with the tantrums. It's when he became violent to both her and Yoav that she considered leaving. The yelling came with slaps, first fairly soft—a sting, a slight reddening—then harder, a loud clap, real pain. Yoav refused to come down for breakfast. Zehava cried to her psychiatrist friend, begged her for a solution. Chaim was a good man, Zehava told me. But the delayed trauma, the dreams, and now the pills. It was unbearable.

The psychiatrist consulted with expert colleagues, who consulted with their expert colleagues. They recommended a six-week hospital stay, followed by a new experimental cocktail of pills—a regiment favored by the Israeli army for the most intractable cases of what we now call PTSD. The treatment brought a halt to the slaps. But it split Chaim into two personalities. Cheerful, warm, weirdly smiling during the day. This was the Chaim I knew. And mean-spirited, irritable, and sarcastic at night—the Chaim Zehava and Yoav endured. Nighttime Chaim refrained from violence but made up for that with cutting insults. Zehava had lost her youthful beauty—the only reason he'd loved her in the first place. Yoav was a total failure. Likely not even his biological son. His friends betrayed him; his university colleagues bored and embarrassed him; his fellow survivors were liars and charlatans; he despised their preening self-pity. The doctors tinkered with his dosage.

The new formula banished the insults. But now Chaim dabbled in Israeli politics. Zehava wasn't sure if it was the drugs or the trauma or a genuine political awakening based on Yoav's Lebanon horror, but now Chaim gave all his rhetorical skills to bashing Israel. He wrote a series of op-eds, most of which Zehava managed to talk him out of publishing. But she had to read his cruel bile. Israel was a criminal nation engaged in illegal wars.

An apartheid state. A brutal occupier. Guilty of genocide on three borders. Neo-Nazi. Ashke*nazi*, a new epithet he embraced. Zehava had sacrificed life with her family in Kansas City to live the Zionist dream. She'd given her soul to Israeli politics. So reading these missives was brutally demoralizing, especially since he ended up not publishing most of them, so it was like he'd composed these screeds for an audience of one—her. It was during this time that he came out publicly against Israeli's invasion of Lebanon. On that issue, he'd assured her, he wouldn't be censured.

Zehava could live with the sudden political radicalism. Israel was a boisterous democracy. Chaim added a particular voice, one that was neither rare nor new. She worried for Yoav—he, after all, had to suffer through the madness of Lebanon while Chaim merely wrote about it. But Chaim could spout off about the Ashke*nazis* all he wanted. It was a free country. At least he wasn't slapping her and calling her a "hag whore." But now there was another problem. Women.

Really, girls. Students. Chaim initiated a series of affairs with young, attractive graduate students. Zehava didn't need to resort to detective methods to discover the dalliances. Chaim bragged about them. He showed her polaroids. Some of them X-rated. He averaged approximately one student a month. Some turned him down, maybe most of them. But there was always someone for Saint Chaim of Auschwitz, the righteous survivor, the Jewish people's Holocaust laureate, Israel's moral hero.

For the final chapter of this sad, tragic saga, Zehava needed another cigarette. She lit one and invited me to stand with her on the balcony while she smoked and finished the story. I hesitated—it was, after all, the scene of Chaim's final moments. But then I joined her, as the wind shifted and carried her smoke away from her flat in the direction of Wadi Joz.

"After a year of this student-of-the-month club, I'd had enough," Zehava told me. "I gave him an ultimatum. One more girl, and I leave him. *And* I go public. Amazingly, he agreed right away. No more affairs. He'd had enough, he assured me. The doctors tinkered with his dosage. Somehow, his libido had been thrown into overdrive. But they'd fixed him. He was over it. He would dedicate the rest of his life to me and Yoav, and also to the people of Israel.

"But he lied. He gave up most of his young lovers. But he held on to one. The difference this time was that he hid it from me. I found out. It doesn't matter how. And this one was the most inappropriate of them all. Shocking. Even for Chaim. Totally shocking. When I confronted him, I insisted we speak on the balcony so I could smoke. He forbade smoking inside the apartment. He told me it reminded him of the crematoria. You see, even today, he's gone more than twenty years, I smoke on the balcony."

She took two quick puffs, then looked at me as the wind shifted directions and a breeze carried her smoke toward Mt. Scopus. I imagined her twenty-two years before—younger, fit, enraged—confronting her wounded, unfaithful, lying husband. Without thinking, I gripped the balcony railing so she couldn't toss me over the side.

"I think you know what happened next."

I nodded but didn't say anything. I wanted her to finish the story.

"I called him a lying bastard. He agreed. But then I said something inexcusable. I told him the ashes in Auschwitz are ashamed of him. You've disgraced those teeth and bones, I said. Your family's dust. The image was too much for him. I could tell what was coming when he flexed his palm. A slap. This time, maybe it would draw blood. Or send me toppling to the courtyard below. Sure enough, his hand reared back. It happened quickly, but somehow, I experienced it in slow motion. I'm told that's not uncommon for battered wives. Time slows down. So I was ready. Before the slap could reach my face, I caught his hand and, without thinking, twisted it as hard as I could. I pushed him away from me, which was toward the railing. Remember his bum knee. His hip. He lost his footing and fell shoulder first onto the top bar of the railing. He looked at me, panicked. For a split second, it looked like he'd be able to retain his balance. But it was almost like a slight breeze pushed him. He rolled to his right, that is, toward the ground. And fell. On his head. There was no screaming, just the weird 'Whoops.' Like he'd dropped a glass. 'Whoops.' Then a thump." She looked over the railing as if she could still see his broken body.

"You killed him," I said. I'm not sure why I needed to state the obvious. Probably, I wanted to hear the words from her.

"I killed him," she agreed. Her voice trembled slightly and oscillated between low and high. "In self-defense." She stubbed out her cigarette on the top railing. Our eyes remained in contact.

"Why not tell the police the truth?"

"I didn't think they would believe me. You remember, Chaim was pretty infirm in those days. I was a lot stronger. But even if I'd ended up cleared, I'd always be the person who killed Saint Auschwitz. That would be the end of my career. Yes, I'm ambitious. I don't apologize. My ambitions aren't only for me. They are for my country."

She gestured, and we walked inside. She pointed to the couch. I sat while she boiled water in the kitchen, brewing yet more tea. She came out with two steaming cups and a full box of cookies. "So listen, Judah," she said, blowing on her tea. For the first time this visit, the Jerusalem night air turned cool. I felt goosebumps on my arm. With the smoke gone, the outside air regained its peculiar tang of garbage and citrus. "I don't know what you think you can do with this information. Of course,

I'll deny that I admitted anything to you. Believe me, no one will back you up, not Michal, not the shopkeeper, not his wife. Not Charlie, no matter what you might think. You'll stir up a cloud of suspicion, certainly, but I've successfully cultivated a lifetime of respect in Israel, and most people here will believe me over a foreign journalist. You know, in Israel, we don't trust the foreign press.

"But there's something more important than a twenty-two-year-old scandal. Judah, you know what I've been doing this past week. I'm about to join the government. This is a real opportunity. I'm negotiating now with the highest levels of the Palestinian Authority. For peace. Real peace. This is an opportunity that comes along once in a century. A genuine coalition for a permanent settlement. But Judah, it's so, so delicate. You're not a fool. You know enough about our backstabbing politics. One mistake, and the religious right-wing crazies who oppose any concessions will undermine all my work. They'll get me thrown out of the government. Right now, I'm the only figure in Israel and the Palestinian territories who both sides more or less trust. But if you cast doubt on my character, peace will die. You cannot publish this story now. Too much is at stake. Peace here means more peace in the world. Think, Judah. We are about to end the longest war in world history. Don't you dare blow that up."

By the time she finished her sermon, Zehava's voice had fully regained its clear tone and high register. She had lectured me for ten minutes, like a professor instructing an introductory class, where the hierarchies of intellect and knowledge were painfully obvious.

I couldn't help but laugh. "World peace?" I said. "That's what I'll screw up if I write my book? World peace is in my hands?"

"Write your book any way you'd like. Just don't write that I was anything other than the faithful companion to the Saint of Buna."

"Pretty convenient that world peace depends on you getting away with murder."

She clicked her tongue three times. "It wasn't murder. It was self-defense. I explained it to you the best I could. I will not repeat my story. But yes. It's convenient for me. It's also everything I've worked and trained for. No one else can do this, Judah. Only me. I've convinced leaders on our side, who've never considered any territorial compromise, to suddenly open their minds. I speak Arabic, Hebrew, and English. I love the Land of Israel—all of it—as much as any lunatic messianic freak. I'm extraordinarily sensitive to our security concerns *and* basic human rights for the Palestinians. No one else has a better grip on all the issues. I can stop a forever war that's killed thousands. Listen, you don't have to take my word for it. Talk to Charlie. He's become a much more important figure here than he's let on. And he's your friend. Now, if you'll excuse me, I have approximately ten thousand phone calls to make." She looked at the box on the coffee table. "Take the rest of the cookies back for Hannah."

◆ ◆ ◆

I surprised Charlie at his office in the Russian compound. He was talking on his cell phone when I ignored the guard and his assistant and barged in. He quickly folded his phone and smiled at me. "One last goodbye?" he said.

I pointed to his phone. "Zehava?" I asked.

He chuckled. "I told her you were smarter than she thought. I guess you didn't leave such a great impression all those years ago when you worked for Chaim." He came around the desk, put his arm around my shoulder, guided me to a chair, and sat across from me. Before I could ask, he confirmed everything Zehava had told me. She'd lied to me from the beginning. She wrestled Chaim off that balcony—killing him. But Charlie believed her when she claimed it was self-defense. From what he'd heard, Chaim wasn't the saintly author of his reputation. He was cruel and violent to those who loved him most. There was no sense in pursuing a prosecution. Anyway, yes, Zehava was essential to the peace process, which had suddenly bloomed. Damage her reputation, and you kill the dream of 2,000 years—Israel, finally at peace with its neighbors.

I nodded. Again—peace is in my hands. I could be a hero or historic villain. The power of my words. I wondered why Charlie continued to lie to me. "Before I decide what to write, or what to leave out, can I ask a few questions? Off the record?"

He held open his hands, prepared to accept anything. "Please."

"The whole business with Alon, Kaplowitz. That was a lie from the beginning, right?"

He nodded his head slowly but didn't comment.

"Neither of them was planning on meeting with Chaim that night. Neither planned to blackmail him. You all just made that up. Right?"

"Listen, Judah—"

"Let me finish. The idea that maybe someone killed Chaim because of his ideas. His theology or his politics. His statement about the Lebanon War. All bullshit, correct?" I didn't wait for an answer. "I suspected you were playing some kind of misdirection game from the beginning. I just didn't know why. You told me you needed me to bring in evidence so you could justify reopening the investigation. But from what I can see, you're pretty high up here. You're the guy who makes the decisions about opening investigations. Really, you wanted the opposite. You wanted to make sure that no one pressured you to investigate Zehava. So you fed me this conspiratorial horseshit about Kaplowitz and Alon. Radical ideology. Blackmail. You knew if I published that, I'd have no solid proof, since it simply wasn't true. And that, here, people would read it as just more biased Israel bashing, typical American journalist crap. It would be a reason *not* to investigate."

"Wow," Charlie said. "You're even smarter than *I* thought. That whole year we lived together, I never saw you go to one class, except for Chaim's. But maybe you did learn something. Look, why don't we—"

"No," I interrupted. "Before we decide what I should write, let me finish. How did you get Alon and Kaplowitz to go along? A right-wing mystic? A religious settler? They don't seem like the types who would protect Zehava."

"Looks can be deceiving." He watched me.

I nodded. I'd known the answer after speaking with Zehava. "They're part of the new peace coalition. Zehava convinced them to join. So they conjured up their little plays to fool me and deflect suspicion away from her. They wouldn't be in any real legal danger because they'd made the whole thing up, and anyway, you controlled the investigation."

Charlie leaned back and grinned. He looked so much like the young, cocky soldier I'd met twenty-two years earlier. *Why*, I wondered, *does everyone I knew look the same here, while I clearly grew older?* You'd think all the stress of living in a potential war zone would eventually carve its way onto foreheads, hairlines, posture. But Zehava, Charlie, Michal, even Yoav—all as young and spirited and restless as ever. I, on the other hand, was so fucking tired. "Zehava is a formidable woman," Charlie said.

"No kidding." I thought for a moment. "And you're part of the coalition too, aren't you, Charlie? You weren't just doing Zehava a favor by keeping me off track. There's something at stake for you too. Right?"

He shrugged. "No use denying it. Yes. I'll be part of the negotiating team. Zehava and I have been discussing this possibility for a long time. For years."

"Really? How did you become so close to Zehava? When we lived together, you hadn't even met her. You only barely knew Michal. I know it's a small country, but it's not that small."

He offered a half grin—an enigmatic Mona Lisa smile—maybe proud of me, maybe condescending. Like a proctor, he waited for me.

"Michal," I said. "After I left, somehow you became friendlier with Michal."

He shrugged. "More than just friendly. I was curious," he said. "You were gone."

"She was married. *Is* married."

"Yeah, well, nothing happened at first. It took a while. But that marriage? I mean, you know. To Yoav? It was a mistake from the beginning."

"So, you've been involved with Michal. For how long?"

"Jesus, Judah!" he said. His forehead turned red, and he clenched his fists. It was the first time I'd seen him angry. It was a scary look. "Not everything in this country revolves around Michal. Israel's not just a receptacle for your youthful heartbreak, your romantic, adolescent memories. For God's sake. We're talking life or death here. War or peace."

"Okay," I said. I held up my hand. "Okay. Fair enough. I see your point." And I did, though it occurred to me that Israel had in fact been a receptacle for the romantic obsessions of Jews for thousands of years. What was longing for Jerusalem, if not a thwarted romantic dream? Wasn't the point of Zionism to finally fulfill our deepest, most mythic longings? "But from my perspective, I'm not the only one with a personal stake in this. You and Zehava get promotions. If I don't publish what I've discovered, you become important players in the government. You're both trying to persuade me not to smash this new, delicate peace structure. But you're also asking me to help advance your own positions. How do I know your interests aren't completely selfish?"

He grinned, a wide, toothy, shiny smile. *The joy of a twenty-year-old*, I thought. I'd never smile that way again. "Judah," he said. "Judah." He waited, as if all he had to do to get me to understand the depths of his logic was to repeat my name, as if the name *Judah* were some secret Jewish code that if I only thought about it for a moment, I could solve. "Judah," he said one more time, almost a whisper, like an incantation. When I didn't respond, he said, "What am I going to do with you? How about this? A deal. Here are the terms. For your part, forget what Zehava told you. There's no evidence. You'll just piss her off, and believe me, you don't want that. Anyway, don't make this some tawdry domestic story—a husband and wife who torture each other, who drink too much, who finally have it out on the balcony. That's not the story. You know that. Stick to theology, to ideology, to myth. That's the narrative Chaim deserves, don't you think? If you do, here's what I'm prepared to offer. Exclusive access to the peace process and the negotiations. You'll be the first to report our success to the world. That's another Pulitzer for you, for sure. Not to mention the money when you publish *that* book. Just lay off Zehava. Let us do our work. What's that John Lennon song? Give peace a chance. Corny, huh? But still a good deal for you. And Judah. If you do publish accusations against Zehava, I can't control her. And I repeat. You do not want her as your enemy." He leaned forward. "What do you say?"

I considered the deal. The mix of threats and rewards was skillfully done. I couldn't ignore either, and he knew it. I was impressed and even a little flattered that he understood me so thoroughly. When I so clearly didn't know him at all. "I'll think about it," I said.

He stood. It was time for me to go. We embraced. I smelled the shampoo he used and occasionally let me borrow from way back then. The nostalgia from the scent nearly knocked me off my feet. "We'll see each other again soon, right?" he said, releasing his grip but still holding my shoulders, looking me in the eye. "We won't let another twenty-two years go by?"

"Soon," I agreed, nodding. I even meant it. Sort of. "I promise."

I never saw him again. Three years after our final embrace, a terrorist bomb blew up his office door, killing him instantly.

◆◆◆

I picked up Hannah at Michal's flat. She was packed, ready for the airport. Her canvas duffel bag bulged. She'd clearly done some shopping. Next to her smaller backpack, I noticed a plastic bag with three thick books. "Presents," she told me. "From Rabbi Kaplowitz. He dropped them off for me. And I guess for you." *Kaplowitz*, I thought. *Giving my daughter books?* But, really, what harm could they do? I asked her if she could meet me outside in the taxi. I wanted privacy to say goodbye to Michal. She amazed me by not arguing. She wrapped Michal in a bear hug, then grabbed her suitcase, backpack, and various loose packages, shuffling awkwardly but quickly out the door.

Michal smiled and sized me up, as if she were examining all of me for the first time. "An amazing daughter. Sensitive. Intelligent. Perceptive. Kind of a smart-ass. You've done such a wonderful job with her."

I looked at the door, as if Hannah had somehow left behind an image of herself. "I wish I could take credit," I said. "Probably the nicest thing I can say about myself as a single dad is that I haven't screwed up that badly. Not yet, anyway."

She laughed, assumed I was joking. "Well, I'd love to have a daughter like Hannah."

Michal was still smiling widely, marveling at her fondness for my daughter, but I wondered if I was seeing regret in her eyes. I knew Michal and Yoav had decided early in their marriage not to have children. I never asked why. It was none of my business.

Now I wondered if she was disappointed, but I didn't ask. Still none of my business.

"I wanted to say goodbye," I said.

She regarded me curiously, wondering exactly what kind of creature she was looking at. "Oh," she said cheerily. "Okay. Thank you. Goodbye to you. *Lehitraot.* Until next time."

"No," I said. "I mean goodbye. Really. Goodbye."

"Ah," she said. Her lips turned down. She wasn't smiling. "That kind of goodbye. But Judah, why? Yoav—well, I think you figured it out. He moved out six months ago. We're getting divorced. So, you know. It doesn't have to be . . . what it was. I'm free."

I thought about Charlie. "I know," I said. "Still. Goodbye."

She watched me, studied my face, waited. She looked so young. *How is it possible?* "Goodbye, Judah," she said finally. When we embraced, I almost succeeded in holding back my tears.

❖ ❖ ❖

As we buckled into our cramped airplane seats, I asked Hannah about the books Kaplowitz gave her. She reached into her backpack, pulled out the thickest of the volumes, and handed it to me. I looked at the title. *"Returning for the Answer: A Guide to Coming Home for the Young Jew."* I raised an eyebrow at her. "He thought it might be what I needed. For my spiritual life."

Seven years later, when she applied and was accepted to rabbinical school, she cited Kaplowitz's book as her most important religious influence. But that was years in the future.

"Your spiritual life?" I asked my fifteen-year-old high school student. "You have a spiritual life?"

She shrugged. "I'm not sure what it means. But I liked the guy. We've got a long flight. I figure I'll give it a try. At least it's not about suicide."

"How are you doing on your project?" I asked. "Did you get enough information from Kamal?"

"My suicide bomber? I guess so. I wanted to know more. Honestly, he was kind of boring. I thought he'd clear up some mysteries."

She shrugged, and we took off. The engine noises drowned out possible conversation, giving me a few minutes to think. When the plane leveled off, and the flight attendant finished her ominous warnings and instruction, I turned to Hannah. "I know you're upset that Mom never left a note. But really, what could she tell you? You were five years old. You wouldn't have been able to read it."

She nodded three times quickly and tightly shut her eyes. A half a tear leaked from the right one. "I know," she whispered. I thought of Michal complimenting me on my fatherly skills. I waited until Hannah opened her red-rimmed eyes, then cleared my throat. But I didn't have anything to say. I put my hand over hers.

"I have a question for you," she said.

"Of course."

"Are you still having sex with Michal?"

The question didn't shock me. It just surprised me. I went through a half a dozen possible responses, from no, never, how could you to it's none of your business. I was about to choose one—I don't remember which—when, seemingly independent of my own will, my eyes closed, and I found myself weeping. In front of my young daughter.

"It's all right, Dad," she said. Now she patted my hand. "Come on, stop. Enough crying already. But how were you doing it? If you were sneaking off to Jerusalem every once in a while, I think I would have noticed."

I took three deep breaths, squeezed Hannah's hand three times, and steeled myself. From my junior year tear-filled night with Michal until Mary took her own life, I rarely cried. Maybe never. But after Mary's suicide, I could cry any time—at movies, silly TV shows, school plays, sad songs. The problem wasn't crying; it was stopping. But I stopped so I could confide in my daughter. "She'd come to New York," I said. "A few times a year. After Mom died." I shrugged. "It wasn't just sex. It was mostly sex. I won't say it didn't mean anything. It did. It meant something. Just not what it used to mean."

"And when you were with Mom? When you were married?"

Tears. Tightly shut eyes. Again.

"Dad! Come on! Enough!"

"Just once," I whispered. "Just once. When you're mother . . ." I couldn't finish the sentence. "Just once," I repeated.

"That was shitty. But I forgive you," Hannah said. "I'm sure Mom forgives you. I just needed to know."

"Thank you for saying that. You know, all this time, I've been worried that you were obsessing over Chaim's suicide. I felt so guilty taking you on this trip. Now it seems like you were more interested in my love affair with Michal."

"Oh, believe me, I'm not that interested."

I laughed. "Of course. And Chaim? Are you still interested?"

"I was," she said. "To tell you the truth, I became less fascinated when I realized it was murder, not suicide. Once I knew that, it was easy to figure out who did it."

"Oh?" I said. "You figured it out? Do you want to tell me?"

She closed her eyes again, and for a moment, I assumed she'd fallen asleep. But I realized she was just thinking things through, worried I might break down again. "I do want to tell you," she said.

I waited.

She told me.

Part 3

CHAPTER 20

September 2023

I took the deal with Charlie. I wrote my Chaim book, but I kept his death a mystery—maybe suicide, for all sorts of possible reasons from lingering Shoah nightmares to ill health, the burden of being Jewish history's most eloquent witness, the loneliness of writing, or the unsolvable vagaries of the human soul. Or maybe a weird accident, a drunken tumble off a seldom-used balcony. Maybe murder—a conspiracy of Israel's various fanatics. These speculations were pure fiction. Most of the book was simply biography that I enjoyed writing, especially when the reporting took me to Cracow, and I reconstructed his youth, including his many love affairs as a teenager. I didn't take Hannah along with me that time. The book sold well enough to rescue my journalism career. I landed at the *Washington Post* but took early retirement when they insisted I leave New York and move to

Paris. My girlfriend was in New York; Hannah, her husband, and her two-year-old daughter lived in North Jersey. I wasn't leaving.

Of course, Zehava never negotiated peace. She and her team held one round of secret meetings with Palestinian negotiators in London. Charlie, holding to our deal, arranged for me to sit in as long as I agreed to hold off any reporting until a final deal was reached, and even then, with no direct quotes. Charlie sat out those negotiations. He had to stay in Israel in case a new terrorist wave broke out. The two sides exchanged maps, Israel offering roughly 95 percent of the West Bank, the Palestinians insisting on the whole thing with a few minor border adjustments to accommodate most of the Jewish settlers. I wasn't allowed to study the maps, but I was able to sneak enough of a glance to see that Pisgat David landed on the Palestinian side on both versions. I wasn't sure what Chaim would have thought about that.

When it came to territory, the two sides were never too far off. It seemed like a promising start. But subsequent meetings devolved into intractable issues like dividing Jerusalem, the right of return for Palestinian refugees, recognition of Israel as a Jewish state, how to connect Gaza with the West Bank, the role of Hamas. What began with a measure of warmth and hope quickly disintegrated into bitter quarrels. Both sides approached me "off the record" and explained in detail why the other side was to blame for the inevitable collapse of the talks, which happened a week after the London meetings. International relations was never my bailiwick, but I wondered if the whole London meeting was a farce—an elaborate play so both sides could insist they were willing to make sacrifices for peace, but the other side was eternally unreasonable. When I finally received Charlie's permission to write about the conference, the *Post* buried it in the middle of the paper. No one cared. Meanwhile, the suicide bombings fizzled out as Israel built its West Bank barrier. But the forever war continued, with Hamas missiles and sometimes flammable kites flying from Gaza, followed, like day followed night, by Israeli bombs and tanks and new settlements. The West Bank quieted but was never free from terrorist violence. Neither was Israel proper. One terrorist bomb, planted outside of the Russian Compound, killed the head of Israel's police homicide division—my friend, Charlie.

Hannah blessedly lost interest in suicide bombers, but the books from Kaplowitz gave her a new obsession: Jewish spirituality. The day she graduated from high school, she informed me she was going to become a rabbi. The news disturbed me for absolutely no rational reason, other than when I thought of rabbis, I thought of Kaplowitz and Alon—black-hatted *haredim*. But she won me over completely thirty seconds into her senior sermon at Hebrew Union College. Confident, tall, eloquent, funny, she urged us to consider Chaim Lerner's theology—a God with infinite love but limited power. She married a millionaire software engineer she met on JDate. After her honeymoon, she showed me how even an old man like me could use a dating app. Six months later, I met Liora, a tax attorney. She became my second Jewish girlfriend after Michal.

Michal, for the most part, honored our goodbye. If she ever visited New York, she didn't contact me, and despite Hannah's urging while she spent her first rabbinical school year studying in Jerusalem, I stayed away from Israel. Michal did send the occasional New Year's greeting, and she friended me on Facebook. She emailed me when Charlie died, and for the first time, I wrote her back, sharing my condolences. Fifteen years later, she messaged both Hannah and me that Zehava had passed away. She urged us to come for the funeral. She had one more thing to tell me, but she could only do it in person.

◆◆◆

Business class beat coach. I wondered if Hannah flew that way all the time. Hannah didn't want to leave her baby for more than a few days, and I just didn't want to stay long. So we only booked three nights at the David Citadel Hotel in Jerusalem, and we'd arrive the morning of the funeral. I was afraid we'd be exhausted, but the bed-sized seats and soft cushions assured a fairly decent night's sleep. Instead of jet lag, I was buzzed with too many cups of coffee when we stepped off the taxi onto the Mt. Herzl cemetery—the graveyard reserved for Israel's most important dignitaries. Hannah held my arm as we walked slowly to the grave. We might have looked like a winter-spring couple, but I felt her odd fear that I might fall, that she was the only thing holding me up.

Hundreds of mourners crowded the grave, maybe thousands. It was late September, cool, sunny, pleasant. But the crowd made me sweat, and I thought about suicide bombers, even though I couldn't miss the dozens of armed soldiers protecting the site. The eulogies were all in Hebrew. Hannah, who'd become fluent, whispered a running translation into my ear. I caught the gist of the first speaker—a grizzled old man, who regaled us with funny stories about Zehava's early years in politics. Then, I tuned Hannah out and just took in the scene. I wasn't surprised, but I was impressed to see Israel's current prime minister, defense minister, and leader of the opposition. The current president—a tall, handsome, youthful guy—got up to speak. He must have been a skilled orator because I heard sniffles from the crowd, and then from Hannah. He made everyone cry. It took a fair bit of squinting, but I spotted Michal in the front row, standing next to Yoav. He kept his face in his hands the whole time. He couldn't stop himself from weeping. I expected a lengthy service. But after the president's eulogy, a crane lowered Zehava's shrouded body into the grave. A cantor sang a few quick prayers, and that was it. Thirty minutes. The crowd dispersed.

"We should find Michal," I told Hannah. I'd lost track of her in the crowd. "Maybe she'll head back to Chaim's house with Yoav. We could get a taxi."

"I know where she is, Dad," Hannah said. She took my arm and pulled me up the hill, past the tombs of David Ben Gurion, Zalman Shazar, Golda Meir, and Theodore Herzl. We came to a narrow path that led to a clump of tall pine trees. Hannah stopped and pointed. "I'm not going," she said. "She said she wants to talk to you alone."

I looked at her, my rabbi daughter, taller than me, and now with a daughter of her own. I'd suspected that she'd kept in touch with Michal, especially during her year in Israel. But I didn't realize, though I should have, that maybe they occasionally spoke about me. I nodded and headed for the trees.

I found a woman sitting on a bench. At first, she was utterly unfamiliar. It was a grieving old lady, sitting on a bench in a quiet part of a tree-lined cemetery. A cliché painting. But friendship imposes a blessed alchemy on time. I looked a little harder, and the wrinkles dissolved. A ghost of luster brightened her hair. Her sad smile when she looked up transported me back forty years. It was Michal.

She stood, but instead of greeting me, she pointed to a headstone. I looked. Part of it was in English. It was Charlie. "He'd be so honored if he knew he was buried here," she said. "With prime ministers and presidents. And now with Zehava."

"Maybe he does know," I said.

She looked at me. "Yes. Hannah told me you've become religious. I can see why you might believe that."

"I think you mean Hannah's become religious. She's a rabbi."

"Oh, I know. But she was talking about you."

I considered that. Liora dragged me to services every Friday night. I sort of enjoyed them. After services, she took me to a home-cooked Shabbat dinner—challah, kiddush wine, roast chicken. *Am I now religious?* I decided not to contest Michal's claim.

"Come sit," she said. "Charlie's parents dedicated this bench. They moved to Israel a few years after he died. I sat with them just three weeks ago."

We sat and stared at Charlie, his stone, his earthly avatar. We shared a silent moment of memory. I thought of Charlie helping me unpack during the confusing first night when I knew no one in the whole country. I remembered spotting his gun and him explaining to me the concept of "purity of arms." Who knows what Michal was thinking. I didn't try to guess.

"He was sad that he lost your friendship," Michal said.

"My fault," I said immediately. "I'm terrible at staying in touch. Even with people I really like. People I love."

"He was afraid it was his fault. Because of, you know. What he withheld from you. What he couldn't tell you."

The cemetery was deathly quiet. No breeze through the leaves. No mosquitos buzzing. Not even the faint sounds of traffic, even though we weren't far from the road, and traffic was ubiquitous in Jerusalem. *Where,* I wondered, *did this silence come from?* Maybe it was just my aging ears. "Is that why you brought me here?" I asked. "To tell me what Charlie couldn't? He's been dead now for many years. Why now?"

"I couldn't tell you while Zehava was alive. She forbade me. Absolutely forbade me. From telling anyone. But especially you."

I put my arm around Michal's shoulder. After forty years, it still seemed an absolutely natural gesture, though there was nothing erotic about it. Michal scooched in closer and put her head on my shoulder. I think she cried, softy. I didn't. I held her for some minutes, maybe two, maybe twenty, maybe forty. Enough time to give Michal the courage to tell me what I already knew.

She slowly lifted her head from my damp shoulder. "Chaim never would have killed himself," she said.

"I know."

"Yeah, you saw that from the beginning. You only spent, what, eight months with him. But you knew him better than most of us. He staked his whole identity on surviving. All the physical pain, the nightmare memories—it was all fuel for survival. I never met anyone more committed to life. He would have lived until his last organ gave out."

"But someone killed him," I said.

She snapped her head sideways to gawk at me, pushing her hips away. "You say 'someone.' But you know who it was. You know it was Zehava. She told you."

"Michal," I said. And now my tears suddenly flowed freely. I don't know why. Maybe just saying her name?

But she was dry-eyed. "Oh," she said. "You *know*. Really know. I told Zehava. I told her you'd figure it out. You knew all along."

I couldn't speak. I nodded. I knew.

"You knew. You knew it was me."

◆◆◆

She told me the story. She was fifteen the first time Chaim came on to her. The two families—Yoav and his parents, Michal and hers—occasionally vacationed together. One time, they spent the day on the beach in Nahariyah. Michal's father and Yoav ran off to explore the dunes; Michal's mother and Zehava left to search for a bathroom. Any moment, any one of them might return, but for now, Chaim and Michal were alone. Chaim peppered her with questions. The boring ones most caring adults might ask: What did she want to be when she grew up? What were her favorite school subjects? What books was she reading? But he also probed her opinion on theological issues, something even her best teachers had never done. He asked her why, in her opinion, an almighty God might allow something like the Holocaust. She suggested that maybe God wanted to help but couldn't. He seemed fascinated by her response. She was flattered, intrigued. He moved closer, asked another question, this time about why some humans, Nazis, for example, perform the most sadistic acts. She answered, with the growing confidence of an excellent student impressing her teacher, that she assumed most abusers had themselves at one time been abused. He was a skilled listener, giving her enough silence so she could complete her thoughts. She was so wrapped up in her explanations of good and evil that she barely noticed his finger on her ankle, slowly moving up her calve. He jerked it away when he saw Michal's father and Yoav returning.

Over the next two years, Chaim caught Michal alone numerous times. He'd be waiting for her at the bus stop. Or he'd arrange for himself to give a guest lecture at her high school and then offer to walk her home. Or he'd just pop in when her parents were gone. They talked philosophy and theology and sometimes politics. Chaim flattered her; he was the celebrity intellectual, but he seemed curious about *her* ideas. But, each time, he maneuvered their bodies enough to touch her somewhere on her person—the back of her neck, her shoulder, her right rib, her knee. The top of her breast. When that happened, she instinctively slapped his hand as hard as she could. Stunned, and stung, he looked around and then wordlessly fled.

For the next three years, he left her alone. She began dating Yoav, fell in love with him. She was a constant presence in Chaim's apartment, but apart from an occasional banal exchange—or, when he thought no one was looking, a wink—he ignored her. This, in fact, was the time she grew closer to Zehava. Zehava taught her to bake, how to dress, how to apply makeup, how to do her hair—all the supposedly feminine things Michal's mother had always ignored. Zehava told her she was the daughter she never had. It made Michal slightly uncomfortable but also truly loved in a way she'd never been by her own often absent mother. During her army service, home for weekends, she grew as intimately close to Zehava as she did to Yoav. It was like she was dating them both. Chaim, in the meantime, kept his distance, so much so that Michal wondered if she'd just imagined the naughty touching.

Things changed her first year at the university, after the army. For one, she and Yoav took a break while he completed his officer training course and then served in Lebanon, and she dated me. But also, Chaim resumed his advances. It started again with Chaim sharing his ideas. He was her teacher, but he called her his colleague. He read her passages from his philosophical articles, excerpts from his upcoming theological book, and his anti-war op-eds. She offered comments, and he often incorporated her suggestions into the published work. Again, she was flattered. One of Israel's foremost thinkers took her advice about his important writing. That's when she'd boasted about him to me. When she introduced me to Chaim and Zehava.

But after a few months, around the time of Yoav's bitter trauma in Lebanon, Chaim leaped over her boundaries once again. This time, Michal wasn't a skinny teenager. She was twenty-one years old, a young woman. Chaim moved faster this time. One day, he touched her forearm while she explained the thesis of the paper she was working on. She was strategizing how to remove his hand when he leaned in and kissed her mouth.

The next several months were a blur. From a distance, she could almost imagine the time as a dark comedy, an adult screwball Tom and Jerry skit. She'd speak normally with Chaim when they were alone—he was, after all, someone she'd known her whole life—but she'd always be prepared to duck and dodge his lips, whisk away his hands, and laugh it off with him. Her pseudo mother-daughter relationship with Zehava deepened, especially since her mother was out of the country. And she fell in love with me, even while, unbeknownst to me, she stayed in touch with the suffering Yoav. By this time, she'd heard the rumors about Chaim's womanizing, often with students. She figured he'd get over her quickly. All she had to do was slap his hands a few more times, and he'd move on to someone more willing, a less complicated relationship.

But, just as she was making the wrenchingly difficult decision to break up with me and marry Yoav, Chaim grew desperate, aggressive, and pathetic. Now he'd grope her, even if it wasn't clear they were alone. She smelled alcohol on his breath when she ducked his kisses. One time, he stole her bike out of her apartment and rode around the neighborhood, forcing her to come fetch it so he could kiss her cheek. Another time, he grabbed a piece of her shirt as she walked out of class. No one noticed, or at least those who saw pretended not to notice. This was decidedly not the #Metoo era. The truth was that many saw, and they simply looked away.

Finally, that night. Zehava invited her over to share a new brand of wine from the Golan. Chaim would be out late. Just us girls, Zehava said. Maybe Michal would even sleep over. In the morning, they'd go together to the *shuk* to look at wedding dresses.

"You can figure out the rest," she told me.

I supposed I could have. She waited for me to finish the story myself. Or to ask. I didn't say anything. I just watched Charlie's headstone. Finally, she continued.

Zehava, she said, already an important political figure, had to take a phone call in her office. Michal waited patiently on the living room sofa, enjoying the excellent Golani wine. Suddenly, seemingly out of nowhere, Chaim appeared. He stood next to her knees, without touching. He grabbed the wine bottle and gulped half of it down. She could also smell some other alcohol on his breath. Maybe gin, she didn't really know. He spoke softly so Zehava wouldn't hear. He told her it was time for apologies.

He'd behaved abominably. He needed to stop. He knew that. She was going to be his daughter-in-law. Even my depravities have limits, he told her. Please, he said. Join me on the balcony. I want to talk in private.

Why the balcony? She had no idea. Like everyone in the family, she'd rarely seen him, or really anyone, ever use that balcony. Probably, he thought it was private enough. Zehava wouldn't hear. Michal didn't think about it. She took him at his word. If he wanted to apologize, she'd let him. She was already desperately tired of their cat-and-mouse game.

As soon as he closed the balcony door behind him, he attacked her. He pulled her into an embrace, kissed her hard on her lips, and touched her breast. After that, everything happened too fast. She blocked out most details. She shoved him away with her right arm. He grabbed her left hand to steady himself and ended up twisting it, yanking it out of its socket. The pain was so great, she reared back her right arm and shoved him hard in his chest. He toppled two steps backward and hit the railing hard. For a fateful instant, his back momentarily balanced on the top rail, he locked eyes with Michal. He extended his hand and reached for her. She hesitated for an excruciating moment. He said, "Whoops," toppled over the rail, and fell on his head with a thump. Dead.

Michal spoke calmly, dry-eyed, clinically. She could have been describing a trip to the bank, an algebra problem, or an urban renewal suggestion—and not the accidental killing of her father-in-law, one of Israel's great minds. Nothing in her story surprised me. Chaim's behavior shocked and appalled me beyond words. But it didn't surprise me.

"How did you know?" she said. She turned from my face and joined me in staring at Charlie's white granite stone. It was as if we were talking to him, explaining everything. The wind picked up a bit, cool and brisk, a hint of Jerusalem winter. But it was still a beautiful day. I could see Hannah in the distance, talking on her phone.

How much to say? I exhaled deeply, then inhaled. "The way you hugged me that night," I said, "when I was leaving Israel. Remember, I stopped by just to say goodbye to Chaim. You told me you had just found his body under the balcony. You rushed up to me. Like a lover. For just a second, I thought you were taking me back. You hugged me. I didn't know why. But it was just with one arm. That's a weird way to hug. At first, I figured, okay that's your 'just friend' hug. But I saw you wince. You were in pain. Something happened to your left arm."

Michal nodded. "Yes. It hurt. Five minutes later, Zehava maneuvered it back into the socket. It was a skill she remembered from early motherhood. She was always such a mother to me. By the time the police got there, I was fine." She turned to face me. "So that's it? You knew right away that I'd killed him?"

I shook my head. "No. Really, at the time, I was too heartbroken to think about anything other than my own pain. I've tried really hard over the years to stop being that selfish. Having Hannah helped. And a dying wife. Anyway, when I allowed myself to think about it, I was like everyone else. I assumed it was another Holocaust-writer suicide story. I wondered about him leaving no note, but after Mary's suicide, I learned that not everyone leaves a note. Later, I figured the Holocaust survivor suicide angle would make a good book. That's why I came to Israel, not to solve a mystery. But when I realized both you and Zehava lied about your alibis, I knew that one of you had killed him. I started with Zehava because, frankly, I hoped it was her, not you. But I thought back to that weird one-armed hug. After that, it wasn't hard. When I found out about the women, the young students, well, I just knew you must have been one of them. I figured you fought back." I shrugged, rather than say the rest out loud. "It just surprised me how far Zehava was willing to go to protect you.

I could have published her confession, and maybe, who knows, she could have been arrested. She risked everything for you."

Michal nodded. "She was always like a second mother to me. I think she felt my mother wasn't up to the job. Or maybe she felt guilty for what Chaim did. But you should know. She was *never* in danger of being arrested. The most you could have done was embarrass us. And I guess ruin Chaim's name. But by the time you were writing your book, I just wanted to forget about him. Oh, and I was also never in any legal danger." She nodded toward the headstone.

"Charlie," I said.

"He would have buried the investigation no matter what you wrote."

"He knew it was you?"

She nodded. For the first time, tears leaked from her eyes. "Of course."

I wondered suddenly if the whole stew Charlie cooked up— with Alon and Kaplowitz—wasn't about peace negotiations at all, at least not for him. I wondered if he was subtly, trickily—he was a smart guy after all, the only one not to underestimate me— pointing me toward Zehava all along to protect Michal. I guessed I'd never know.

"He loved you," I said, as if it had just occurred to me.

She took several tissues out of her purse. But she didn't need them. She'd already stopped crying. "And I loved him. Oh, Charlie. I really loved him."

CHAPTER 21

Excerpt from *Here There Is No Why: The Death and Life of Chaim Lerner* by Judah Loeb
2005

The following is an excerpt from an interview Nobel Prize–winning American Jewish author Nathan Rothstein conducted with Chaim Lerner. It's taken, with permission, from Rothstein's award-winning volume Writers from Hell. *Rothstein published the book about a year after Lerner's death and dedicated the volume to his memory. The interview was conducted on Lerner's balcony less than a month before his fall.*

NR: Why do you think you survived?

CL: That is a difficult question, fraught with possibilities for misunderstandings, hurt feelings, and even a sort of, yes, blasphemy. But I'll begin with the least controversial reason. Luck. Because I fled to the forest early in the war, I had several years away from the camps. So I was among the last to face the Auschwitz machine. Its jaws opened, yes, but the Germans lost before they could clamp shut on my sick but not dying body. And, of course, you know I had a skill that the Germans valued; I was a chemist, and Auschwitz included Buna, a rubber factory that aided the German war effort. Of course, I did zero chemistry during my time in the *lager*. I schlepped heavy barrels of toxic materials from here to there—something for which my body type was uniquely unsuited. But no chemistry. Still, the degree no doubt saved my life when I arrived at the selection. Also, yes, I knew German. Fluently. I could understand the mad orders from the lunatic guards, and that helped me avoid several beatings. I've never seen an academic study, but my guess is that those who were fluent in German survived at a higher rate. Still, yes, most of them died. And now I arrive at a place where I hope not to be misunderstood. My purpose is not to hurt anyone's feelings. I've heard it said, and this makes some sense to me, yes, that the worst of us survived. By that, I mean you needed some innate selfishness to cheat the Angel of Death in the *lager*. You had to have the proper instinct to know when to push yourself into the right line and perhaps, yes, push someone else out. You couldn't share your bread too often, and if you did, only with a partner who was healthy enough, yes, to help you, to reciprocate. I tell you this because you are a writer, and writers seek truth. This is a truth that is not often admitted, for obvious reasons, yes? But you and I, we don't flee from truth.

NR: So that's it? You spoke German? You had your chemist card? You were selfish?

CL: Certainly. But I have to add one more element. And here, yes, I touch on the blasphemous. I hesitate to discuss these matters. They hint at surrealism, or even, yes, myth and madness. My reputation suffers. And yours, also, yes, if you publish this. Nevertheless. We will be brave. There is a kabbalistic concept known as *chayut*, from the Hebrew *chai*, which means life. A deep idea, impossible to explain fully in this format, or, yes, any format. It has to do with the four levels of soul—soul here meaning the life force shared by all created things. Actually, there are five levels. This is the riddle and wordplay in the Kabbalah, yes? Four levels, but really five. Never mind. *Chayut*, or 'vitality', is the fourth level, the highest level available to human beings. The fifth level is, yes, God's level, but let us call it the mythic level, or the transcendent level. And then, let's forget about it. It's not accessible and only exists on an undiscoverable plane. But the fourth level. *Chayut*. Yes? Now, I've discussed the phenomena of the *musselman*, German for Muslim. Strange choice of words. No one knows who coined the term. The *musselmen* were walking zombies. They'd surrendered their souls. Their eyes were blank. The *haftlinge*, the prisoners, recognized a *musselman* right away. The life force was gone. It would be only a matter of days. Either that *musselman* would keel over and die, yes? Or be shot for not obeying. Or selected. The *musselman* was a human without a soul. Even the lowest level. My theory—and this is kabbalistic theory, therefore, impossible to prove, and, frankly, dangerous to share, yes? My theory is that those *haftlinge* who become *musselmen* were born with low levels of soul. Or, shall we say, *I* prefer to say, God, for mysterious reasons, granted them lower levels of soul, of the life force. As for the survivors? God gifted us with extra measures of *chayut*. I insist on claiming this was an explicit creative act from God. It is not genetics. My father became a *musselman*. So did my brother. It is not reward and punishment. I tell you, with every fiber of modesty, that my father and brother were better men than me—stronger, more intelligent, more generous. And yet. *Chayut* is the mystical answer to your inquiry. Which is to say that, ultimately, it is meaningless. Totally without meaning, yes? Still. Important. To me.

NR: But if the survivors were, shall we say, 'blessed' with *chayut*, how do you explain the phenomenon of the Holocaust writers who took their own lives? Let's call it the Paul Celan syndrome. The survivor/poet/suicide.

Long pause.

CL: To articulate is to free the monster? Writing reveals the truest depths of human evil, at the cost of the poet's life? How do I respond to this question? As you know, none of these brilliant writers utilized an ounce of their brilliance to compose a single line regarding their suicides. No suicide notes. From writers, no less. A glaring absence. No explanation for their most consequential decision. Perhaps their work is their note.

NR: It sounds like you're criticizing them.

CL: Not at all. The Shoah leaves me without judgments of conscience. I simply ask the questions. Why no note? Why? Sometimes, there is no why.

CHAPTER 22

September 2023

Déjà vu hit as Hannah and I buckled ourselves in for the return flight to New York. The sound of the seat belt click carried me back eighteen years. A powerful feeling, for sure, but not transformative enough for me to ignore the obvious, blessed difference: first class. No more scrunching against each other to catch a few hours of restless sleep. No straining for leg room. No sharing two cramped, smelly bathrooms with hundreds of coach fliers. *A rich daughter,* I thought. *All that was missing from my life, back then.* Except for everything else.

Hannah must have been struck with a similar déjà vu because, after clicking on her belt, she remarked, "It seems like we have our deepest conversations stuck next to each other on long flights."

I chuckled. She obviously had something to share because I had zero interest in debriefing her about my conversation with Michal or being debriefed on any conversation or insight Hannah might have gained from Zehava's funeral. I was truly, blessedly finished with the Lerners. The plane took off. I reached next to my seat for the latest Stephen King novel but kept it unopened on my lap. I waited.

"What's the worst thing you've ever done?" she asked after twenty minutes of flying.

I snuck a sideways look at her. *A grown up*, I thought. *A mother. When did this happen?* The ghost of her five-year-old self sat on my lap as I pondered her ridiculous question. "I'm supposed to tell you?"

"Yes, Dad. That's why I asked. You're supposed to tell me."

"I'm pretty sure you know the answer," I said. When I first admitted the worst thing I've ever done to Hannah, tears exploded on my cheeks. This time—I don't know why—my cheeks stayed bone-dry.

"Your affair with Michal while you were married to Mom?"

"It wasn't an affair. It was one time. And your mother—"

"Okay, okay. And that's the worst thing?"

I shrugged. "I'm a pretty boring guy." I touched my Stephen King book. "Is there something you want to tell me?"

She nodded, and I noticed her lips were tightly pursed, a sign since she was a toddler that she was fighting back tears, and that she would fail. "Hannah?" I said.

"It's time for me to tell you. But I'm afraid. You're going to be so mad at me."

She was thirty-two years old. A beloved spiritual leader. As competent as her mother and just as engaging a personality. Married, a parent. We hadn't lived together since she'd moved to Mt. Holyoke her first year of college, fourteen years before. *What could she possibly have done to me?* "Hannah . . ."

"I brought something with me," she said, breathing rapidly. I had to strain to hear her diminished voice over the drone of flying engines. She reached into her backpack. "I've been meaning to show it to you for, oh, let's say twenty years. Maybe longer." She took out a letter-sized envelope. It was as white as new, unwrinkled, as if she'd just ironed it.

I recognized the handwriting on the front an instant before she placed the envelope in my hand. It said, "Judah and Hannah." In Mary's handwriting. Talk about ghosts. My heartbeat raced. My stomach grumbled then froze. My eyes yawned open. But no tears. "What on earth?"

"The note," Hannah croaked out. "Her note."

"Hannah?"

"I found it," she said, steadying her voice. "On the steps. When I found her body. I could barely read, but I recognized my own name. I told myself it was for me. I'm not sure I even knew your first name. Or, probably, I did, but I wanted it to be for me. I don't even remember why." She took my wrist and held tight, as if rescuing me from flying out the window. "Honestly, it wasn't until I was twelve that I realized, I mean really realized, that this was for you also. But I couldn't show it to you 'cause I knew you'd be mad that I'd hid it all these years. I sort of forgot about it till I was fifteen and we took that trip, and I wrote that horrible report about suicide bombers. I almost told you about it then, but I got so sad, and I thought again, oh, he'll be mad. And then every year—every day—that I didn't show you, the sin became worse, so I couldn't tell you. Or, shit, I don't know. Maybe I always wanted to keep it from you. I wanted it to be mine. Mine alone. I don't know why."

"Hannah," I said. I breathed in through my nose and blew the breath out with my mouth, a calming technique Mary had taught me. "I'm not mad. Really. Not mad." I wasn't. She was five years old. How could I be mad? Tears flowed down her grown-up cheeks. I pointed to the envelope. "Should I?"

"Yes, yes!" she said. "Read it."

I removed the thrice-folded page from the envelope with extraordinary care, as if I were handling an ancient, sacred text. The date was at the top: May 11, 1995—that was the day Hannah found the body. Mary wrote it on that same day, in her clear, careful hand, with black pen.

> *Dear Judah and Hannah,*
> *You know why I have to do this. I'm so, so sorry for the hurt this action causes, but hurt and pain and tragedy moved into our lives many months ago, and this now makes it easier for all of us. Be strong for each other. Help each other. Love each other always, as I love you.*
> *Mom (Mary)*

I refolded the page, carefully placed it back into the envelope. For a moment, I considered keeping it, but then I handed it back to Hannah. "She didn't mean for you to find it," I said.

She shook her head. Her eyes were tightly shut, but I couldn't spot any tears.

"You weren't supposed to be home that early."

Another head shake.

"It's a pretty short note."

A nod.

"That was it, right?" I asked. "There were no other notes? Nothing else?"

"No," she said, her voice carrying just above the engine noise.

I thought about Mary's message. It was so short. I basically memorized it after reading it just once. I'd have thought a long-lost (lost to me, anyway) missive from my dead wife would fill me with love, longing, and nostalgic melancholy. And it did, but only for a second, and it didn't last past the "Dear Judah and Hannah." Instead, I felt an unaccountable irritation growing from my belly. "It's pretty short," I repeated. Hannah finally opened her eyes and turned them toward me. "And she tells us, 'Be strong for each other.' Well, of course we're going to try to be strong for each other. What choice did she give us? And 'Help each other'? What else were we going to do? And she writes, 'tragedy moved in?' I don't even know what that means. And I definitely haven't the slightest idea why she'd think killing herself would make it easier on us. Six months in rehab? That wasn't easy. Oh, and how can she say, 'You know why I have to do this'? Honestly, I *don't* know why. There were treatments we hadn't tried yet. Sure, her chances weren't great, and the treatments were awful, but we would have helped her. Even you, five years old. You helped both of us get through that horrible year. So, no, I don't understand why. Do you?"

Hannah, young mother of my grandchild, smiled. My daughter, discussing her mother's suicide, smiled. Five minutes after handing me a suicide note she'd withheld for twenty-seven years, she smiled, like Mona Lisa, like Buddha. It was a pretty smile. "'Why' is not the right question," she said. She touched my finger. "It was never the right question."

EPILOGUE

Hanukkah 2023

Three months later. I'm sixty-one years old, entering old age, and suddenly, I'm surrounded by Jewish things. It's the eighth night of Hanukkah; candles are burning bright. Tiny plastic dreidels in many colors are spread out on the table in front of me. Pictures of golden menorahs decorate the walls. There's a mezuzah guarding the door to the hall. I'm wearing a multicolored *yarmulke* on my gray head and a flowing white tallit around my neck. I can't keep it from sliding down my shoulders.

Most importantly, I'm standing under a *huppah*, the marriage canopy made from four poles and my late father's wedding tallit. Next to me, wrapped in her own violet and red tallit, is my fiancé, who is minutes away from becoming my wife. The white-robed rabbi, my daughter, is reading from our *ketubah*, the decorated, poster-sized marriage contract where we promise, among other things, to care for each other, even in old age—at this point in our lives, not an idle pledge.

Toward my left, under the canopy, stands my sister, smiling proudly, eyes shining like jewels. My granddaughter plays with my son-in-law in the corner of the room. They laugh loudly. Hannah moves through the ceremony like the pro she's become. At her instructions, I lift Liora's veil. We exchange rings, sip the sweet wine once, and then sip it a second time. With a shaky voice, fear, not anxiety, I speak words of love. Liora responds with similar words; then Hannah speaks. Hannah sings.

Now she's explaining the breaking of the glass. She explained it to me privately weeks ago. The shards, she told me, symbolize our broken world. By smashing the glass, I invite sorrow into this moment of our greatest joy. I couldn't help it. I thought of Mary. I thought of Michal. I thought of Yoav and Charlie. I thought of Israel. I thought of Chaim.

Hannah kneels in front of me and places the handkerchief-covered glass under my foot. Unbeknownst to her, I've practiced at home a few times, destroying three thin wine goblets—wedding presents from my first marriage.

She rises. She nods at me, smiling. I take a breath. I smash the glass into a million pieces.

www.ingramcontent.com/pod-product-compliance
Lightning Source LLC
LaVergne TN
LVHW041753060526
838201LV00046B/989